THE SCRYING

Book One in The Scrying Trilogy

JACI MILLER

Solitary Pen Press

The Scrying: Book One
The Scrying Trilogy
Copyright © 2017 by Jaci Miller
Solitary Pen Press
Cover Design by Streetlight Graphics

Print ISBN: 978-0-9988069-0-7
Ebook ISBN: 978-0-9988069-1-4
Library of Congress Control Number: 2017478856
First Edition: 2017

This is a work of fiction. Names, characters, places, and incidents are either a product of the author's imagination or are used fictitiously. Any resemblance to actual persons, living or dead, business establishments, events, or locales is purely coincidental.

www.jacimiller.com
www.solitarypenpress.com

To Sherry, for always making me believe.

"And thou shalt be the first of the witches known."
– Charles G. Leland, 1899

CHAPTER 1

February 9, 1985

H E SAT AT THE OLD walnut desk, the ancient parchments strewn across its worn and scratched surface. Picking up one of the fragile pages he scanned the words written on its yellowed surface, the pitch-black ink highlighting the perfect script of his ancestors. The letters seemed to waver as he read the only line it contained—*one world born from another will share an equal fate.*

His brow furrowed as he contemplated those words, their meaning still escaping him after all these years. It had been the first parchment he'd discovered, hidden between the pages of an old leather-bound book containing his family genealogy. He found it on his thirteenth birthday, the same day he'd experienced the vision.

His green eyes glazed as he thought back to that day in Braemore Woods forty-three years ago. A day, which began his obsessive search for answers and fueled an unyielding desire to uncover the truth behind his family's legacy.

He'd seen the Elder Oak in his dreams weeks before he ventured into the forest to find it. It beckoned to him, a silent shadowy figure in a moon-filled night. He had gone to the tree without hesitation, easily finding it hidden deep in the woods. When he touched the tree's trunk, the vision was instant. Suddenly, he found himself immersed in another time and place. Lost in the forgotten energy of a distant universe that was far beyond anything the imagination of a thirteen-year-old boy could construct. Everything about the universe was surreal, its magnitude overwhelming, its realms so dissimilar yet eerily cohesive in their existence. The realms were uninhabited, each blanketed by a haunting silence. Their pasts, faded memories shrouded by the emptiness leaching from their surfaces.

The vision had ended with the image of a young woman, standing atop a magnificent waterfall. Her long dark hair flowed lazily behind her and piercing green eyes staring vacantly. She held a familiarity and he sensed she was somehow a part of him, but he hadn't known who she would be until now.

He pushed the parchment aside and picked up the birth announcement from where it leaned casually against the desk clock. His hand shook as he held the paper. "IT'S A GIRL!" was scrawled in white across the card's surface, a message that had a profound meaning to his family. One month ago, the identity of the young woman from his childhood vision was revealed. With her birth came the realization his family legacy was no longer a myth; bedtime stories handed down through generations. Those words held an undeniable truth. He knew now the reason for his childhood vision. It was his responsibility to guide her, to help her uncover her connection to that mysterious world.

He put down the birth announcement and began to gather up the fragile parchments, sliding them carefully into a slim leather folder. Securing the flap with a thin leather string he wrapped the folder in a black velvet cloth and positioned it at the bottom of the small wooden chest, placing the other items he'd collected over the years, on top. Finishing the note, he sealed it in an envelope and taped it to the inside of the chest's lid.

A glint of light flashed in his peripheral vision, and he turned his attention back to the desk. The medallion hung from the desk lamp, its green stone reflecting the artificial light as it gently swung on a long thick chain. He reached for the ancient medallion, removing it and placing it his palm. This medallion was the key, and she would need all the help and guidance he and their ancestors could provide when she faced the uncertainty of her future.

He thought about the vision again and the strange shadow he'd seen in the young woman's eyes. Initially, he was confused by its meaning but as the years passed and he'd revealed the truth behind the family legacy it had become apparent. It was the shadow of separation; the mark representing a splintering of a person's identity and a sign of a fractured destiny. The young woman's future could not yet be written because two different destinies awaited her and only she could choose, which of them would unfold.

Lost in thought, he tightened his grip on the medallion, feeling a slight pinch as the stone embedded in its face dug into the skin of his palm—*destiny had been forging a path through time, and it was nearly upon them.*

CHAPTER 2

January 9, 2016

Everyone has a destiny. It isn't always glamorous, it doesn't always lead to greatness, but it is a destiny nonetheless—a fate designed specifically for one individual. Unfortunately, Dane Watts-Callan's destiny was also her biggest secret. It was her thirty-first birthday and like all the others over the past eighteen years, it marked the beginning of another year of deception.

Her mood had darkened over the past few days as it always did around her birthday. With the weekend festivities her friends planned about to commence, her mood had progressed to sullen.

Stevie insisted they do something special this year since it was Dane's thirty-first and thirteen years since the six of them became friends; a numeric inversion Stevie could not ignore. She'd reluctantly agreed because she didn't want to disappoint everyone but truthfully, she would just as soon ignore this birthday like she attempted to do every year.

Sitting at the kitchen counter, the morning cup of tea still warm in her hands, she stared at the pictures on the wall. Twelve beautifully framed images of six women, one for every year of their friendship, taken at each of their annual get-togethers. They'd met through a random set of circumstances, a strange link of occurrences happening in a very short time-period. Essentially, a domino effect—one girl meeting another and then that girl meeting the next until six strangers connected and ultimately became lifelong friends. Recounting those odd circumstances always made for good fodder at their annual girl's weekend, but Stevie liked to sum up their chance encounters with one word —*destiny*.

She glanced back at the twelve photos. Soon number thirteen would hang beside them, another painful reminder that her best friendships were based on secrets and lies.

The ring of her cell phone startled her out of her thoughts, looking down she saw it was her mother calling. "Good morning mom."

"Morning honey. Your dad and I thought we should give you a quick call, it's not too early, is it?"

Dane laughed, "No, Tyson, and I have been up for a while now."

Upon hearing his name, the bullmastiff at her feet lifted his head, big brown eyes widening in curiosity.

"OK, good. We know how you feel about this time of year, but your dad and I still wanted to wish you a happy birthday."

"Hi sweetie," her father chimed in from another line. "How's my birthday girl? Looking forward to your girl's weekend?"

"Yes. But keeping who I am from them is more difficult

under these circumstances and you know I hate to have to lie to them." She sniffed, unwanted tears stinging her eyes. Silently, she cursed herself for getting so emotional.

"We know honey, and we are sorry," her dad soothed. "It's a difficult price to pay because of your family legacy, but you know it's a necessary one. Don't look at it as lying, instead consider it, not oversharing."

She could hear her mother whisper a scolding at her father's failed attempt to joke.

"You know it's how it has to be Dane, discretion is how our kind has been able to survive for centuries without detection," her mother reminded her.

"I know mom, I just can't help feeling maybe it could be different with them. That they would understand."

"Maybe they would, but revealing your identity as a witch to anyone, not like us, is forbidden. You know this."

Witches, Dane mused. She had known she was a witch since her "awakening" at thirteen; the time when a person born with magic gains their powers. Unfortunately, she never grew comfortable with her identity as a magical being, especially when she was constantly having to hide her active powers from mortals. "I know, but it would be easier if I could just be me for a change."

"We wish things were different, and they were like us, but your father and I have met them plenty of times, and although Stevie would make a brilliant witch, none of them have the aura. You know the rules," her mother said, carefully reiterating what she told her daughter on numerous occasions over the years.

The aura, Dane thought, *the specific light and scent a witch gives off, her magical calling card and something only other witches can detect.*

"I'm sorry Dane, I know this secret is a heavy burden, but your destiny was written long ago," her father interjected, his calm voice showing the deep affection he had for his only child. "You come from two of the oldest families of witches in Europe. It's your birthright."

"Thanks for the reminder Dad," she huffed.

Her mom sighed, "We love you, Dane." She was used to the stubbornness her daughter exhibited on a regular basis but seeing her only child in pain because of her heritage was never easy. The Watts and Callan families had, for centuries, readily accepted their magic and the ensuing responsibility but Dane had always been more apprehensive. It was like she carried the burden of that responsibility for everyone and was afraid to disappoint.

"Have a happy birthday honey and enjoy the weekend with the girls, we will see you all next week."

"Thanks, mom, dad, see you Wednesday," she said hanging up the phone and wiping away the stray tears clinging to her cheek.

Glancing up at the wall of images she noticed year five was hanging slightly crooked. Lifting her hand, she gently flicked her fingers watching as the frame righted itself into a level position.

"I suppose being a witch has its advantages," she said looking down at Tyson and winking, the bullmastiff's tail smacking against the floor in agreement.

Making herself another cup of tea, she headed into the bedroom. Sitting on the floor by her bed she reached underneath and pulled out a wooden box. The lid was carved with an elaborate pentacle, a gift from her grandfather on her eighteenth birthday. Opening it, she removed a small scroll from its contents, unrolling the fragile parchment she read the lines out loud.

A witch shall practice their craft, unseen by the eyes of mortals.
A witch shall devote their life, to accepting the anonymity of their gifts.
A witch shall never divulge their true identity to any mortal being but stay solely visible only to those who possess equivalent powers.
A witch must remain equal to mortals as understood by mortal law, practicing their craft only in secrecy.
A witch must never use their powers against mortals even in their own peril or that of others.
A witch must be guided by the Rule of Three, never succumbing to the lure of dark magic and the negative energy associated with it.
A witch must always live by the ethics of the Wiccan Rede so that their gifts never provide them with an advantage over the mortal world.
This is the burden, the destiny, and the oath a witch must uphold under the sanctity of the Protection of the Coven.

The Protection of the Coven were 'the rules' her mother referred too. A sacred doctrine, which those who possess magic are bound by. Enabling witches to remain undetected when practicing their craft. An oath that is recited by every new witch during their circle ceremony; a ritual where the coven elders welcome them into the family coven.

Reading the oath became a ritual for her and one she ceremoniously repeated every year right before her birthday. It was a way to remind herself to never get too close to anyone, for she was never going to have a normal life always having to keep a part of herself secret.

In the beginning, Dane had no idea how much of a burden being a witch would be or how much her life would need to change because of it, but as her powers grew, so did the responsibility to protect her secret. As a result, Dane's life as a witch became a constant deterrent to her relationship with mortals. Although she quickly found a balance between her two lives, the walls she built to guard her family secret had formed an impenetrable barrier around her heart. A change, which resulted in an independent and private individual who found it difficult to show weakness but easy to keep people at arms-length.

She put the scroll back in the box and pulled out her family grimoire; a book containing pages of spells, potion recipes, family anecdotes, stories, and legends, all from and about her ancestors. The large leather-bound book was thick and heavy, its surface worn and slightly tattered, and it constantly smelled like herbs and burnt incense, but it was her most-prized possession.

Passed down through generations of Watts women, each added their own insights into the craft before passing it on. As a healer, her mother had filled pages with healing potions and spells, before giving it to Dane on her eighteenth birthday. By that time, she was already a highly intuitive empath, had developed telekinesis, the ability to move objects with both her mind and her hands, and possessed an innate ability for spell writing and incantations, so she was able to both learn from and contribute to the grimoire.

Her hands caressed the soft leather, careful to open the aged book gently. The spine cracked slightly in protest as she flipped past the pages containing her family history and genealogy, stopping when she reached the myth from her dad's side of the family. A story which had been a bedtime staple when she was a child and one that she herself documented in these pages.

It is said, the Callan Clan were an ancient family of powerful warlocks who possessed archaic Celtic magic. Descendants of a primordial mythical tribe of sorcerers known as Warlicians. The Warlicians, the legend holds, were an elite group of magical warriors existing in a time long before mankind. Their heroic feats passed down through generations of Callan sons were legendary— magical knights protecting the ancient realms from evil. It was said, they possessed powerful warrior magic and were dominant in battle, having the ability of foresight, which made them almost unbeatable.

When Dane was younger, she'd longed for the power her father's ancient ancestors possessed, mesmerized by the romance of their quest. Unfortunately, as her father pointed out many times, the Warlician legend was founded in ancient Celtic myth, not reality. Putting the grimoire back in the wooden box, she replaced the lid and pushed it under the bed, thinking about the myth and how much she wished it to be true.

Tyson had followed her into the bedroom and was now curled up on the rug beside her, his large brown eyes watching her intently. She stroked his head absently as she thought about the coming weekend.

The girls were all gathering at Stevie's house tonight, to hang out, hike, and relax for the next two days. This girl's weekend was shorter this year as Stevie's job as a make-up artist had taken her out of town for the past two weeks, and she wouldn't be back until today. In hindsight, staying in town instead of traveling, like they normally did for their annual girl's weekend, was a good idea especially since a winter storm was due to hit the area by early evening.

She loved these weekends with her friends, but they were always a little more difficult as the years passed. As the relationships became more important, she found it increasingly problematic to maintain a comfortable distance. It was at these times when being a witch was more of a curse than a blessing.

She headed into the bathroom leaving Tyson looking after her with a furrowed brow and a scowl. "I'll be out in a minute," she said over her shoulder as he stood up and lumbered over to her bed, climbing up and stretching out in the middle, giving her another scowl. She smiled and shook her head at what Tyson perceived to be an act of defiance, his way of throwing an enormous temper tantrum without exerting too much energy.

Looking in the mirror, she noticed the dark circles emerging under her bright green eyes. She looked tired, or stressed, she couldn't decide which, but she hoped a hot shower would help. She'd been having difficulty sleeping the past few nights, tossing and turning for unknown reasons. When she did sleep, it wasn't restful, and it certainly wasn't helping her appearance.

She turned off the faucet and stepped out of the steaming shower already feeling less gloomy. Reaching for her towel she quickly dried herself and pulled on her robe, grateful that it was still slightly warm from its tumble in the dryer.

She was meeting with the mayor at ten-thirty, and she didn't want to be late. The city hired her to be the official photographer for the June 2017 Founder's Day celebration, marking Brighton Hill's three hundred and fiftieth birthday. Normally the mayor did not work on a Saturday, but she wanted to meet with her to go over the decisions the Chamber of Commerce and the city board members had finalized last week. The mayor was leaving town on Monday for a two-week family vacation and today was the only time she had open on her schedule.

This job was a large one and was going to require her full attention for about six months prior to the event but came with an almost unlimited budget. The city had been planning for this celebration for decades, and they were sparing no expense. Although, she often missed her career as a photojournalist, getting this job gave her an opportunity to once again capture a story using images, documenting the history of a town she now called home.

Pulling on a casual outfit of leggings, tall leather boots, and a long sweater, she quickly looked outside at the thermometer before adding a scarf, down vest, and gloves to her ensemble. Calling for Tyson, who'd moved from the middle of the bed to the end, she grabbed her laptop case and headed out the door.

He immediately darted after a squirrel that dared to take up residence on the front lawn. After a few more circles around the base of the tree in a futile attempt to find the squirrel who'd scurried up the trunk, he finally gave up. Trotting to her Wrangler he jumped into the passenger seat and panted out his enthusiasm.

"Proud of yourself?" She asked sarcastically before backing out of the driveway.

A few blocks from City Hall, she turned into a gas

station. Pulling up to a free pump, she waited patiently for the attendant to finish with the car in front of her.

"Fill it up?" The attendant asked running his hand through his tousled hair.

"Yes, thank you," she responded reaching past Tyson for her wallet.

As she waited for the attendant to fill her tank, something out of the corner of her eye caught her attention. Turning to the right she saw a very striking young woman walking up the sidewalk toward the gas station. She was tall and thin, and her long straight hair was a brilliant fiery red. She was wearing tight black leather pants, leopard print booties, and a chunky black turtleneck sweater. The long black trench coat she wore open, flowed behind her in the wind. Her eyes were covered with oversized black sunglasses and as she walked past the station she slowed, her gloved hand reaching up and pulling them down onto the bridge of her nose. Turning her head slightly she locked her dark eyes on Dane as a small smirk crawled over her crimson lips. She shivered as the woman's penetrating stare caused a cold chill to crawl down her spine.

"Lady, did you hear me? I said that will be $27.89."

"Yes, sorry," she said breaking eye contact with the strange woman and handing the attendant her credit card. She quickly looked back in the direction of the redhead, but she was nowhere to be seen. Thanking the attendant, she put her credit card back in her wallet and took a long deep breath. The sky was beginning to darken menacingly, an indication the predicted winter storm was approaching.

Starting the Jeep, she drove out of the gas station as an uneasy feeling settled over her.

CHAPTER 3

AETHER, GABBY'S METAPHYSICAL STORE WAS Dane's favorite place in the Brighton Hill shopping district. A small, eight hundred square foot space she named after the ancient classical element, alchemists believed filled the universe above the terrestrial sphere. It catered to those who practiced new-age religions or subscribed to a non-traditional lifestyle. The store's inventory consisted of incense, oils, magical elements, divination tools, healing stones, tarot cards, books, jewelry, everything a new ager could want.

Stevie, of course, was her best customer since Dane purchased most of her supplies out of town. The store was only two blocks from City Hall, and since her meeting ended early she decided to surprise Gabby with lunch.

As she drove, Dane went over the details of her meeting with the mayor. It had gone well, and she loved the direction the planning committee wanted to go, highlighting the dark side of Brighton Hill's history in their celebration. Like

Salem, where her parents lived, Brighton Hill was a town infamous for its history of witchcraft.

The hysteria associated with witchcraft and Satan, which ran rampant throughout Europe in the sixteenth and seventeenth centuries had eventually found its way to the New World. The Puritans became the catalyst that flamed the fires of this unreasonable hysteria in America. As organized religion took hold, the furor surrounding God and Satan created an environment ripe for hysteria. Magic was deemed the devils work, a belief, when combined with ignorance and fear and propagated by religious strongholds, developed a foundation where reason and logic were discarded. A heretical frenzy, which resulted in numerous women and men being unjustly accused of practicing witchcraft and killed as punishment.

The Salem Witch Trials were the most infamous, but the fear and ignorance defining that era did not leave Brighton Hill unscathed. Instead, this type of irrationality provoked a singular witch hunt; accused and condemned an entire family and ended the legacy of one of the most influential people in the town—darkening its history forever. John Dunham, whose father founded Brighton Hill in 1667, was put to death—hung in the town square along with his wife, his four sons, their wives, and their six children; the youngest being born only months before.

The hysteria that claimed the lives of the entire Dunham lineage would eventually be traced, by historians, back to John Dunham's business partner, Samuel Lewin. The entire families' demise left no living heir, so John Dunham's considerable assets reverted to his business partner as his next benefactor. Lewin's greed and jealousy were the catalyst that fueled the town's hysteria, igniting an already fearful and tense environment. All logic, compassion, and rational thinking were thrown aside and without much in the way of evidence, the town elders took the lives of every living family member, citing their crimes as an allegiance to Satan. John Dunham's final words, as the noose was laid around his neck—*It is not the devil you have to fear but God himself, for your souls will suffer his wrath.*

The City was planning on commemorating the Dunham family by formally exonerating them in the City's Charter and erecting a memorial listing each of the family member's names. As a witch who was once again in hiding, she appreciated the gesture and tolerance but was unable to shake the feeling that things would not be as amicable if mortals knew there were those born with magic, living among them.

The mayor also wanted to feature the old flour mill in the commemorative promo package. It had been abandoned for decades, but the mill was an integral part of the town's history. Over the years, the Brighton Hill Chamber of Commerce talked about renovating the property into upscale apartments, offices, and retail space but had yet to finalize a plan or approve a budget for the three-story, 45,000 square foot red brick building.

Built in the 1800s, the mill sat abandoned on the outskirts of the city. It was a historic landmark, but its fading and sagging exterior coupled with the overgrown landscape, cemented its unfavorable reputation as an unsightly blight on the surrounding area. It was this very image the mayor wanted to market; the forgotten past—the foundation for an exciting vibrant future. She requested Dane take photos of the mill immediately and have them ready for her approval when she got back from vacation.

It was just before noon when she pulled into the parking lot beside Gabby's shop. This street was the most popular spot in town and was always busy, especially on a Saturday. The Chamber of Commerce spent a lot of money five years ago laying cobblestone over the asphalt and changing the streetlights to electric versions of centuries-old gas lamps. Many of the stores and restaurants that lined this street were locally owned and operated and boasted an eclectic variety of products and services. As Brighton Hill was a historical tourist destination, the shopping district project had been justified and was very popular and lucrative during the town's multiple tourist seasons.

The sign on the door said, 'Closed for Lunch' so she knew there wouldn't be any customers in the store. Unclipping Tyson's leash, she pushed open the front door, watching with amusement as he lumbered his way through the display shelves looking for Gabby.

She was standing at the checkout desk and once he knew he'd discovered her whereabouts his entire body wriggled with happiness. She turned just as Tyson pushed his thick skull into the side of her leg.

"Well hello Tyson," she laughed, gently stroking him behind his ear as he pushed his head further into her leg.

Dane walked toward her carrying a white takeout bag, "I brought lunch."

"Hey Dane, this is a surprise, I was just getting ready to close up for the weekend." She said, walking over to hug her friend.

"I thought you weren't closing until three?"

"That was the plan, but with the pending storm business has been slow, so I decided to close at one."

"Well, my meeting got out early, so I brought lunch

from Peleto's Deli," she stated, holding up the white paper bag in triumph. "Enough for three."

"Three?"

She nodded pointing to the front door. "Stevie," she said, as Gabby once again heard the entry bell ring as her roommate walked into the shop.

Dressed in her normal attire of skinny jeans, motorcycle boots, and a leather bomber jacket Stevie Jacobs embodied casual chic.

"How do you do that?" Gabby questioned, as Stevie waved and headed in their direction.

"Do what?" She asked reaching into the white bag and pulling out takeout containers.

"That!" demanded Gabby pointing in the direction of Stevie. "Knowing things before they happen!"

"I knew she was coming. I talked to her earlier, found out she was already on her way home and told her to stop here for lunch."

"Well I spoke with her as well, but it doesn't mean I know the exact second she will walk through the door!" Gabby stammered.

She shrugged and smiled at her exasperated friend, stifling a laugh. Her empath abilities allowed her to feel energy from substantial distances and because she was so familiar with her friends' individual energies, she always knew when they were near, even if they were not yet in sight.

"I give up!" Gabby said in desperation as Stevie sauntered up.

"What did I miss?" Stevie asked, noticing the frown on Gabby's face.

"Nothing much," Gabby responded. "Only Dane doing

her weird mind stuff again."

Stevie looked at Dane a smirk on her face. "Predicting the future again?"

"Not exactly," she chuckled. "Gabby thinks I can, but I'm just a good guesser."

"Guessing!" Gabby huffed. "Is that what you call it?"

"Intuition," Stevie interjected, grabbing the white bag from Dane and quickly changing the subject. "What's for lunch, I'm starving?!"

The three women chatted for a while, catching up on the happenings of the past two weeks since Stevie had been out of town. Reluctantly, Gabby looked at her watch and noted the time; she needed to reopen the shop. She excused herself for a moment, heading to the front door to switch back to the 'Open' sign as Stevie and Dane cleaned up the lunch mess.

"Have we heard from Kai?" Gabby asked returning to where they stood.

Dane nodded, "I spoke with her on my drive here. She's coming in as soon as she finishes up a few things at the marina and makes lunch for her dad. He's worried about the weather and wants her in town prior to the storm starting."

"That's a good idea considering how much Kai loves snow!" Stevie said sarcastically.

Dane smiled, nodding in agreement "I also spoke to Elyse and Marlee this morning, they have their charity committee meeting this afternoon but will be over after."

"Then let the festivities begin!" Stevie said in triumph laughing as the entry bell rang in response.

When Gabby went to help the customer who just entered, Stevie turned to Dane, a serious look on her face.

She knew that look; it was the one Stevie used when she wanted to say something but was unsure if she should.

"What is it?" Dane asked.

Stevie hesitated slightly before answering, "I got a call on the way home, it was Alex."

"Who?"

"Alex," Stevie repeated. "The handsome guy you met at my Christmas party, the chef."

She rolled her eyes. "Oh right."

"He was wondering if you would be interested in going out for dinner, or a drink," Stevie said quietly knowing the response she was going to get.

"No."

"But he's a nice guy and you haven't dated anyone since you and Mason broke up. It's been over a year."

"Thanks for your concern, Stevie, but I am fine single."

Dane could count the relationships she had engaged in over the years on one hand. None of them lasted more than a few months except Mason who'd stuck around for almost two years. He was an attorney she met through her friend Elyse. He worked long hours, and she barely spent any significant amount of time with him, which was probably the reason he lasted longer than the others. She liked her alone time and her independence but becoming emotionally intimate with someone was risky, especially because she would never be able to divulge her secret.

Short-term relationships were more her style or no relationship at all. There were many reasons she didn't excel in the romance department, being a witch just happened to be one of them. Her mother even tried to set her up with a few warlocks over the years, but those went downhill quicker than her relationships with mortal men.

Everyone had pretty much given up trying to fix her up, except Stevie, which was the oddest part considering she herself didn't like committing to anyone long-term. She remembered Stevie telling her once, serious relationships stifled her free-spirit and disrupted her chi.

Dane took a deep breath and gave Stevie a withering look.

Stevie threw up her hands in defeat. "Fine, no Alex."

As Stevie and Gabby made last-minute additions to their to-do lists she took the garbage to the back room. She was just coming back into the main area when the store's entry bell rang. Kai walked through the door followed by the same red-haired woman she'd seen earlier at the gas station.

Retreating into the doorway of the backroom she watched as the woman made her way through the store nodding to Gabby as she circled the perimeter. She never really stopped to look at anything just walked slowly, running her index finger along the shelves like she was checking for dust. The closer she came to where Dane was standing, the more the cold dread creeping over her skin, intensified.

"Dane, are you OK?" Kai was standing in front of her frowning, blocking her line of sight to the strange woman.

"Yes fine, just a bit of a headache," she replied, smiling at her friend.

"Are you sure? You look a little pale."

She nodded as she moved past Kai, her eyes searching the small store for the redhead. She saw her at the counter speaking with Gabby, their voices low. The phone rang, and Gabby excused herself to go answer it. She felt intrigued by this mysterious stranger, yet leery that the feeling of dread seeping over her when she was in her presence, was a warning. The longer she continued to stare at the redhead, the more uneasy she felt.

As if she knew she was being watched, the red-haired woman turned around slowly, her dark eyes locking onto Danes, as a faint smile appeared on her crimson lips. Her eyes were hypnotic; dark endless pools drawing Dane toward them. Her empath abilities were trying desperately to connect with this strange woman but there was nothing surrounding her, no emotion whatsoever, just a hollow emptiness.

The redhead continued to stare at Dane, her eyes never blinking, until Gabby hung up the phone and turned her attention back to her. They spoke for a few minutes more and then the redhead quickly left the store without a backward glance.

Gabby came over to where Kai and Dane were standing. "What's going on?" she asked, noticing Kai was anxiously watching Dane.

"I'm not sure," Kai answered.

"Who was that?" She asked, still staring at the front door.

"I don't really know. She said she's in town looking for someone. Why?"

"I was just wondering."

Kai frowned. "Do you know her?"

Dane shook her head, the feeling of dread still lingering heavy on her skin. "No, I just thought I saw her somewhere before. Who is she looking for?"

"She didn't say, an old friend apparently. She came in here to buy mugwort, but as you know I don't carry it. You are the only person who ever wants it." Gabby said, looking at Dane. "Don't you make a special tea with it when you have headaches?"

She nodded.

Not exactly for headaches, she thought, thinking about the main ingredient in her family's mystic tea recipe; a special brew used for altering the state of consciousness during astral projection or when opening the inner eye to another plane of existence—her families' ancient art of scrying.

"Anyway," Gabby continued. "I told her I only special order it, but if she wanted some I could have it in a couple of weeks." Gabby looked back at Dane, a frown creasing her brow. "Are you sure you're OK?"

She smiled, reassuring her friends she was fine.

Convinced, Gabby and Kai headed back over to Stevie, who had been walking around the store filling up her small shopping basket with incense, oils, a couple of books on dream interpretation, and a new censer for burning sage.

Dane watched her friends as she thought about the strange red-haired woman and the uncomfortable way she made her feel. Who was she and why was she in Brighton Hill? Who was this 'old friend' she was looking for and why did she want mugwort? If she was a witch, and by the way she made her feel possibly even a dark witch, why could she not see her aura?

She'd never met a dark witch, as they were more relevant in the time prior to the witch hunts, but her mother told her a few still existed today.

Dark witches were tainted by cursed magic and because of this they often made pure witches anxious, nauseated, or worse, when in their presence. They were also known to be barren, cold and unfeeling, void of any true emotion, which would explain why she could not sense any emotional energy from her. If she was a dark witch, she was cloaking her aura and if that was the case she was using very powerful magic indeed.

She recalled what her grandmother had told her about dark witches. They often practiced dark magic, ancient rituals, and sacrifices. Thinning the boundaries between life and death. They did not worship the gods and goddesses as pure witches did, instead, worshipping daemons; soulless entities existing in the dark space between planes, feeding off the pain of others. Apparently, some witches burned at the stake in Europe were dark witches who cared little about hiding their magic from mortals, instead, screaming out curses as the fires ignited their flesh.

If this woman was a dark witch, and that was a big if, there was a reason she was in Brighton Hill and it likely wasn't good. It was important Dane find out more about her.

CHAPTER 4

KAI WAS STANDING OUTSIDE THE front door of Aether when Dane walked out, staring at the dark gray sky that threatened to erupt at any moment and send feet of snow cascading down upon them.

"Oh, my goodness!" she huffed. "More snow! Will winter ever end?"

Dane stifled a laugh knowing how much her friend hated the cold weather. Kai was at her happiest when the weather was warm, and her toes were in the water. Her father, Admiral Jason Parker, had been stationed in Hawaii at the U.S. naval base, Naval Station Pearl Harbor. It was there Kai was born and where she lived until she was sixteen when her father retired and moved his family back to his hometown of Brighton Hill, NY. Kai was horrified at the prospect of living in a small town with a lake as their only form of water. Her bleak future was only slightly enhanced by the fact that her father purchased a marina, so she would be living, like she did in Hawaii, on the water. Brighton Hill eventually grew on her, the cold had not.

Agreeing to meet at Dane's house in an hour, Kai went to buy wine and pick up a part her dad needed for a boat.

Dane decided to drive by the old flour mill on her way home and take some pictures at dusk. She turned on to the old mill road, just as the sun began to sink in the late afternoon sky. She loved the unremarkable insignificance of this road and how quiet it was now. Since the town built the new highway, joining the downtown area with the outer subdivisions, like the one she lived in, hardly anyone drove this old county road anymore. Of course, the new highway didn't have the simple tranquility or nostalgic appeal of the old mill road. It was one of the reasons she still chose to travel it instead of the highway, that and the compassion she held for the old flour mill sitting abandoned in a large field, forgotten.

She liked the stark loneliness of the old flour mill and understood its seclusion. She felt a kind of kinship with it because, like her, the old mill had a secret.

The area surrounding the mill was full of spectral energy. A fact she'd discovered when she was in college. Her abilities as an empath were not limited only to the living, she was just as connected to the energy of the dead. An individual's energy is unique, and each person leaves a specific marker in the physical world when they pass on. For those who become stuck their markers manifest into a dense spectral energy known as imprints, lost and confused energy trapped in a place known as the veil—*a dark unforgiving space* between life and the afterworld.

The veil surrounding the old mill contained a combination of spectral energies; individuals who knew they are dead, and those who didn't. Those who know walked through the veil shrouded in a haunting sadness unable to move away from whatever was keeping them tethered to this world. For the others, they were caught in a loop, fated to repeat their final moments over and over unaware their life had ended.

She could always sense the energy of those who died violent deaths. It was an unstable erratic essence scarred by the dark act that snuffed out their lives. She felt these types of energies all over Brighton Hill because of its violent past, but for some reason, they were always the strongest at the old flour mill. The place seemed to draw these unstable energies toward it, consuming their sorrow and confusion in an attempt, to maintain its own stagnant existence. The abandoned mill seemed to have unwittingly created an unseen pocket in the veil, the energies falling prey to its depths unable to move away from its eerie emptiness, forever caught in the unforgiving space.

Over the years, she had connected with a few of the imprints caught here. Gaining insight into the reason for their inability to leave the veil and helping to release the emotional tether anchoring them to the physical plane. Unfortunately, most were unable to escape the perpetual void that was the veil. Doomed to exist in this space forever. Those were the ones she felt the most empathy toward—an eternity of emptiness and sorrow trapped in an aimless void, unable to escape their final reality.

Pulling up in front of the old mill, she got out of the car, drawing her coat tighter against the bitter wind. The temperature continued to drop as the storm front neared the city.

She scanned the mill's windows; the blackened arched frames staring out expressionless. The mill had always projected an unsettling image, like something sinister, was hiding behind its aging brick walls. With the dark clouds of the storm front overhead and the last of the setting sun igniting its shadows, the image was reinforced.

She lifted her camera and snapped a few photos, moving around the property to get interesting angles and capture the mill's silent baleful presence, highlighted by the dimming landscape. She finished just as the last of the fading sun disappeared, a shiver creeping up her spine as she reached the Jeep.

There was a subtle difference in the air around the mill tonight, it seemed more chaotic than usual. She recognized the different spectral energy as they floated aimlessly around her, imprints of the past caught indefinitely in the fabric of this world, but there was something else. Most of the energy she encountered here belonged to mortal innocents and sometimes those with a darker aura. Tonight, there seemed to be others—imprints manifesting traces of malice, an energy that didn't belong and was somehow disrupting the veil.

Suddenly, her cell phone vibrated, causing her to jump slightly. She got in the Jeep and read the message from Kai notifying her she was already at her house. Quickly, she started the Jeep and drove away from the mill.

As she turned onto the old mill road, she caught a glimpse of the mill's dark silhouette in her rearview mirror. A deafening silence seemed to saturate the night air with trepidation.

Kai was standing in the driveway looking miserable when she pulled up. The snow had started, and it was beginning to come down hard.

"You guys remember I despise snow, right?" She said, following Dane through the front door, wiping her jacket clear of snow. She was not thrilled that this year's girl's weekend revolved around winter activities. Ski weekends were one thing but hiking in the snow.

"I hate being cold, I look terrible in hats, and hypothermia is a real issue in these parts," she grumbled.

Dane laughed and rolled her eyes at her friend as she grabbed the bag she packed this morning, her snowshoes, and some food for Tyson.

"You look cute in hats," she joked. "Anyway, are you forgetting Stevie has an enormous back deck with a fire pit and hot tub? After a couple of bottles of wine, a few hot toddies, and an hour in warm soothing water, you won't even know you are surrounded by snow and ice."

Kai scrunched up her face and shook her head, "I doubt that, but it might make it a little more bearable."

Laughing they headed back outside to load their snow-shoes and bags into the Jeep. She whistled for Tyson who had vanished behind the house. He came bounding out of the dark, covered in snow, shaking excitedly as he reached them, covering Kai's pant legs with the wet flakes.

"It's going to be a long weekend," Kai groaned, getting in the Jeep.

Ten minutes later they were driving up Stevie's long tree-lined driveway that ended at her perfect little log cabin in the woods.

Stevie bought the old cabin years ago, at an estate auction, spending the last few years renovating it. She'd updated the plumbing and electricity, put in new windows and doors, a fireplace, and added an addition that housed a huge master suite and bathroom. She knocked down a wall between the two existing bedrooms and created a new larger bedroom and walk-in closet, which was now Gabby's room. The kitchen update was completed six months ago and boasted gourmet appliances, granite countertops, and a large island for additional counter space.

Stevie's home was beautiful, cozy, inviting, and located in the most tranquil setting at the edge of Braemore Woods. Her breath always caught when she rounded the final corner of the drive and the honey-colored cabin came into view. Regardless of the season or the weather, the sight of the beautiful pine logs highlighted by a lush green backdrop or a pure white snowy landscape always mesmerized her. She also loved Stevie's home because it was so different from her own modern suburban townhouse.

The Christmas lights framing the cabin's roofline and covering the bushes twinkled brilliantly as the snow began to fall harder and the darkness closed in around the cabin. She pulled the Jeep in behind Stevie and Gabby's vehicles and was quickly met by Stevie's dog Diego, who could not contain his excitement. Tyson was equally ecstatic and greeted Diego enthusiastically, the two of them running and playing in the front yard, oblivious to the rest of the world.

"Best friends," Stevie said, as she came out of her house and walked across the deck, motioning to the happy canines romping in the new-fallen snow. She carried two copper mugs in her hand containing a wonderful warm amber liquid that gave off a strong toffee and nutmeg aroma. Offering the concoctions to Kai and Dane she smiled and said, "Welcome to girl's weekend. Come on in, Gabby's in the kitchen."

Dane stood quietly, looking out the large front window at the falling snow, absently playing with the new pendant hanging around her neck; a gift from her friends. As requested, the girls kept her birthday celebration to a minimum. After Marlee and Elyse arrived, they enjoyed an amazing creamy shrimp pesto pasta, birthday cake, and a lot of laughs.

The gift was a surprise, and not one she expected. It was a beautiful silver handcrafted pendant; a long flat rectangle etched with a crescent moon; a small diamond embedded into one of its points. At the bottom, the numbers six and thirteen were engraved—*a symbol of their friendship.*

She looked back at her sleeping friends, who had all succumbed early to the fatigue of the after-dinner snowball fight, the hot tub, and multiple glasses of wine. The house was quiet except for the crackling of the fire, and she was glad for the alone time.

The clicking of the clock was a reminder today was not just another birthday. It was her thirty-first and for witches, it meant the possibility of a second awakening. Most witches never experience one, staying in their first awakening for their entire lives. But for the rare few that do, a second awakening usually means gaining additional powers and abilities and a significant shift in one's destiny. The likelihood of this happening to her was almost nil for she only knew of one witch who had experienced a second awakening in the last century. A coven priestess from Italy, who ten years ago gained the power to give life to plants and crops. Apparently, she travels the world now, helping famine-relief victims.

She glanced at the clock on the wall, it was ten thirty-eight and the witching hour would soon begin. If she was to be gifted with a second awakening and gain any new powers or insight, it would happen before midnight.

She left the snow-encrusted window and tiptoed through her sleeping friends to the large armchair by the fireplace. Curling up in the chair and pulling a blanket over her legs she stared at the clock on the wall, waiting patiently for it to strike twelve.

CHAPTER 5

THE FOG ENSHROUDING HER WAS thick, stifling her breathing and coating her skin with a chilling dampness. It was late. The air was tinged with the unforgiving bitter sting that only existed in the wee hours of the morning.

She was surrounded by trees, their looming shadows evident in the fog. The ground was covered with leaves, brown, withered, and faded from time. They crunched under her feet, the sound rebounding off the dense fog.

She searched for something recognizable in the mist as she continued to walk carefully, her surroundings never seeming to change no matter how far or which direction she ventured. Her senses were useless. She felt lost and confused as the mist pressed in on her.

Somewhere in the distance, she heard a faint sound, an incessant rhythm echoing through the fog. She tried desperately to find the source of the noise, but the fog's thickness masked its direction, and she continued to stumble around aimlessly.

As quickly as it began, the sound ceased, and the fog began to dissipate. Warmth began to spread through her, pushing out the chill. She could feel a strange energy flit through the air as the fog slowly disappeared. As her eyes adjusted, she realized she was standing in the middle of a clearing. In front of her stood a massive tree its bulk wrapped in the silvery light of the moon, a strange energy emanating from it. There was a familiarity with this tree, its strength, and power comforting. A memory flitted carelessly on the edge of her awareness as she stared at its rough bark, its twisted branches, and its full lush canopy. As she tried to grasp it and pull it forward, the memory disappeared into the recesses of her mind.

The wind picked up as the tree began to groan, its branches making the same sound she had heard earlier echoing in the fog. It was a soft whisper that encircled the entire tree and as she approached it intensified.

Instinctively reaching out, she placed her palm gently on the rough bark and closed her eyes, concentrating and letting the tree's energy flow through her. Soon the incessant whispering calmed, revealing a word repeating over and over—a*waken.* She removed her hand and began backing away from the tree as the word reverberated in the surrounding air. Suddenly, a flash of green light exploded from the tree, and she felt herself losing consciousness.

She awoke in a cold sweat and sat bolt upright; the heaviness of the fog still embedded in her skin. As her eyes adjusted to the dimming light cast by the fireplace, she looked at the clock as it ticked drowsily on the wall —*midnight.* She must have fallen asleep.

It was just a dream, she thought as the feeling of disorientation lingered and the erratic whispering echoed faintly in her ears.

She glanced around the room at the other five girls still sleeping soundly. The house was quiet and as her birthday ended, she felt an overwhelming sadness as she realized her secret desire to one day inherit the ancient mythical powers of her father's ancestors was just a silly childhood fantasy. Any chance of myth becoming a reality had just passed with her thirty-first birthday. Feeling a small sense of disillusionment, she curled up in the chair, wrapping the blanket tightly around her.

Closing her eyes, she listened to the fading crackle of the fireplace. As her body slowly succumbed once again to her exhaustion, she felt a slight twinge in the deepest recesses of her mind.

Nine inches of snow had fallen overnight. It was still coming down hard as the girls emerged from the house for their hike. The old gnarled tree in the middle of Braemore Woods had become a special place for them during their thirteen-year friendship. They had hiked to it often and on occasion had spent the weekend camping in the clearing surrounding it. Stevie's idea of hiking up to the tree as part of this year's girls' weekend was less about the adventure and exercise and more about Stevie feeling sentimental about the occasion.

"This should be interesting," Gabby claimed as she clamped on her snowshoes her head motioning toward an exasperated Kai. Her disgust at the snow that had fallen overnight and the steady stream of flakes continuing to fall heavily to the ground was already apparent.

"Are you sure this is a good idea?" She asked pointing at the dark, ominous clouds hanging thick over the forest. "What if we get lost or stuck?"

"Lost!" Dane huffed, shaking her head. "You have hiked to this tree so many times even you should be able to get there and back with your eyes closed. Anyway, the snow won't be as thick or heavy in the forest, the canopy will hold out much of it. You will be fine Kai."

"Come on, let's get a move on," Elyse called from where she stood at the entrance to the forest.

Stevie, grinning mischievously and unable to resist a chance to tease her friend, picked up a snowball and tossed it at Kai. "Suck it up Parker," she yelled. Her aim was perfect, the snowball disintegrated against the back of Kai's head causing everyone to howl with laughter. Kai groaned outwardly once more for emphasis, brushed off the clinging snow, and reluctantly trailed Elyse into the forest. Laughing the rest of the girls followed. The dogs, unaware of the teasing rituals of humans, romped ahead blissfully enjoying their canine shortcomings.

The girls hiked through the gray-lit forest for an hour before they reached the rock outcropping that indicated the opening to the clearing. Several years ago, on the inner side of the rock face, Marlee had written all their names in a circle; a symbol of infinity and never-ending friendship. As they passed the spot where the names were written, Dane noticed the ink had faded slightly and time had melded the names even closer together. Gently she brushed her finger-tips across the writing as she passed.

The clearing was covered with a brilliant array of fallen leaves, their autumn colors forever captured by the cold, frozen in time. The snow could not penetrate the thick canopy, so the clearing was lost in another season. Near the back was the old, enormous, and unusually shaped tree; its thick trunk twisted and its tentacular branches spreading out in every direction. Some reached skyward, others bent awkwardly to the ground, thick limbs skimmed the surface crisscrossing with the large roots that exploded from the earth only to dive back underground a few feet away. Thick green moss carpeted the base of the twisted trunk covering the protruding roots with a vibrant green mat. The moss covering the higher branches was long and thin dangling in clumps from the crooked limbs and swaying gently in the winter air.

The girls settled in around its base, unpacking the lunch they'd brought and opening steaming thermoses of hot chocolate. Tyson and Diego circled the tree's base sniffing and scratching at the ground. Curious, Dane followed them.

This tree was the one in her dream last night, and she was curious as to why. She moved around the massive trunk until she reached the back where a long scar defaced the thick bark. It was about a foot in circumference, the edges of the bark frayed and forming a callus outline around the margins of the scar. The interior was smooth, layers of bark missing, exposing the fine-grained wood underneath.

She placed her palm at the center of the scar, curiosity dictating her movements. The bark began to warm under her touch igniting a slight tingle that vibrated from the trunk's interior. Closing her eyes, she blocked out the sounds in the clearing, concentrating only on the feel of the bark under her hand.

Suddenly, she could hear voices, whispers of a thousand souls, but unlike those encircling the old flour mill, these imprints were from a different past. The whispers were inaudible, but she could feel how time stretched around the spectral voices. These were not ordinary people, their energy was different, it was stronger, more balanced somehow.

The whispers continued to increase in volume as the warmth from the tree intensified. Unexpectedly, a green light flashed through her mind, and she heard a voice whisper—*awaken.*

Recoiling from the tree, she stood trying to catch her breath, the shock vibrating through her bones, as her heart pounded wildly in her chest.

"Dane, are you coming to eat?"

"Yes," she answered, as Stevie came around the left side of the massive trunk.

"What are you doing back here?" She murmured, noting the dogs were sitting quietly, one on either side of Dane.

"Nothing, I was just reminiscing." Forcing a smile, she grabbed Stevie by the arm dragging her back to join the others.

The hike back was uneventful, and the girls made it in record time thanks to Kai, who constantly remind everyone they had not brought provisions and would not last long if the darkening sky caught up to them. Shaking off the remaining snow from their jackets the girls headed into Stevie's house just as dusk began to fall. After an hour in the hot tub and a hot meal, the girls had begged Stevie to perform some Tarot readings.

Dane was amused at how fixated her friends were on the readings and how excited they got with the information Stevie would reveal about their futures. She did not partake in any form of fortune telling performed by a mortal for fun. Witches prided themselves on their ability to gain insight into the future using tarot cards, tea leaves, stones, crystal balls, and other magically infused items but the ancient art of scrying was always practiced with the utmost respect for the hand of fate. Witches perfected their art of divination through years of practice, as well as superior knowledge of their own self, unlike mortals who interpreted the future—inaccurately—with irresponsible abandon. Stevie though had respect for the power divination wielded and for a mortal, she practiced the archaic art very well indeed, which was not surprising considering her heritage.

Stevie—short for Stefania—came from a long line of Romani people known as Roma or gypsies. Both her grandmother and mother are *chovihanis*, herbal healers and fortune-tellers who emigrated from Europe shortly after Stevie was born, to live with her American father in Brighton Hill.

Dane adored Stevie's grandmother or *bunica* as Stevie affectionately called her. She was full of Roma gusto; a robust and domineering woman who spoke her mind and had great influence over Stevie's upbringing. Stevie learned everything she knows about the Romani ways from her grandmother, an extremely superstitious and spiritual individual, grounded in old-world tradition.

Stevie embraced the carefree attitude of the gypsy way, her family culture, and its beliefs integrating it into her modern life. She also maintained a strong metaphysical belief system and for that reason alone, Dane gracefully declined every time Stevie inquired if she wanted a tarot reading. She had no desire to be outed as a witch by a deck of cards.

A few hours later, Dane was finishing up the dinner dishes.

"Are you sure you don't want me to do yours?" She heard Stevie call in her direction.

She shook her head, a smirk spreading across her face. "I think you know the answer to that Stevie," she replied, looking at her over her shoulder.

Stevie laughed and nodded, immediately packing up her tarot cards.

It was almost ten and everyone was tired. As the girls were packing to head home, Stevie went into the kitchen and pulled Dane aside making sure she was out of earshot of the others before speaking.

"Something is going on with Gabby," she whispered.

"What do you mean?"

"She called me a couple of days ago when I was in New York City, it was late, really late."

"What did she want?"

Stevie leaned in closer. "She wanted to know if I was OK."

"Why?"

"Apparently, she had a dream. She was really upset because the dream was about us and it was very similar, to the vision she experienced when she first met us."

She stared at Stevie remembering when they had found Gabby, battered and disoriented stumbling around on County Road 5, thirteen years ago. "The shadow?"

"Yes, only this time we were in the forest, and the shadow was coming in from all sides, surrounding us."

"Did she hear the same voice whispering?"

"Yes, and the same message, *save them.*"

She looked over at Gabby, who was laughing at something Marlee had said. "She's probably just dreaming about the old memory, right?"

"That's what I thought until she admitted she has been having strange dreams for about a week now."

"Strange? In what way," she asked her brow furrowing at Stevie.

"Just images really, vivid images. Places, landscapes, nothing she recognized, although she did say after she woke she was left with a feeling of familiarity like she should know something about them."

"Do you think she's remembering?"

Stevie hesitated. "Her past?"

She nodded.

"Maybe," Stevie said, quickly ending the conversation as she saw Gabby moving toward them.

CHAPTER 6

G ABBY YAWNED AS SHE PUT the key in the lock and
opened the front door of her store. She didn't
get much sleep last night, and she felt like she
might be coming down with something.

Banging the snow from her boots she entered the store
and turned on the lights. City workers were still fighting to
plow the streets and sidewalks clear of the twenty-six inches
the storm had dropped over the past two days. It had eventually let up overnight and now only scattered snow showers
were in the forecast. The downtown was quiet. She didn't
expect many customers today so decided it would be a good
time to start her year-end inventory.

As she passed the large gilt-framed mirror hanging
behind the front counter, she caught sight of herself, stopping a moment to gaze at her reflection, piercing blue
eyes staring back. Her platinum blond shoulder-length
bob was razor cut, hanging in jagged pieces around her
pale face. The black streak that ran from her part down
the front left side was an anomaly, a fluke in her genes but

now highlighted the dark circles forming under her eyes. Dismissing the reflection, she settled onto the stool behind the front counter, sipped her coffee and opened the inventory ledger. There were no sounds filtering in from the street outside as the storm suffocated the entire city, leaving behind an eerie quiet. It was a quiet she knew well.

She could smell the coldness in the air as its chill embedded itself in her skin. The earth was damp beneath her fingertips as she lay there quietly, waiting, listening. Slowly, she opened her eyes squinting against the light evading the trees, their uppermost leaves swaying lazily back and forth.

She could see the blue-gray of the sky as it peeked through the canopy. Snow falling languidly toward her, fluttering slightly as the breeze caught its flakes. The eerie quiet of this place shrouded her in its emptiness as she closed her eyes and waited—a single tear sliding silently down her cheek to the cold earth below.

The pain started with her toes and worked its way up her legs, into her lower back, across her abdomen and up through her shoulders, ending with an explosion inside her head. Letting out a violent scream, she convulsed, as the pain tormented her entire body with vicious spasms. She screamed for what seemed like an eternity until the pain subsided to a dull ache and her voice and body went numb.

Hesitantly, she opened her eyes, squinting against the dull daylight. Tears blurred her vision as she turned her head painfully to the side. The forest floor was a beautiful rich brown, delicately covered in places with a blanket of newly fallen snow. Pine needles and leaves were piled up at the trunks of the trees from where they had fallen.

She moved tentatively, gradually managing to get her broken body into a sitting position without passing out. Her breath came in shallow gasps as she forced her body to move. After a few minutes, she pulled herself onto her knees and painfully got to her feet, her breathing labored, as she surveyed the area. She was surrounded by tall trees, which seemed to stretch in each direction indefinitely. She had no sense of direction, no idea where to go. Her mind was blank, no memory of where she was, how she got here —*or who she was!*

Steadying herself, she picked a direction and started walking, agonizing pain surging through her body with each step. After what seemed like an eternity she heard the faint hum of engines, cars on a road somewhere up ahead. She slowly made her way to the edge of the forest where the dense trees opened into a small clearing. Beyond she could make out the pale gray of an asphalt road.

With what little strength she had left, she forced her bruised and battered body to the edge of the road. She heard the roar of an engine and saw the gleam of a bumper as the car got closer, turning into the curve in the road up ahead. Waiting, she willed herself not to submit to the blackness desperately fighting to take hold. As the car finished rounding the corner she painfully threw herself into its path, facing the oncoming vehicle.

The car raced towards her until suddenly, there was a squeal of tires on the pavement as the brakes locked and the car screeched to a halt just feet from where she stood. She collapsed onto the asphalt in a bleeding heap, all her energy spent. Through the dark fog that had begun to overtake her consciousness, she heard car doors slamming, footsteps running toward her, and voices speaking to each other in panicked tones.

"Oh, shit I almost hit her, where the hell did she come from?"

"I don't know, but we need to get her to a hospital. She looks to be in pretty bad shape."

She could hear their voices, but the warmth of the pavement was comforting. All she wanted to do was sleep.

"Stay with me," she heard a voice say, "help is on the way."

Her eyes fluttered open fighting to find the source of the voice. As her vision cleared she saw them, two young women, looking anxiously down at her. One was kneeling beside her the other was pacing frantically behind her, speaking to someone on a cell phone.

The pain wracking her body began to pull her once again into unconsciousness, but this time she welcomed it. Through the oncoming haze, she saw something surrounding the girls—a dark, smoky shadow slithering unnoticed around them. Suddenly, an eerie silence fell over the area and the shadow began to close in, its wisps reaching out to touch them. She wanted to call out, to warn them, but she was unable, her body numb and unresponsive, the haze pulling her down into darkness. As she faded into oblivion, she heard a whisper flutter through her mind, *save them.*

She stood and walked to the front window. The wind had picked up, and the snow was beginning to drift, small gusts swirling through the empty streets. That memory was one Gabby would never forget, for it was her first and had been haunting her for thirteen years.

She had no memory prior to that day. Her past was a mystery, summed up in an inch-thick file marked 'Jane Doe' and stuffed in the cold case archives of the Brighton Hill Police Department. If it hadn't been for Stevie and Dane finding her, she may not even be alive. She often thought about that fateful day and how all her friends, strangers back then, had helped her.

In the beginning, it had been terrifying, but they were always there. Supporting her, giving encouragement, even being strong for her when she felt weak and lost. As the years passed, she gained confidence in her new identity. She had embraced her new life as Gabby Winters, eventually developing and identifying with this new person. But her missing past was always with her, and she wondered if the dreams she had been having lately could be lost memories resurfacing.

The dreams had started about a week after Stevie had left for New York City on assignment. At first, they were just brief images of places and landscapes, a view of some-where she did not recognize. There was nothing extraordinary about these landscapes, just unknown places, which was why she wondered if maybe she was dreaming about her lost past. Then the dreams started to change, the landscapes more imaginary, the imagery leaving her with a feeling of recognition every time she woke up. It was unset-tling, but nothing compared to the feeling of fear she felt after the last dream. The image of Stevie and Dane walking through a forest and suddenly being surrounded by a menacing dark, shadowy fog had caused her such anxiety she had called Stevie immediately to see if she was OK. There was something about the dream. How it reminded her of the shadow she had seen surrounding them thirteen years ago. It had left her with a sinking sensation that something bad was going to happen. A feeling she hadn't yet been able to shake.

CHAPTER 7

THE RED GLOW IN THE dark room amplified the black and white images hanging on a clothesline at the back of the room. She used the tongs to move the white paper, floating aimlessly in the developer tray on the bench, until an image began to appear. Dipping the new print into the stop bath and the fixer trays she hung it with the others, standing back and studying the haunting photos of the old flour mill.

It had been a while since Dane had used film as she mostly shot in digital these days. But with the entire campaign based on the historic essence of Brighton Hill, she wanted the old mill's story to be captured perfectly. She knew the grain and limited tone of film would enhance the haunting emptiness that emanated from the mill in a way the crisp clearness of digital couldn't.

She stood back and studied the images. There was something different about the one she had just developed. The image seemed to be blurred, a small section of the mill distorted. Had her lens been dirty? A smudge that had shown up on the image.

Moving in closer and picking up her magnifying glass, she focused in on the distorted part of the image. It was not a smudge but rather an outline of something, something that seemed to be standing right in front of the mill, something not visible to the naked eye. She felt a chill run down her spine as she continued to inspect the image, moving the magnifying glass back and forth across the photo.

The mill itself was darker in this image, its outline highlighted by a faint shadow encasing the entire structure. She inspected a few more of the images but none of them contained the blur or the faint shadow that appeared in this one image. Checking the darkroom clock, she flipped off the lights and left the room, determined to get to the mill before dusk.

"Tyson, I won't be long," she said grabbing her coat and heading out the front door, the bullmastiff lifting his head only briefly before going back to sleep.

As she drove toward the old mill road, she felt a chill, not in reaction to the cold, but one more foreboding. There was something wrong with the mill's energy, she had felt it two days ago when she had taken those pictures and now it was confirmed by the strange distortions that had shown up in one of those photos. Something was causing the mill's unique energy distress, and she needed to discover what.

Driving a little faster she arrived at the mill's entrance just as the sun was disappearing behind the horizon. She turned into the driveway, the wrought-iron entrance gates were rusty but stood open, a gaping hole beckoning her in. One had fallen from its hinges and leaned at an odd angle against the brick column to which it was once attached, the other creaked loudly in the wind, its rust-covered hinges screeching as it moved.

She drove slowly down the unkempt drive, her Jeep shifting back and forth as the wheels dug into the mud and sunk into the numerous potholes littering the lane.

The mill loomed up in front of her, a hulking shadow waiting in the waning twilight, its worn brick crumbling in places where the mortar had disintegrated or cracked. There were no streetlights or houses on this part of the old mill road and in the fading light, with only the moon's reflection casting a dim glow on its facade, the mill looked more ominous than usual.

Only its outline was visible in the fading light. A solitary smokestack protruded above the mill's roof, its long, dark mass casting a menacing silhouette in the sky. In the dying twilight, the mill looked dejected, its neglected appearance causing a pang of empathy in her as she pulled up to the loading dock and parked.

The air surrounding the mill was erratic, and she was having a difficult time identifying any of the imprints moving through its space. Their energy caught in an odd, unbalanced atmosphere. Exiting the Jeep, she opened the back and grabbed a flashlight from her emergency kit. The wind had picked up and its chill swirled around her, howling as it raced in and out of the mill's broken windows. The abandoned building groaned in displeasure as a loose shutter banged against the exterior. Everything about the mill's energy was wrong. There was a mix of panic and confusion in the air, permeating the menacing chill being spread by the oncoming night.

She turned on the flashlight, pointing its beam toward the massive structure and sweeping it back and forth. She could sense something strange floating just below the mill's surface, an unknown energy echoing its displeasure at her presence. Staring up at the old mill she shuddered as the sweeping motion of the flashlight's beam illuminated its worn facade. Most of the windows had been broken years ago, the vacant black holes now just lifeless unseeing eyes staring blankly out from the dilapidated building. With a slight hesitation, she walked cautiously to the side entry door, hoping the city had not fixed the lock since some teenagers had broken in a few months back.

As she neared the door, the air changed. She stopped as she was suddenly encased in an eerie silence that hung directly over the mill. A suffocating blanket wrapping itself tightly around the exterior. The wind died down, and she realized there were no longer any sounds in the evening sky, just an uneasy nothingness. She searched for signs of the erratic energy that pulled her here. Pushing her empathic senses further up and out into the night sky, but it too was gone. She could feel the energy of the dead caught in the veil. Their imprints were constantly moving, surrounding the mill, but they were infused with a restlessness—a distracted flow that distorted their movement and interrupted it somehow. The fear and confusion she felt saturating the air moments before were emanating from them, something was causing them distress.

Dark magic, she thought, moving slowly to the side door.

The large padlock was still broken. The door stood slightly ajar. She pushed it open and was immediately assaulted by a damp, musty scent wafting out from the old mill's stagnant interior. Covering her mouth and nose with one hand she pointed the beam of her flashlight into the dense darkness, sweeping the light back and forth.

Nothing greeted her but emptiness.

Taking a deep breath of the chilly but clean outside air she slowly entered the darkness of the mill's interior ignoring the unsettling caution prickling her skin.

Her eyes adjusted quickly to the dimness inside the mill, but the musty stale heaviness in the air continued to assault her nostrils. Breathing through her mouth, she continued to walk toward the back of the building where she knew the back stairs leading to the basement, were located. Luckily, she had done a photo shoot here a few years back and was vaguely familiar with the layout, making walking around the abandoned building at night a little less daunting.

Moving as quickly as she dared, she wound her way around grinders and millstones until she reached the stairs, careful not to trip on any of the debris that lay scattered over the concrete floor. The mechanisms running the exterior water wheel protruded from the wall just before the stairs, and she almost collided with them as she made her way through the darkened warehouse.

Cautiously, she descended the rickety wooden steps into the dank below, the pull of a strange energy getting stronger with each step.

The back steps led to a small storage area still full of old wooden packing crates stamped on the side with THE GRISTMILL FLOUR CO. A haunting reminder of the mill's once vibrant past as the industry that built Brighton Hill. The air down here was dusty and heavy, and Dane found it difficult to breathe. But underneath the lack of freshness, she could smell something that did not belong. There was a faint smell of rotten eggs and charred wood, seeping out from somewhere up ahead.

Moving past the dusty crates she headed to a small door

located at the far end of the room, the peculiar smell intensifying and making her gag as she approached. Pushing open the door she recoiled at the stink radiating from inside. The small room was filled with the stench of decay, a stagnant, petrified odor flooding its stifling aroma outward through the now open door. A mustiness seeped out of the shadows, and she shivered as it too carried the stench of dirt and decay. Covering her nose and mouth again with her gloved hand, she entered the damp room.

Other than a small table there was nothing else in the room except a dozen or so small white candles littered throughout the empty space. She picked one up smelling the wick.

Sulfur, she thought, *would explain the rotten egg smell.*

She swung her flashlight around the room, checking every corner. There were no windows or doors other than the one she had entered through and the floor was dirt, caked and cracking from years of neglect. She moved to the small table, shining the beam on its surface. There, burned into the top, was a pentacle, the odor of charred wood still floating in the surrounding air. It was rudimentary, crooked and asymmetrical. It looked as if it had been produced by a child in a hurry. As she moved the flashlight beam closer, she could make out something, a fine powdery substance, caught in the burn pattern. Wiping her index finger through the dust she lifted it to her nose, the smell of rotting eggs wafting in her nostrils.

There seemed to be sulfur all over this room, but why? Sulfur was normally used for protection and purification spells; spells that included countering magic or banishing unwanted spirits or entities.

What was this room being used for?

Someone had been here recently, she could sense the tendrils of magic that lingered, embedded in the surfaces of the room. The magic essence was subtle, but she could feel it. Its energy staining the hot dense air with its hollow mark. There wasn't enough residual left for her to try to reveal the nature of the source with her own magic, but the hollow stain that remained could only mean one thing—it was tainted with dark magic.

Turning the beam to the other side of the room, she noticed part of the dirt floor behind the door looked disturbed. She crouched down to get a closer look at the strange symbol had been drawn into the dirt floor. It was an odd shape and not something she recognized. It looked like a sigil the way the lines sloped, crossed and intertwined, but not one she was familiar with.

Removing her cell phone from her coat pocket she took a picture of it. Walking back to the small table she took a shot of the charred pentacle as well, and then left the small, dank room.

Hurrying through the dark building, she reached the side door, taking a deep cleansing breath as she exited. The night sky had quieted, the imprints seemed calmer. She sensed a fragile stability remained within the veil, but everything seemed to be almost back to normal. She was sure now someone was using the abandoned mill for their own purpose and it was somehow causing a tilt in the energy of the dead surrounding it even if only temporarily.

As she took another deep breath of the cool night air, she felt a prickle creep up the back of her neck—*someone was watching!* Her eyes searched the dark property but all she could make out were the shadowy silhouettes of the mill's smaller storage buildings.

Under the watchful stare of unseen eyes, she walked quickly to her Jeep, started the engine, and drove away from the abandoned mill. Glancing back in the rearview mirror she thought she saw a glint in an upstairs window. Slamming on the brakes she quickly turned around, nothing but blackness greeted her, the window was as dark as the rest of the mill's gaping holes.

A shiver ran down her spine as the clammy hollowness of the mill seemed to reach across the field, saturating the night air with a trepidation that seemed to follow her as she drove away.

On the drive home, she thought about the remnants of magic she had felt in that room. The white candles anointed with sulfur and the different symbols carved into two of the room's surfaces. It had a ritualistic feel and Dane was convinced that the redhead who just appeared in town was somehow involved. The emptiness of the magical essence clinging to the air in the basement was a characteristic of cursed magic, and she was sure that essence belonged to a dark witch.

The redhead watched from the mill's darkened window as the black Wrangler drove away. She was not surprised the witch showed up at the mill for she knew sooner or later she would figure it out. Blocking her aura from the witch was exhausting but necessary. Unfortunately, it was much more difficult concealing the essence of the magic she'd been practicing, and she knew she was at risk of being detected.

Thankfully, the damn witches' aura was so strong she could smell her stench coming and had been able to get out of the basement room before she entered. If she'd been caught there her plans might have been compromised, as she was still unable to determine what abilities the witch had and how powerful she was. She'd made the mistake before of taking on a witch more powerful than she and barely made it out alive, she would not make that mistake twice.

The noise her heels made on the old wooden planks echoed through the abandoned space as she walked through the upstairs rooms. She'd searched for years to find the right magical bloodline. Enduring unspeakable pain because of what the witch's ancestors had done to hers. Now that she'd found her, the one she'd been seeking for so long, she was going to enjoy her revenge.

CHAPTER 8

THE SUN BLAZING ITS EARLY morning rays through the crack in her bedroom curtains woke Dane minutes before the alarm. Tyson snored loudly beside her, barely moving as she got out of bed and headed to the bathroom. She had decided after the strange dream and her peculiar experience at the tree she would snowshoe back up to the clearing. Her parents were arriving tomorrow morning so today was the only free time she had.

After her shower, she dressed, packed the last of her items into her backpack and double-checked she had everything she would require. She wanted to revisit her connection to the tree without any additional distractions, so she had not told any of her friends about her plans. Since it was Tuesday, they were all working except for Stevie. She didn't expect anyone to notice her missing for a few hours.

She had spoken to her parents last night. As expected they had asked her about her birthday eve, subtly referring to the witching hour and inquiring whether there were any signs she had experienced a second awakening. She assured them her thirty-first birthday was nothing but ordinary, deciding not to tell them about the strange dream or her experience at the tree until she could make more sense of what it meant.

Dane carefully made her way past the rock cropping. The excessive snow that had fallen over the weekend made it difficult to traverse the narrow passageway leading into the clearing. Pulling Tyson gently along by his leash she managed to maneuver her way past the massive drift attempting to block her path.

The thick canopy that encircled the clearing had kept most of the snow out, only a dusting scattered across the bright mosaic created by the fallen leaves. A silence pulsated through the clearing as the sun that broke through the trees trickled down in bright beams. Strands of its rays surrounding the old misshapen tree, washing the forest floor in a brilliant warm glow.

She walked over to the trunk and took off her backpack, placing it on the ground as she bent down to clip off her snowshoes and brush the snow from her pants. Opening the backpack, she pulled out her compass, noting that the tree stood at north.

Taking out a small black cloth she laid it at the base of the trunk where a large root pushed up aggressively from the ground, arching into the air slightly before disappearing once again into the earth. She needed a portion of the tree inside the protective circle and the arch in this root would allow her to close the circle beneath it.

Carefully, she removed the remaining items laying them

gently on the cloth in a specific order. When she finished, she sat down facing the tree. Calling Tyson, she had him lay behind her instructing him to stay. His massive frame curled up tightly, his back touching hers, his entire body relaxing under her calm, confident energy. Her intent was to use her powers to connect to any magical essence that existed in this space or within the tree, and she wanted to ensure that Tyson was inside the protective circle with her when she cast it.

Picking up her athame she carved a wide circle around them in the ground, ensuring that it included her altar and a portion of the tree root. She placed small votive candles at each of the cardinal points representing north, south, east and west—*the Watchtowers*. Selecting the small silver jar from the items on her cloth she opened the lid and using her fingertips spread the prepared salt mixture inside the dirt trench she had just created. Lighting each votive as she passed it. To cleanse the protective circle, she sprinkled drops of witch hazel at the cardinal points and spritzed salt-water throughout the air with the tips of her fingers. When the circle was ready, she lit the sage bundle waving it above her head, the smoke languidly drifting through the cool air, cleansing the space and removing negative energy.

Closing her eyes, she recited the protection spell she had written earlier that morning, the incantation echoing in the quiet clearing.

Thrice around the circle's round.
Sink all evil into the ground
A magic circle pure of light
Banishing that intent on harm or fright
And cleanse this circle to make it sound

Thrice around the circle 'til bound.

The salt circle began to glow as a pale white light crept slowly from the circle's edge. It continued upward and inward until it resembled a sphere surrounding Dane and Tyson in a protective bubble.

Encapsulated in the protective space she reached for the thermos and unscrewed the lid, steam rising from the hot liquid inside.

Tranquil Tea—she thought, her nose crinkling at the odd aroma that rose from the open thermos.

This tea was an old family recipe handed down through the Watt's family for centuries. It was a mystic tea, a natural concoction that had sedative-like abilities. The putrid aroma was just one of its many unappealing qualities; it also had a tart bitter flavor that left an unpleasant aftertaste in the back of one's throat. These, fortunately, were greatly outweighed by its one redeeming quality—its hallucinogenic properties. Many of the seers and healers in her family used it to calm their minds and open their inner eye to the emotions and energy of others and to connect with the metaphysical energies that pulsated in the fabric of the universe. It was a way for a witch to focus her conscious mind on a different plane and to bring her subconscious closer to awareness.

She was hoping that it would clear her mind enough to allow anything magical about this tree or this clearing to freely enter her mind while in a conscious state.

It only took a few minutes before she felt the familiar euphoria; a naturally induced lethargic feeling that cocooned her entire body in a warm, hazy embrace. As she drifted slowly into a peaceful calm, she reached out and laid one hand on the tree root inside the protective circle and the other on the bare ground focusing intently on the feel of the rough bark and the cold earth beneath her palms. Each of her senses instinctively intensified as every fiber in her being became aware of the tree's energy, a vibrant pulse running through its bark.

As the effects of the tea continued to surge through her blood embracing her in a magical intoxication, she could feel the tree respond. A shudder rippled under its bark as it awakened, shaking off the vestiges of an eternal slumber. The hand resting on the tree's root began to tingle, a warm vibration that burrowed into her palm as the haze lifted from her mind and the tree's energy was revealed.

First, a chorus of whispers entered her mind; spectral energy that seemed to be marked by a different time and place. She could sense an extraordinary power, a strength that pulsated around them. Images began to appear—vast landscapes of lush green forests, magnificent waterfalls, and dusty barren rocks. Breathtakingly beautiful landscapes that did not mimic any in her memory. As the images faded from her mind, they were replaced with a strange symbol— a silver dagger, its blade encircled by a green sphere of energy. The image hovered momentarily as if burning itself into her memory and then it slowly disappeared until nothing, but blackness and a deafening silence remained.

She could still feel the tree's energy as it flowed through the root into her hand, but the tea was wearing off, and she was losing the connection. Just as she felt her heightened awareness slipping away she heard a solitary whisper —*awaken*.

Dane's eyes flew open as her hand jerked away from the tree root, unnerved by the intimacy that had accompanied the whisper. Her abrupt reaction to the voice left her gasping for breath. She still sat safely inside the protective circle, and she was alone in the clearing, so where had the voice come from? She remained still for a few more minutes, calming her mind and allowing her breathing to steady as her body continued to flush the remaining hallucinogenic properties from her system.

Dane could feel Tyson's warm body pressed up against her back, his rhythmic breathing helping to calm her. Pulling in one last deep breath of the cold afternoon air, she carefully opened the protective circle, released Tyson from his spot, and thanked the goddess for her protection.

Packing up her belongings, she placed the backpack against the base of the tree beside her snowshoes, stepping back to inspect the old tree. Her head tilted slightly to the side and her eyes narrowed as she studied it carefully. The tree seemed more vibrant than it had on the weekend, its canopy greener, its bark rougher, the moss that clung to its surface seemed to move slightly, a faint up and down movement as if it were breathing. She walked a slow circle around the tree, inspecting its trunk and low hanging branches, stopping when she reached the scar in the back that marred its thick surface. Her fingers traveled leisurely over the blemish, a tingle following their path. Frowning, she backed away from the tree, shaking her head of the remaining fog that still clung to her mind.

Strange, she thought.

Looking around for Tyson she found him nosing and pawing the ground at the side of the tree's trunk. Curious, as to what had caught his attention, she quietly moved closer to him. His tail was stiff, the hair on his back raised, and he expelled a low whimper with every swipe of his paw.

The ground he was intent on digging up was a small patch of dark soil at the base of the tree. Nestled in between two thick roots and partially concealed by the bright green ground cover—small white flowers still flourishing in the frigid winter months. She knew of only one moss that could withstand cold temperatures and flowered year-round— Irish Guardian moss, but it was normally only found on the peaks of mountains in Europe.

"What's wrong buddy?" She asked watching him snort a few times into the ground before frantically clawing at the soil. Grabbing his collar and pushing him gently away from the spot, she knelt on the ground and placed her hands on the freshly disturbed earth, surprised by the warmth that she felt emanating from the soil. Tyson was panting, leaning over her shoulder, a small whine coming from his lips as he pressed them closer to her ear in reassurance.

Ignoring him she brushed off the remaining loose dirt and frozen leaves revealing the surface of a flat stone buried beneath the soil. She removed the flashlight from her coat pocket and shined the beam on the stone's face. Etched into the surface was a symbol. At first glance, it looked like a star with ten points but as she looked closer, she saw that it was two pentacles, a smaller one overlapping a large one. Around the edges were etchings, a series of arching lines and dots that reminded her of a glyph or rune. She took a picture of the face of the rock with her phone and quickly covered it back up, making a mental note as to its location.

As she stood, a strong breeze blew through the clearing and the tree's limbs creaked and groaned as they shuddered in its wake. A strange feeling swelled inside her. She could feel the tree's essence deep in her mind, the images and whispering echoing somewhere in her memory as a strange feeling of knowing flooded her senses.

Grabbing her backpack and snowshoes she ran from the clearing, with Tyson on her heels. As she disappeared around the rock cut the breeze faded and an eerie silence fell over the clearing as the old tree began to glow.

CHAPTER 9

THE REDHEAD SNEERED AS SHE saw the witch across the street. Her temper flared as the breeze carried her stench across the pavement. The very sight of her caused a rush of anger to flood over her, but she remained calm. She had to. If she lost control for even a minute, all she had planned could be ruined.

She knew the witch had spotted her, so she hurried her step. She was not interested in speaking with her nor having a confrontation. There would come a time when she would make the witch aware of their fateful connection but now was not that time. Now was the time to observe, to study, to find out what she could, and keep her distance. To concentrate only on what she must do to ensure that the witch got what she deserved.

She increased her speed as she felt the witch start to track her. Sneering once again she quickly darted around the corner and disappeared.

The moment Dane got home she picked up the phone, absently dialing her parent's number and listening to the monotone ringing at the other end.

"Hello," her mother said, her voice soothing her frayed nerves even through the phone.

"Hi mom," she sighed, "Do you have a minute?"

"Oh, hi Dane, of course, I do sweetie, what is it?"

She spent the next ten minutes filling her mom in on everything that had happened in the past few days—the dream, the experiences with the tree, the mysterious red-haired woman, and the strange energy that seemed to be altering the imprints surrounding the old flour mill.

"The dream seems prophetic Dane, are you sure that nothing happened on your thirty-first birthday? You know during the witching hour?" Ella Watts asked.

"I'm sure mom, it was uneventful. I had a dream that's it."

"Well this connection you seem to have with this tree in the woods shouldn't be ignored, your empathic abilities seem to be sensitive to it, but it's the voice that you keep hearing that causes me some concern. Your abilities only allow you to feel energy and emotions, it does not allow you to hear voices. What if there is someone else out there with your father's power?"

Dane's father, Nathan Callan, was known to Celtic witches as a *Timestopper;* a witch who possesses the power to stop and move time, both in the real world and in an individual's mind. It was an ancient form of ocular telepathy and a unique gift, which had, for decades been instrumental in erasing the memory of any mortal who accidentally witnessed magic being performed.

Her father was the only Timestopper left in the modern

world and the only one in his family history that had ever possessed the antiquated power. She had not developed any powers mimicking her father's ability but her telekinesis, also an antiquated and rare power, was considered an ability that came from the realm of space and time manipulation.

Her father's power was unique as it allowed his conscious mind to inhabit the space between the memories and thoughts of an individual, undetected. A power that for many was against the witch's creed for it influenced the free will of an individual. Her father was very aware of this negative assessment of his abilities and therefore only used them if absolutely necessary.

Although her father's gift was powerful, it was limited, his ability in the real world could only stop and move time back a few minutes. When he entered someone's mind he could only see and replace memories that were tainted by magic. He did not have the power to converse with someone inside their head, nor could he invade someone's REM sleep.

If her mother's concerns were valid and the voice she had heard whispering *awaken,* was real and not just part of the dream, it was not a Timestopper, but someone who possessed a very powerful verbal telepathy. A magic that had been extinct from the modern world for hundreds of generations.

Changing the subject, she asked her mom about the red-head and the strange dark energy she could sense hovering around the edges of the veil. "I feel like they are connected."

"It seems likely, tell me again what happened when you ran into her today."

"I was coming out of the Java Bean Market and I saw her across the street, she was exiting the hardware store carrying two large brown paper bags. I was curious, so I followed her until she vanished around a corner and disappeared. I was left with that uneasy sensation but this time something was different, I could feel the essence of dark magic floating in the surrounding air. She has to be a dark witch, right?"

"I am not sure Dane, dark witches are extremely rare, it is more likely she is a pure witch that has lost her way. Whatever the case may be, one thing is definite, she is using some very strong magic to cloak her aura from you. Please be careful, if this woman is using dark magic, only trouble will follow her."

"I will. Can you show something to dad for me?" She asked "It's a photo of some sort of symbol or insignia. It looks like a pentacle with a smaller pentacle on top encircled with glyphs or runes. I believe it is of Celtic origin, but I am not sure. I'm hoping Dad might have some insight."

"Of course, sweetie. Text me a picture and I will have your dad look at it when he gets home. He's working late tonight at the hospital but should be home in a few hours."

"I will mom, see you tomorrow." She thanked her mother and said goodnight, texting her the picture the moment she hung up.

She took Tyson for a long walk, the cold night air soothing her troubled mind. After unpacking her backpack, she started a load of laundry, vacuumed the house, put fresh sheets on the guest bed, and washed the dishes. As she dried them she thought again about the images she had seen during her vision at the tree and the strange sense of knowing that seemed to filter through her entire being afterward.

Suddenly, a flash of green light exploded in her head. She could hear the glass break as it fell from her hands, but she was powerless to do anything about it as the silver dagger once again appeared in her mind. Just as suddenly, an image of the old gnarled tree in the middle of Braemore Woods appeared and a strong, deep voice echoed in her head—*awaken!*

She stood unmoving, as the voice faded from her mind. Gasping for breath she reeled from the loss of energy the vision had sapped from her. She looked down at the shattered glass around her feet, completely unnerved by what just happened. Invoking a vision through divination is one thing but having one naturally was a power that only seers possessed; witches with the gift of premonition.

Hearing a low whine behind her she turned to see Tyson staring at her, his body rigid. Concerned about the confusion she could see in his eyes she reached down to reassure him that everything was OK. He gently licked her hand nibbling on her fingertips like he used to do when she first rescued him. It was a quirk that he exhibited when he was unsure about something, a way to expel nervous energy, but he hadn't done it in years. She crouched down until they were level. Gently she took his face in her hands and kissed the top of his nose.

"I'm OK, Ty," she whispered softly in his ear noting his tail wag slightly in response.

She carefully cleaned up the broken glass, acutely aware of the strange sensation that pumped through her veins.

Making a cup of hot tea she curled up in bed, mentally and physically exhausted from the visions she had experienced today. Just as she was falling into a much-needed sleep she was aroused by the ping of her phone, notifying her of an incoming text. Yawning, she picked it up and looked at the sender, it was her father. His text said that he didn't recognize the symbol, but one of the glyphs looked familiar.

Glancing at the bedside clock she saw that it was after midnight. She thought briefly about texting her father back but abandoned the idea quickly. Exhausted, she didn't want to think any more about it tonight. She would find out what her father had to say in the morning.

Putting her phone down and snuggling in beside a snoring Tyson she watched dreamily as the room filled with a silvery glow, the moonlight finding its way through the large bank of windows on the far side of the bedroom.

CHAPTER 10

I T WAS JUST PAST ELEVEN-THIRTY in the morning when her parents walked through the front door, her father carried a small intricately carved wooden chest.

Dane looked at him quizzically. "Did you meet a pirate on your way here, dad?"

"Funny girl," he said, smirking as he laid the chest on the ground in the living room. She hugged both her parents, allowing Tyson to get his share of attention before bringing out the coffee and muffins she had made this morning.

"So, mom told you everything?"

"Yes, she did." Her father nodded, taking a sip of his coffee as a strange look passed between him and her mother.

"And does any of it make any sense to you?" She questioned, hoping he would have some answers. Her father's side of the family was much more versed in the darker side of magic.

Celtic history was full of references to creatures that

were more malevolent than nice; fae, goblins, and water horses were all portrayed as devilish in Celtic lore. Legends also depicted the Druid priests as devil worshipers who used the power of nature in their practice, but her father believed that this negative stigma was untrue and that the Druids were in fact, a powerful force for good.

"Maybe," he said hesitantly, pointing toward the carved wooden chest at his feet.

"What is it, dad?"

"It belonged to your grandfather," he explained, a sadness coating his voice as he spoke of his late father. "I only opened it briefly at the time and didn't think it contained anything of importance, so I put it in the attic with the rest of his belongings. It was mostly old papers, family genealogy, spells, some sketches and quite frankly I had forgotten about it until last night when your mother showed me the picture you sent. Not the symbol itself but one of the runes, it was something I had seen before."

"You know what it is?" She asked excitedly.

"No, but maybe this chest will help you find an answer," he said slowly turning the chest toward her so that the front side of it faced her.

Her eyes swept over the dark, grainy, mahogany wood. Its surface was worn and scratched but the intricate carvings on its exterior highlighted the craftsmanship. The carvings depicted a multitude of Celtic knotwork and symbols; triquetra's, crosses, endless knots, and triple spirals, all contained in a delicate border that reminded her of a mass of tangled ivy and thorns. As her eyes continued to take in the beauty of the wooden chest, she noticed the flat brass lock on the front. It was simple, a standard latch lock with a large brass padlock securing it, but it was what was above the lock that caught her eye.

Engraved into the brass panel was one of the glyphs from the symbol that she had sent her father. The symbol that had been etched into the rock at the base of the old tree.

She stared at the chest a few seconds longer and then gazed up at her parents, both anxiously waiting for her reaction. "What does it mean?"

Her father took a piece of paper out of his pocket. "I believe it is a character that represents the earth element," he said handing her the paper.

She looked at the crudely drawn image, it was the same as the one engraved above the lock—a crescent moon with two dots inside its arc. Just below the drawing, in her grandfather's handwriting was written, *earth*.

"What's in the chest dad?"

"After your mother showed me the picture you sent her, I remembered where I had seen that glyph. I went to the attic and re-opened the trunk. That paper was sitting on top. I didn't really go through it when my father died, so I took a better look this morning."

"What is it, dad? What did you find?" She stammered.

Nathan Callan reached into his pocket and pulled out a tattered envelope which he handed to Dane. "This used to be taped to the inside lid, it must have fallen off at some point, so I didn't see it when I opened the chest the first time."

She stared at the back of the envelope. It was firmly sealed, but some corners were bent, and a slight fraying had damaged one edge. Discoloration and smudges marred the envelope's crisp whiteness, the fragile paper unable to hide its age. Turning over the envelope she saw her name, clearly written in black ink in her grandfather's handwriting. There was a date scrawled in the top right-hand corner—her birthdate. Carefully, she opened the envelope, anxious to see what was inside. Pulling out a note card, she slowly read the words her grandfather had written thirty-one years ago. As the last word crossed her vision, she took a deep calming breath and read it again.

The first-born daughter of the Callan lineage has been born today—to my son. Never in our history has a female child been born first to a Callan male for we are a lineage of male-dominated magic. Our destiny has now taken on a new direction. My granddaughter's birth represents the beginning of the end—the ancient Warlician prophecy, one that our clan thought legend for centuries, has been revealed as truth. My own path, forged decades ago, led me toward this new beginning and now that it is upon us, I must guide her to her true destiny, whatever that destiny is to become.

Nathan Callan stood up and came over to where his daughter sat on the sofa, taking her hand in his. She handed the note card to him watching silently as he read it quickly and then handed it back.

"What can you tell me about this prophecy that grandfather speaks of," she asked.

She could feel her father tense as he thought about the words on the note card pausing only for a moment before he spoke. "You know for centuries my family has been a male-dominated lineage with very few females being born into it, but what you may not know is that there has never been, a female born first to a Callan male. You Dane, ARE the first."

"OK, so kind of odd but do you really think it has any significance?" She said, waving the note card around.

"Apparently, your grandfather thought so." Her father's brow furrowed as he tried to bring the old memories forward. "The bedtime stories I told you as a child Dane, were the same ones your grandfather told me. I thought it was all part of the Warlician myth but apparently, my father thought differently. It was always important to your grandfather that my brother and I understood and respected all aspects of our family lineage, true or otherwise, but I never thought that he took the legend seriously." Nathan Callan shook his head in disbelief at this sudden revelation.

"The prophecy dad—*what is it!?*" She demanded, her voice rising slightly.

"The Callan legend, as you know, reveals my side of the family to be descendants of a mythological group of magical warriors—an order known as the Warlicians. It is a story that has been passed through generations of Callan sons and one that quite frankly we have always assumed to be fabled—like the Greek Gods. These Warlician warriors were said to be a male race, derived from the most powerful warlocks of the age. Apparently, the first-born sons of these dominant tribes were promised to The Order in return for peace and prosperity. The magical sons were trained to become elite warriors sworn to protect the magical realms and their people. Legend tells, the Warlicians harbored peace among the realms differing races for centuries, until the Great War when an ancient evil almost destroyed the realms and their magic."

Her father looked over at her mother, who nodded, encouraging him with a faint smile.

"Anyway," he continued giving Dane a somber look. "There have been stories about an ancient prophecy whispered through my family for generations. Most of us just assumed it was part of the lore. It foretold of a female, born first to a Callan son. She would be destined to become a fierce warrior—an immortal that would lead an army of supernatural beings in a fight to save mankind from extinction. The story changes slightly over time as many myths do but that is basically the basis of it."

He looked at his daughter, her lack of reaction causing him to shift uncomfortably. "This so-called prophecy was just part of our heritage Dane, no one actually believes it to be true. I am shocked to find that my father might have. Your grandfather was entrenched in the magical community, a pillar of it. He was extremely active in its preservation and often secretive about it, but you knew him, Dane he was a man of great integrity he was not delusional even if this does seem a little far-fetched."

"Do you think that there is a possibility that the myths are based on truth? That perhaps the prophecy is about me?" She asked curiously, her inner child relishing the fantasies of her childhood and the possibility that they still may come true.

"I don't know Dane, I doubt it," her father said, a weariness making him seem older than he was. "Your mother and I will try to find out more about this prophecy and the myths surrounding the Warlician legend when we get back to Salem, but this is a big surprise to all of us. My father never spoke of this to me, I had no idea. I have a feeling that he meant to pass this on to you himself, but unfortunately never got the chance."

She nodded tears welling up in her eyes as her father's words brought up painful memories of the sudden death of her beloved grandfather.

He squeezed her hand. "There is a lot of paperwork in that old chest, maybe you will find something useful. Something that will reveal the nature of the dreams and your connection to that old tree. In the meantime, try not to read too much into these tales, any truth behind them is highly implausible even for our kind. I am sure it is not as ominous as your grandfather's note makes it out to be." He looked back at her mother another guarded gaze passing between them.

"There is something else," he said gently.

"What?" she asked, the heaviness of the air in the room causing her breathing to shallow.

He reached into his other pocket and withdrew a small leather satchel. "It's a medallion, a very old one. I have never seen anything like it. I found it tucked in a corner of the chest. There was a note with it, written in your grandfather's handwriting."

He hesitated, and she felt a sudden chill crawl down her spine as she waited for her father to continue. "The note said—*For Dane when destiny finds you.*"

Swallowing loudly, she took the small leather satchel from her father, holding it gently in her hand. The softness of the rich, thick leather was unexpected as the worn weather-beaten surface looked rough and aged. The pouch secreted a musky scent, which mingled oddly with the strong aroma of an herb, one that she knew well—sage.

The satchel was tied with an intricately braided cord the ends encased in small metal tips.

Opening the pouch, she removed the ancient medallion surprised at how dense it felt in her hand. It was a large silver disk, approximately an inch and a half in diameter, its metal tarnished. She held it between her thumb and forefinger the attached thick linked chain falling between her other fingers. The front of the medallion was slightly convex and intricately crafted and detailed. A pentacle encircled a stunning green gem, its five points reaching out toward the delicate Celtic knotwork that edged the metal's outer circumference. Just inside the knotwork, carved in a circle were the words—*spiritus, aura, caminus, aqua, and humus.* She recognized the Latin words immediately--spirit, air, fire, water, and earth.

"The elements," she whispered, feeling her parent's eyes upon her.

Carefully she turned over the medallion, the front now facing down in her palm. The back of the disc was unremarkable, its surface was flat and smooth displaying none of the craftsmanship detailed on the front. There was a small brass plate welded to its middle and as she looked closer, she could see that a figure protruded out slightly from its center—*the glyph*—the same as on the latch of the chest.

She stared at the medallion in her hand, the glyph staring back at her like a silent omen. Was it an ancient symbol for the element earth, a message her grandfather never had the time to reveal, or a warning of things to come?

CHAPTER 11

THEY WERE HAVING DINNER AT *Valentia*, the local American-Italian restaurant located a few doors up from Gabby's store. Everyone had made it, including Cal, Ethan, and Kai's father, Jason Parker who was currently talking football with her dad. Her mother was chatting incessantly with Kai and Stevie about wedding plans and teasing Ethan about being outnumbered by the five women in Kai's life. Dane looked around the table at her extended family, a warm feeling coming over her as she basked in the smiles, laughter, and loving energy of the most important people in her life.

"Happy Birthday Dane!" Marlee said, holding up her wine glass in a toast, the others cheering and joining in.

Smiling she raised her glass in response. "Thanks for coming. I love you all."

The evening was going exactly as it always did when they all got together, her mother fussed over all the girls worrying if they were eating right and getting enough sleep. Her father and Mr. Parker finalized their March golf trip by loudly wondering if they should allow Cal and Ethan to tag along again. The girls amused everyone with stories of their many escapades together, each girl remembering a slightly different version and arguing over details until they broke out in fits of laughter.

A waiter came to clear the dinner plates and inquire if anyone would care for coffee and dessert when she felt an empty, emotionless energy crawl over her skin and sink deep into her pores. The menacing chill was followed by a wave of uneasiness and discomfort, a sensation she recognized immediately. Her eyes darting around the restaurant searching for the red-haired woman.

She spotted her, casually drinking a glass of red wine at the bar, the rim of the glass stained with her signature bright red lipstick.

The conversation noise at the table became muted as she blocked it out, focusing her attention on the woman, eyes boring into the back of her head. Dane knew the red-haired woman could feel her eyes upon her. She seemed to delight in the game of avoidance, casually taking another sip of her wine.

She continued to stare at the woman intently, every one of her senses directed toward her. Slowly, as if she just realized Dane's eyes were upon her, the redhead put down her wine glass and turned leisurely around, dark eyes penetrating, her face distorted with resentment.

Dane felt an unfamiliar twinge deep down in her being, as a strange wave of familiarity rose from the depths, flooding her with an unnerving feeling of déjà vu. She managed to maintain her gaze until the redhead turned on her heel and walked toward the exit, leaving her slightly breathless and encased in a cold, clammy chill.

Excusing herself, she left the table catching her mother's worried look as she ran after the woman. Her mother knew what that woman was, it was there in her eyes, she too must have sensed the suffocating void surrounding the dark witch.

She burst through the restaurant's front door, apologizing to the young couple who were just heading in. Scanning the street, she found the redhead turning into the back alley behind the restaurant. Running, she followed her into the shadows.

The alley was dimly lit. A fog had started to descend into its thin corridor, but she saw the woman just up ahead. Moving quickly, she closed the gap, grabbing her by the arm, and forcing her around, so they were face to face.

Suddenly, everything before her eyes went black, as nausea rifled through her body and visions erupted in her head. A young red-haired girl being beaten by a drunken man, his breath laden with the smell of whiskey, his clothes soaked with stale sweat. The girl's cries were drenched with pain and sorrow as she cowered in the corner, her frail little body crumpling under his abuse. Then, a young teen appeared, her red hair tied back in a tight ponytail, tears streaming down her face as other kids her age mocked and ridiculed her, calling her worthless, poor, and trash. The images morphed again as chants echoed through a dark forest. A coven of dark figures surrounding an altar, a menacing tone to their voices as they performed their ritual, the redhead, a young woman now, at its center.

Her head throbbed as the images hurled through her mind until finally, she saw the red-haired woman cloaked in black velvet robes staring vacantly out a window of the old flour mill, its dilapidated exterior shrouded in a decadent red glow. The ferocity of the last image was so intense she immediately released her grip on the woman's arm, their eyes locking, confusion saturating the surrounding air.

"Who are you?!" She demanded as the redhead stood gaping in disbelief at Dane, her cool disconnected veneer cracking slightly.

She knows what I saw, she thought as she repeated the question again.

The force of her voice cut through the quiet night echoing off the brick walls that surrounded them. The woman tensed briefly as if startled by her sudden aggression but managed to regain her composure, her face quickly returning to a flat, unemotional canvas. Her dark gaze fixed coolly on Dane, unadulterated disgust flickering deep within her irises.

Seconds ticked by as the two witches continued their silent stare, the glow from a single streetlamp filtered into the dark foggy alley, highlighting the tension that propagated between them. The redhead's face began to contort as her cool facade slipped replaced by a cruel sneer and a tortured shadow that darkened her gaze.

"Lilith" she hissed, hatred dripping off her tongue as she answered the question, her eyes boring into Dane with such fury that she felt herself recoil slightly. "Remember that name," she spat. "For it will be your undoing."

Without a backward glance, she turned and hurried off into the darkness of the alley. The sound of her high heels clicking against the pavement and echoing back toward her was the only thing Dane heard as the fog swallowed her up.

"Lilith," she whispered staring down the alley, her gaze obscured by the thickening fog that slowly descended over the passageway.

She felt a twinge pull at the base of her mind as a surge of nausea rifled through her head causing it to spin in response. Her hand reached out, feeling the rough surface of the restaurant wall. Leaning her forehead against the cool brick she closed her eyes as the uncomfortable feeling swelled.

Through the pain in her head, she heard a voice calling her name, but she couldn't respond as another wave of nausea overtook her. The voice echoed through the alleyway, worry coating its tone as she felt her mother's familiar energy and her comforting arms wrap around her.

Carefully, she opened her eyes, her mother's familiar face directly in front of her, the dim light highlighting the worry in her eyes.

"Dane, are you alright?"

"I'm fine," she replied wearily, feeling exhausted but managing to push herself off the wall into an upright position.

Nodding her mother took her arm, gently guiding her out of the alleyway and back toward the restaurant.

As the cool night air brushed past her flushed cheeks, she began to feel better; the general sense of malaise subsiding. They walked back into the restaurant an unspoken understanding drifting between them. Her mother casting worried glances, which she tried unsuccessfully to disguise with a forced smile.

The party was just breaking up as they sat back down at the table. Glancing at her watch she realized she had only been gone about fifteen minutes and no one at the table, other than her parents, seemed concerned about her disappearance. She stood as Cal gave her a big hug goodbye making her promise that she would come over for dinner with the rest of the girls soon. Agreeing, she waved as he, Elyse, and Marlee left the restaurant.

Kai's father handed her a small gift-wrapped box, "I made it for you," he said kissing her cheek and winking, as he followed Kai and Ethan out of the restaurant, the rest of the girls leaving shortly after.

Dane sat quietly at the table, sensing her parent's eyes on her as she wrestled with the strange feeling growing in the pit of her stomach. Anxious she was not, but the overwhelming sensation that ran through her veins was a little too unfamiliar to ignore. She was acutely aware of the incessant pounding in her head.

Why do I feel like I am hungover? She thought to herself, finally raising her eyes to look at her parents. They both sat quietly, their eyes full of curiosity more than concern.

Finally, her father spoke. "Is your blood racing Dane?" He asked, "Your head pounding? Do you feel slightly out of sorts?"

She frowned at him wondering why he was asking such odd questions. Nodding she closed her eyes and rubbed her head, wishing for these strange feelings to subside.

Her father spoke again, "You will be able to absorb the after-effects once you learn how to control the visions."

Her eyes shot open suddenly as the entire room began to close in around her. "How did you know about the visions?" She asked her voice shaking slightly.

Smiling, her father took her trembling hand. "Because I saw them as well."

She was speechless. She had just experienced a connection with a dark witch, something, unlike anything she had experienced before. What was her father talking about?

Her father's curious gaze stared at her from across the

table as her mother leaned over and whispered in her ear. "Let's go home, you need your rest. We will talk tomorrow."

It was almost midnight as Dane pulled back the comforter on her bed and climbed beneath it. The box that Kai's father had given her still sat unopened on the edge of her nightstand. Curiously, she took the small package and untied the bailing twine that was wrapped around the bright green wrapping paper. Opening, the lid of the small white box, she read the card that lay inside—*life's roots will always bring you home. Love J.P.*

Smiling at the sentiment she lifted the card from the box to reveal a beautiful wooden carving, an intricately sculpted heart that surrounded a tree, its branches reaching toward the top of the heart, its roots filtering to the point. Dane knew that Mr. Parker had taken up whittling as a hobby a few years ago but had no idea how good he had gotten.

She gently pulled the carving from the box. The hearts sides were attached to a slim black leather strap. Carefully, she tied the leather bracelet around her wrist, closing the lobster clasp to secure it. Running her fingers softly over the polished wood, she closed her eyes and yawned, allowing exhaustion to take over.

The red-head slammed her purse on the table, sending dust flying in every direction. The old flour mill groaned in response as the wind whistled through its emptiness.

She paced back and forth, her head exploding with confusion. How had the witch gotten inside her head? The things she had been able to see. Her secrets, memories she kept locked up deep inside were suddenly exposed by that witch. *But how?!* Had she misjudged her power?

Her mind was reeling as she went over the events of the night in her head, trying to find an answer. Suddenly, she realized something, the witch was different, her stench had changed slightly. She now possessed another layer to her already complicated aura. It wasn't noticeable at first, but the witch seemed more powerful, her energy balanced, and there had been something unseen sizzling in the surrounding air.

It had been unsettling, and it had distracted her, and for a moment she felt helpless, like the little girl she had left in the past, paralyzed by an overwhelming fear.

Her pacing decreased as she thought about the witch. This was not a power that she had considered. It was not one that she could easily outmaneuver, but it was one that could derail her plans. She would need to figure out quickly, what had changed and why, so she would not fall prey to the witch the next time.

She could not afford to underestimate her, for she had been cultivating her plans for years, waiting for the exact moment when she would make that witch pay for what her ancestors had done.

CHAPTER 12

T HE SMELL OF COFFEE GREETED Dane as she walked into her kitchen the following morning. Her mother and father sat at the breakfast bar, mugs of fresh hot brew in their hands. They smiled uncomfortably as she entered. Tyson, happy to see them, wiggled over pushing his head into their legs for attention.

She avoided their concerned stares until she had made herself a cup of tea, turning she scowled at her parents. "Would one of you like to tell me what is going on?"

They looked at one another, fidgeting, as she waited impatiently for either of them to answer.

Her father spoke first. "I asked you those questions last night because I know what happened. We already suspected after you told your mother everything about your encounter with the tree and the visions, but last night confirmed it."

"Confirmed what?"

Her mother's voice was soft, her eyes gentle as they looked deep into hers. "Dane, you did have a second awakening. It now seems you possess at least some of your father's powers."

She gaped at them, unsure of what she heard. She thought back to the strange vision she experienced when her hand had touched Lilith's arm. It was not like the visions or dreams she had experienced in the past few days, it was as if she were in Lilith's head, seeing things only Lilith could know.

"How can you be sure?" She managed to choke out, the blood roaring in her ears.

"Because I was in her head as well." Her father was calm as he answered. "I felt your presence immediately. I saw the same things—the child being abused, the bullied teen, the old mill shrouded in an eerie red glow. Those weren't visions Dane, they were her memories, every single one of them tainted by dark magic. You connected with her mind when you touched her. A link that severed when you released her arm."

He hesitated for a moment, allowing her to process the things he was saying. "Your mother sensed the dark witch just as you did, so I entered her mind, which wasn't easy, she is definitely cloaking her aura. But the memories, you found those and brought them forward, she had hidden them well, and you surprised her at how easily they became unhidden."

She stared at her father, barely able to comprehend the words that were flowing from his lips. A second awakening, it couldn't be true, she felt the exact same.

"Dane, you do have the power of telepathy but whether you have gained my ability to manipulate time and space is yet to be seen."

She shook her head in disbelief. So much had happened

in the past twenty-four hours, and she suddenly felt overwhelmed. Her grandfather's chest, stuffed with papers she had yet to review, a mythological prophecy that may or may not be true, strange dreams she couldn't control, a dark witch who apparently hated her, and a second awakening giving her telepathic powers.

What was going on?

The knot of apprehension in her stomach began to tighten—there was something wrong in Brighton Hill, and she now had no doubt that she was part of it.

"Honey, are you OK?" Her mother asked, looking at her daughter with concern. She nodded softly, her mind churning as her heart fell, the ever-present feeling of loneliness rearing up its ugly head as her life as a witch just pushed her further away from her mortal friends.

She sighed and looked at her father. "The feeling I experienced after the vision, like I was hungover, exhausted mentally and physically, does that happen to you?"

"It used to, in the beginning, but you will learn to absorb the effects, so they become minimally invasive. I am confident that you will be able to separate them as you do with the emotions you pick up using your empathic abilities."

Her father was referring to her innate ability to easily feel and identify specific individual energies and emotions without experiencing the overwhelming loss of her own emotional identity. Many high-level empaths suffer when connected to an emotional spectrum not their own, but she did not experience this turmoil. Her mother called it segmenting—the ability to recognize and separate your own emotions from others and digest or channel them without experiencing physical consequences.

He reached over and touched her hand. "The new power caught you off guard Dane, so your body reacted like a foreign antigen had invaded, making you feel sick as it attempted to neutralize its presence. When you understand and learn how to control your new power, your body will accept the side effects more easily and the symptoms will begin to cease."

She smiled slightly at her father's clinical explanation. *Even the warlock talks like a doctor,* she thought.

"I think you really need to look at what your grandfather left you in that chest," he continued. "A second awakening is extremely rare and does not happen without reason. As history has dictated, the rare few of our kind who experienced one have found themselves entrenched in our magical history, for good and bad. Your second awakening will come with its own destiny Dane and possibly a great price. You must be respectful of the gift magic has given you but wary of what it requires in return."

She took a deep breath, pushed back her shoulders and smiled at her parents, watching as their worried faces seemed to soften slightly. She had been a witch most of her life and had successfully intermingled her magical life with a mortal one. Nothing was going to change; she would learn how to control this power as well and use it to the best of her abilities. Whatever was happening, whatever her new destiny, she would find a way to make it work within the mortal spectrum. She had no choice.

"Your father and I really want to stay, but he is working third shift tonight. They are short-staffed in trauma." Ella Watts gazed at her daughter with an apologetic look on her face.

"Mom I will be fine, really you don't need to worry."

Her mother gave her a tense smile. "It's my job."

She smiled weakly, her mind racing as she tried to make sense of it all.

"Your father will go through the rest of your grandfather's things, see if there is anything else that can shed light on what's going on. I will speak to both sides of the family, maybe someone knows something or there is talk within the magical community. We will figure this out," she said squeezing her daughter's hand affectionately.

"Thanks, mom, dad, I appreciate it."

She had an overwhelming desire to be alone right now, to collect her thoughts and think through all that had happened. It was difficult to think clearly when her mother was hovering over her. Silently, and with a little guilt, she thanked the goddess that her parents were leaving soon.

After breakfast, she helped load the car, hugging them both before they got in to start the long drive home. Although she was glad to be alone with her thoughts an aching emptiness blossomed in her chest as she watched their car drive out of sight. Her eyes pricked with tears as the anxious energy that squeezed her heart reminded her of how much lonelier it was going to get.

As she turned to walk back into the house, she felt an uneasiness spread through her. Quickly, she scanned the area but only the normal neighborhood activity greeted her.

Tyson had gone to greet Mr. Avery, her next-door neighbor, who was out walking his dog. She waved as he gave Tyson a treat

The uneasiness began to fade. Pulling her phone from her pocket, she checked the text messages that had come in this morning, one from Kai and one from Elyse. Ignoring them she turned her phone off and glanced again around the neighborhood unable to shake the stubborn feeling that someone was watching.

Whistling for Tyson she walked back into the house determined to spend the rest of the day trying to get some answers.

There was something different about the witch. The surrounding air sizzled with an unusual energy. Unlike before when all she felt was contempt toward her, there was now a strange sensation of uneasiness and distress that reared up inside her. It was an uncomfortable feeling and very worrisome. She could not afford to be dealing with this type of chaos when so much was a stake.

She pushed her red hair off her face as the cold biting wind blew the long strands aimlessly about. Peeking out from the corner of the bus stop shelter, she watched as they walked to the car.

The parents, she thought, as they got in and drove away. *They were more than she had expected.*

After calming down last night, she realized the witch was not the only one with the power to see inside her mind. She had felt another presence, although it was harder to detect, for unlike the witch it was calm, in control, and almost invisible. There had been a hint of Celtic magic left behind, the old-world kind and rare in modern times. A shadow of a past that had faded when magic became feared.

She knew it wasn't the mother, for she could see in her aura the calming white energy tinged with faint blue and yellow. An indication of a longstanding lineage of British healers. If the witch's parents were from the bloodlines of two of the oldest magical families remaining in the modern world, then they would both be extremely powerful and knowledgeable. A possibility she hadn't considered.

She shifted her position when the witch's eyes began to search the neighborhood, her gaze almost on her before she pulled herself back in behind the shelter. She could feel the witch's energy as it reached out probing. It was strong, confident, and much more powerful than it was at the gas station and then again on the street downtown, days earlier. It was now tinged with something older and darker, an invisible essence entwined in the witch's magical aura, pulsating erratically around her.

Peeking around the bus-stop again she watched as the witch went back inside. Taking a deep breath of the cold winter air, she turned and walked back to her car, fighting to control both the vitriol that raged inside her and the panicked voice in her head that told her to run.

CHAPTER 13

HER GRANDFATHER'S WOODEN CHEST SAT waiting in her office, its subtle pine scent drifting through the small room. Striding to her desk, Dane opened the small metal box containing the ancient medallion and its corresponding note, feeling a sudden rush of sadness as her grandfather's handwriting came into view.

This would be so much easier if he were still here to guide her, to explain what all this meant, and to tell her what to do. She cursed under her breath, hating the drunk driver who had stolen away the man she admired. That fateful day had taken more from her than she had known at the time, for now, it seemed that her grandfather may have had vital information of an ancient past that could very well affect her future.

She looked at the framed picture on her desk. Her grandfather was such a regal looking man, his bright green eyes highlighted by dark lashes, his salt and pepper hair cropped short, his beard trimmed neatly. He had been her rock always there to provide guidance and wisdom during her younger years. His constant presence always managed to keep her grounded even through the tumultuous times.

She had not always been an easy child, especially after her awakening when the burden of her legacy threatened to expose her at every turn. She had become withdrawn and distant with her parents, but her relationship with her grandfather flourished as he always seemed to understand her differently than the rest of the family. Her parents expected her to accept her gifts as part of her birthright, but her grandfather understood how difficult it was for someone like Dane, so entangled in the mortal world, to accept that she was different.

Her grandfather had guided her through those years, taught her the ways of her new reality, and allowed her to feel what she needed to without judgment. Because of him, she had grown into a powerful and resourceful witch. Then suddenly he was gone, and everything changed.

After her grandfather died, she abandoned being guarded about her secrets and closed herself off completely to mortals, concentrating only on her work, her magic, and ensuring that those closest to her were kept emotionally at arm's length. She was still everyone's rock—loyal and reliable, but she no longer let anyone in and because of that her romantic relationships suffered, and her circle of friends diminished. Her parents and her five best friends remained the only ones she stayed close with, but even they were unable to gain access to the innermost sanctum of her heart. Her self-imposed solitude was her way of ensuring her own emotional survival. She had gotten very good at keeping everyone at a distance, and they had all finally accepted her lack of emotional availability.

She shook off the painful memories of his death

concentrating instead on the old chest that sat on the floor at her feet. Turning the brass key, she heard the lock click. Slowly, she opened the lid revealing a mess of papers, clippings, and notebooks all jammed haphazardly into the chest.

She spent the next hour taking everything out and sorting through it, piling the items into some type of organized system. Making a stack for spells and incantations, another containing anything to do with the Callan lineage, and a third pile for antidotes and family recipes. Piled neatly to her left was a stack of small notebooks; all of which seemed to contain her grandfather's journal entries.

As she slowly emptied the chest placing its contents into corresponding piles, she realized how much her grandfather had crammed into the small wooden box. Most of it was family history, interesting but not of any value to the task at hand. The spells and incantations were curious; some dated back thousands of years and exposed a different type of magic than what existed today. She smiled when she read the variety of ingredients and oddities witches used to perform magic in the past.

As she pulled out the last of the papers, she noticed a black velvet cloth wrapped around something at the very bottom of the chest. Carefully, she picked it up from where it lay, surprised by the weight of the unseen item. Removing the black cloth, she saw a long, narrow, leather-bound folder tied tightly by a thin leather string, its length wound around the folder multiple times, secured with a double knot. To her delight in was emblazoned with the same glyph as the chest.

"The real Callan legacy, perhaps?" She whispered, gently tugging at the knot and unwinding the leather string.

Opening the leather flap, she carefully pulled out the contents spreading them out randomly on the floor. The pages contained in the leather folder were not like any of the other papers founded in the chest. The paper was thin, a delicate parchment that threatened to crumble if touched too harshly. Many of the pages had discolored and bore the yellowish tinge of age. The writing was in old script, the black ink faded and bleeding slightly. Some corners of the parchments were torn and dog-eared, but all were thankfully legible. Judging by the age of the parchments she assumed they were passed down through the Callan family. She also assumed that her grandfather had intended to pass them down to her father until she was born and his suspicions about the ancient prophecy were confirmed.

Carefully, she looked at each page, most of the information on them made no sense. There were vague descriptions of other worlds, realms governed by the elements where magic flourished. There were no specifics, no names or dates, so she had no idea when in her family's history they were recorded. Some entries seemed older than others and depicted different scripts indicating the possibility that a multitude of generations had contributed their knowledge and ideas to these pages.

She continued to shuffle through the parchments, finding references to the Warlician legend, but nothing that she had not already learned as a child.

Picking up the last few pages, she immediately noticed a difference in the weight, color, and thickness of the parchment. Studying it closer she realized that it was not as old as the others, it was a modern stock that had been manipulated to look antique. She recognized the handwriting that filled the pages as her grandfather's. He had sketched some small diagrams impeccably in the body of the writing and others he had scribbled hastily into the margins.

Flipping through them quickly she stopped as something familiar caught her eye. Holding up the page she studied the pencil drawing, its shape, contours, and identifying marks all exact—it was a sketch of the old distorted tree in Braemore Woods. Beneath the diagram, her grandfather had written one word followed by a question mark —*portal?*

The other pages contained much of the same, diagrams with one-word questions, or thoughts that her grandfather must have wanted to remember. At the back, there was a small parchment attached with a paper clip to the one in front. It was no bigger than a greeting card and its delicate thin surface was mottled with ink splats. Written across its center, in a perfect ancient script, was one sentence—*One world born from another will share an equal fate.*

She stared at those words, a feeling of despair creeping up from inside her as something in her subconscious seemed to understand its meaning. She pushed the small parchment to the side and returned her attention to the drawing of the tree.

What did her grandfather mean by portal?

Carefully she turned the parchment over and written in the bottom corner in the same handwriting was—*the past is the key.*

Obviously, her grandfather thought the old tree in Braemore woods had something to do with unraveling the truth behind the family legacy and as she read through the parchments again, she began to think so too.

As she climbed into bed that night, she was more determined than ever to find some answers.

Dane heard her name whispered among the treetops as she carefully made her way through the woods. The air was tainted with the smell of burning sage and there was a slight calm that seemed to follow the night breeze. The whispering came from somewhere up ahead, and she carefully made her way through the dark toward it, guided only by the soft light that filtered down from the full moon.

As the whispering intensified, an ethereal glow suddenly penetrated the dark woods up ahead. The warm caressing light beckoning her toward it. When she entered the clearing the whispering ceased and the air quieted, and she could see the glow emanated from the trunk of the old tree.

She felt a sudden shift in the erratic energy that flooded the clearing as a calm strength pulsated from the stately tree, the ethereal glow seeping from its cracked bark. The white light spilled onto the forest floor, slithering toward her, pulsating and morphing its shape as it drew closer. Crackling with intensity, the light expanded upward and outward, stopping when it hovered only a few yards from where she stood. It shifted and sparkled in front of her, in constant motion crackling and spitting small shards of light in every direction.

She stared at the light; the center began to dim as a shadow slowly emerged from its core. The brilliant white light giving way to whatever was moving through it. Unable to look away, she watched in awe as a man emerged from the light's center to stand calmly in front of her, his piercing green eyes gazing curiously into her own.

She looked the man up and down comforted by the calm strength he exuded and the quiet warmth in his eyes.

He reminded her of a knight, a fierce warrior from another time. Dressed head to toe in black, his dark armor was polished to a high sheen. The hooded black cloak that cascaded down his back was fastened at each shoulder with a large cloak clasp; round medallions that bore an interesting mark and one that she had seen before—*a dagger protruding from a sphere.*

At his hip hung a large sword; the intricately carved hilt sticking out from the edge of his cloak was capped with an iridescent green stone. It glowed with ferocity under the dimming light still pulsating from the tree. The blade was long and thick pushing his cloak hem up at the back. It too was polished to a perfect sheen and glinted brightly in the shadows.

His strong, handsome face was tanned, his jaw angular, and laugh lines spread out like a web from the corners of his piercing green eyes. His hair was silvery white, cut short yet still tousled by the evening breeze and his perfectly trimmed goatee ended in a point two inches below his chin. He had a thick scar that ran from the corner of his right eye down his cheek, ending just before it intersected his goatee.

He stood very still staring at her, his green eyes acknowledging her confusion as a slight smirk appeared on his lips. After a few more minutes of silence, the man reached out and laid his gloved hand gently on her shoulder. Suddenly, she heard his voice in her head; a voice that matched the power that this man's appearance evoked. It was deep, steady, and familiar and made her feel safe and comforted.

"Your destiny awaits Callathian. Here the answers you seek will be revealed but first, you must unlock the past. Find the key."

With those words still vibrating in her mind, the man

lowered his hand and walked into the waiting light. As she watched, the light receded back into the tree, leaving her standing alone in the cold, dark clearing. A strange wind began to howl snaking its way through the shadowy forest as the trees once again began to whisper.

CHAPTER 14

DANE HAD WOKEN EXHAUSTED, HER mind hazy with lack of sleep. She felt like she was walking through sludge, her body tired and sore. She had experienced another strange dream last night, and it had again sapped her energy. Sitting at her office desk, she tried to recall details of the dream, only retrieving bits and pieces from the thick fog that dulled her memory.

Taking her grandfather's medallion from the metal box, she held it gently in her hand twisting the thick chain around her index finger as she studied it. There was something bothering her about the medallion. Ever since her father had given it to her she had experienced a nagging feeling that it was something more than just a piece of jewelry to hang around her neck. The cryptic note her grandfather had included with it also made her think it was of importance.

Holding it in her hand she turned it over and over examining its surfaces for the umpteenth time. It was obviously very old, the etching on the front had tarnished slightly; a dark gray appearing in the thick metal's crevices.

Her finger slowly traced the words that were delicately carved into the metal, feeling each letter as it passed under her fingertip. Its front was detailed and beautiful, but it was the simplicity of the back that kept drawing her attention.

The glyph that protruded slightly from the brass plate on the back was small but very defined. The lines were rigid and square and the metal curiously unblemished by time. She tilted it back and forth certain that there was something she was missing. Her fingers continued to search the medallion's surfaces looking for anything out of the ordinary. Suddenly, her finger hit a slight bump on the edge of the medallion. It was subtle but seemed out of place, like a flaw or afterthought not part of the overall design. Turning her attention to the side of the pendant she saw a small round button, no larger than a pinhead, protruding above the base metal. Grinning, she pressed the hidden button.

A series of clicks sounded and the brass plate on the back of the medallion loosened. She grabbed the edges and pulled the plate from the back revealing a small key hidden inside. Her grandfather's words written at the bottom of the old parchment now made sense, maybe the medallion was the past and this key was the one she was meant to find.

Suddenly, she remembered last night's dream and the words the mysterious man had spoken. This key must have something to do with the past, and the answers must be at that tree. Carefully, she placed the brass plate on the back of the medallion and pushed, hearing it click into a locked position.

Jumping up from her desk she ran down the hallway.

She was going back to the old tree where hopefully she would find answers regarding the past and the prophecy. She quickly got dressed and sent a text to Stevie saying that she would not be able to meet her and Gabby for lunch. Grabbing her backpack and calling for Tyson to follow, she headed to the trailhead parking lot.

The sun was shining brightly in the late morning sky as she parked the Jeep in the lot. There were a few cars parked in the far corner but none she recognized. Hurrying, she moved onto the shadowy trail. The temperature was cooler inside the tree line, and she shivered as she walked, Tyson running up the path ahead, as a squirrel caught his attention.

The path to the old tree was clear, most of the snow compacted from use, and she made decent time getting to the clearing. Cautiously, she walked around the rock cropping with Tyson close behind.

Entering the shadows of the clearing, the hair on her arms bristled as a chill ran down her spine. It was extremely quiet.

Too quiet, she thought to herself, hooking Tyson to his leash and clipping the handle to her belt loop.

As she moved deeper into the clearing the breeze picked up, the low branches of the old tree scraped the forest floor, a slow methodical movement that made her shiver in anticipation. The overhead branches, groaning in protest, swayed back and forth allowing sunlight to seep through the thick canopy and ignite the old tree in a soft sparkling light.

Abruptly, the breeze subsided. She heard a faint hum emanating from the tree. Taking a step forward she placed her palm gently on the trunk feeling a slight vibration. Her palm prickled slightly as the vibration quickened, flowing into the ground and causing the area she was standing on to shudder. A faint glow began to flow through the depths of the tree, light leaking from the cracks in the bark, and oozing downward.

Startled, she removed her hand and back away from the tree watching as the glow intensified, pushing through the cracks in the bark, light flowing toward the massive roots protruding from the ground. Stepping further away from the tree she pushed Tyson behind her as the light continued its descent down the trunk, across the roots, and onto the forest floor.

It slithered silently toward her, the light getting brighter. She lifted her hand, shielding her eyes from the sudden glare. The closer the light got, the calmer she felt. She could feel her own magic pulsing through her veins, curious about the strange familiarity that emanated from the light. Her heart pounded as the light drew closer and a sudden deep sense of knowing flooded through her.

Expanding, the light rose upward in front of her, pulsating erratically as it took shape. A subtle shadow darkening its center, growing until it blocked the brightness of the erratically pulsating light, completely.

As quickly as it appeared the light receded back into the tree and standing directly in front of her was a man—*the one from her dream!*

He was tall and dressed all in black; his tanned face surrounded by silvery white hair. His burnished armor caught the glinting reflection of the midday sun. The long blade of his sword extended from his left hip, disappearing under his long black cloak. Everything about the man standing in front of her was just as she had envisioned it.

She stood staring in awe at this stranger, her mind trying to make sense of his sudden appearance.

Her eyes moved down to Tyson who was sitting quietly beside her, his eyes curious but his body exhibiting no signs of fear or distress as he stared casually at the stranger.

She waited but for him to speak and after what seemed like a long period of silence he did, his voice deep, calm, and controlled.

"You received my message," he said, his strong voice filling the quiet that still enshrouded the clearing.

"Who are you?" She asked her voice cracking slightly.

"You may call me Sebastian," he answered pragmatically. He hesitated slightly before continuing, "Your attention is not easy to get."

"So, I wasn't dreaming," she said to herself more than to Sebastian.

"Not exactly," he responded, a smirk briefly appearing on his tanned face, his piercing green eyes twinkling as they looked at her. "Your second awakening gave you the power of telepathy, and foresight, both ancient powers that are common to our kind. Once the channel was open, I only needed to enter."

"Channel?"

"It is a bridge within the mind, a way our kind contacts and communicates with one another."

"Our kind?"

Sebastian smiled. "I am a Warlician warrior, one of the few that still remain after the Great War transformed my world. You by birthright are one of us." Sebastian stated simply.

"I thought Warlician warriors were a myth. A make-believe part of my family's history. You are telling me they were real?"

"The Warlician Order is very much a part of our history. Unfortunately, history fades with time, turning truth into memory and memory into legend but our world was once a great place of ancient magic, powerful realms, and mystical beings. In this world, we may be a myth but our existence comes from truth."

She stared at the intimidating man in front of her, his calm demeanor slightly unnerving. "What does this have to do with me?" she asked thinking back to her grandfather's papers and the prophecy which he was so sure she belonged to.

"You are a descendant of a long line of extremely powerful Warlician warriors," Sebastian said slowly taking a few steps toward her. "Your family's legacy is strong, the oldest clan in our race. You are a Callathian and your bloodline connects both our history and our future—the future of our kind and others like us."

She stopped for a moment when she heard Sebastian say Callathian, remembering that he had called her that in her dream as well.

"What is a Callathian?" She asked.

He stared sternly at her. "Not what, but whom—your ancestors."

"But I am a Callan," she said slightly confused.

Sebastian nodded, "Mortals have a strange way of changing their birth names over time. The Callathian name of my time has become Callan in yours. Your immediate ancestors in this world are Callans, it is true, but your ancient ancestors, those from which your power derives, have claimed the Callathian name for thousands of generations."

"What did you mean when you said others like us?"

"Our race is not the only magical one, there are five realms within our universe, each home to a different magical kind. Warlicians are witch-warriors, descendants of an ancient race of powerful sorcerers and enchantresses. But there are others—mystical beings born of magic and ruled by the elements, each race singular in its identity and yet connected to each other by the threads of magic."

"I still don't understand what this has to do with me?"

"It's your destiny to reunite the races and bring our worlds back to greatness," Sebastian said, a shadow of sadness passing over his sculpted features. "A destiny that must be initiated to save the future of this world."

"My grandfather mentioned a prophecy, he thought it was about me. Is this the destiny you speak of?"

Sebastian's green eyes searched deep into hers, his face softening as he placed a strong hand on her shoulder. "Your grandfather was a smart man, he believed like no other before him. He knew what your future held, accepted what you would become. He had seen your destiny long before you were born. His was to guide you to it. I know he never got that chance and I am sorry."

"You knew my grandfather?!"

"In a way."

The shadow of an old memory passed across his features. "Your grandfather figured out what your true destiny was and now so must you. But first, one's destiny is better understood if they realize their past. Let me start from the beginning, your beginning," he said taking a deep breath.

"Your ancestors are from a magical universe located in another time and place. It is called *Thanissia*—a universe that is home to the Five Realms; magical worlds that were once inhabited by six powerful supernatural races. For centuries, the Warlician warriors defended the realms' parameters, keeping peace among the different races. Known for their potent warrior magic the Warlicians were a deadly fighting force. Each race ruled its own specific realm, but all were overseen by one neutral entity—the Guardian of Deities, the most powerful of all the supernatural entities. For thousands of years, the people of the Five Realms lived in peace and harmony until the Great War. Enticed by the powerful magic that thrived in the Five Realms, a violent predator from a distant universe came. It attacked the realms one by one, a decaying smoky shadow that fed off the life forces of each world and weakened the magical powers of its inhabitants. We called it the *'ancient dark'* for it was unlike anything we had seen or known. Its hunger was insatiable. It was void of mercy. It decimated ancient kingdoms and hunted and slaughtered thousands without forethought or remorse. Its power grew as the magic of the Five Realms depleted, turning once vibrant and potent lands into dark, dying wastelands. Your ancestor, I, and hundreds of other Warlician warriors struggled to stop the extermination of our home but it was not to be. Our end was upon us."

"What happened?" She was entranced by Sebastian's story.

"Faced with extinction the Guardian of Deities harnessed and combined the Five Realms remaining magic and used it to create a new universe, in another time —*earth*," Sebastian said, lifting his hands to indicate this world. "The surviving inhabitants of the Five Realms escaped to the new world through magical portals; gateways in the ether. The Guardian created mortal man, a non-magical entity whose ordinary energy acted as a shield, camouflaging the supernatural being's magical auras and hiding them from detection."

"Wait," she interrupted as pieces of Sebastian's story clicked into place. "This Guardian of Deities created earth and man—are you saying that your entity is this world's, *God?*"

"I believe that is the name mortals have adopted to refer to him. But he is anything like the image man has created." Sebastian replied, quickly continuing with his story wary of the passing of time.

"Without the magical essence of the races, the realms began to recede into dormancy; this deprived the ancient dark of its power source, weakening it. Using this to our advantage we trapped the ancient dark on the largest of the realms, in the deep caverns located on its furthest edge; a barren place known as the Dead Lands. The evil was trapped but the Thanissia Universe lay dying, its magic disappearing leaving the remaining warriors weakened and vulnerable. In a final sacrifice, the Guardian of Deities used his life essence to conquer the ancient dark, encasing him in an underground tomb far beneath the newly created world. A sacrifice that cost the Guardian his physical form and much of his power but ending the Great War."

"Hell," she whispered, referencing the Christian belief system again.

Sebastian nodded silently. "With the Guardians powers depleted and many of our warriors' dead, we were no longer able to protect the realm's people. Our time was over. The realms fell into stasis, their magic dormant. The guardian forbade the realms surviving inhabitants from using their powers in the new world, for fear their magical presence would unleash the ancient dark entombed far below it. Confident that the remaining survivors were once again safe in their new surroundings, the Guardian of Deities remaining essence disappeared into the ether. With his winged protectors, he watches over the earth, mankind, and the ancient dark to this day."

"I still don't see how any of this relates to me." She said, confused as to her role.

"During the Great War, a powerful seer foretold of the Second Rising; a time in a distant future when the ancient dark would break free from his confines and rise once again. He spoke of the *Arcanists*, blood descendants from each of the six ancient magical races. Mortals who would claim immortality and control the power of the elements, emerging to battle the ancient dark for the souls of mankind. One of these descendants would be from the Warlician bloodline, a powerful witch that would lead the others in their quest to once again defeat evil. That descendant was to be a first-born female, born to the eldest son of the oldest of all the clans—*The Callathian Clan*. You see Dane, your destiny was written long before the time of man and it is now coming to pass."

"And you are sure I am one of these Arcanists?" She asked her mind struggling to wrap itself around everything Sebastian was saying.

"Your second awakening gave you an ancient gift. Only Warlician warriors can communicate telepathically with one another through this power. Once your gift was granted I recognized your energy immediately and therefore had the ability to communicate with you. There is no mistaking who you are Dane for you carry the blood of a great family and your acceptance of that birthright must be unyielding. The prophecy, as it pertains to the Arcanists must be realized or all will be lost, and it begins with you."

CHAPTER 15

S EBASTIAN WAITED PATIENTLY FOR DANE to respond. His green eyes stared into her own. She stood motionless, her mind processing what he had said while trying to comprehend the magnitude of the information he had just provided.

This was much more than being a descendant of the bloodlines of an ancient race or gaining telepathic powers. The prophecy expected her to claim a birthright which would send her on a path to possible death and destruction. If an entire universe of magical beings could not defeat an ancient predator, then why would anyone believe that she and five others could?

Her mind reeled, and her palms began to sweat. Taking a deep breath, she looked around the clearing unsure if she should stay or walk away. She needed to think, to digest the information, it was all too surreal. She was beginning to wonder if any of it was true or all a bad dream.

Sebastian could sense her hesitation and the uncertainty

surrounding her. "Maybe it is better if you see the past for yourself, to feel the weight of its memory."

Holding out his hand he gestured for hers. "The past you are about to see will be repeated if the prophecy does not hold true. If the Arcanists do not rise, the earth will suffer an equal fate. Your destiny is unquestioned, it is both salvation for my world and survival for yours."

Closing his eyes, he began to murmur under his breath, his hands tightening around hers as the air stilled. She could feel an unseen presence in the air, a strange energy swirling around them. Suddenly, Sebastian's memories slammed into her mind, and she was catapulted into another time.

She was immersed in a vast galaxy, billions of stars littering the infinite darkness. She could feel its life force, the invisible magical essence that weaved itself through every layer, breathing life into all it surrounded.

Images began to flow through her mind; a powerful waterfall, its spray pounding noiselessly under the sparkling light of two moons, rivers of red lava snaked through black rock canyons, ice towers protruded from crystal blue waters, a mist hovering just above their surfaces. Enormous white mountains surfaced in her mind, their tips sparkling against a stunning purple sky, a thick majestic forest lit up by a thousand twinkling lights, a golden-hued cloud bank hovering low over a sparkling city in the distance. As the images passed through her mind, she felt a heavy sadness and a longing for these long-lost worlds. Their individual beauty marred only by their stark emptiness.

Suddenly, she was overwhelmed by a sense of fear, a chorus of whispers erupted in her mind as a dark shadow crept over the tranquil lands. She could feel a multitude of emotions rush through her, flooding her senses with pain and fear, an unfathomable anguish that suffocated her from the inside. She watched as the beautiful lands, their colors so vivid and pure, turned to ash. Fires raged through the countryside, buildings crumbled, and thick gray smoke floated like a canopy above the land. She could smell the stench of decay, taste the coppery acidity of blood, and feel the fading life force as the world died around her.

She stood on a hill overlooking a muddy field, bodies of the dead scattered across its surface, a feeling of helplessness and failure slicing through her. It began to rain, torrents of water poured from the sky turning the surrounding ground into red rivers, cutting a desolate path through the wasted land. The rain's wake washed away the life that had once animated the faces of the dead, their bodies now lay broken before her, vacant eyes staring into the distance, begging for vengeance.

"Breathe," Sebastian said holding Dane by her shoulders so that she could catch her breath and regain her strength. "You are not versed in our ways yet, and the powers you now possess can sap your energy if you do not know how to deflect."

She gazed into the eyes of this stranger, her empathy for him growing as her mind now fully realizing the horrors he had seen. Those images were his, memories forever burned into his tortured mind, a universe lost in an unforgiving past. She had been looking through his eyes, as his home, his people were decimated by evil. She felt his sorrow, his helplessness as his inability to stop the carnage became apparent, but most of all she experienced his thirst for a vengeance not yet quenched.

"The past will be repeated if you do not accept your true destiny, only this time, those dead eyes staring up at you will be of those you know, those that you love, and the world ignited in hell will be this one."

Releasing her hands, he took a step back, his voice softening.

"I am sorry, but I needed you to feel the anguish that stains our lands, know the veracity about your ancestral home and its fate so that you can understand the magnitude of what is coming and what it means for mankind. You and the other Arcanists are the only hope for the future, of this world and ours."

"Who are the other Arcanists?" She asked curiously.

"That I cannot tell you, as only you can reveal their true identities."

Her eyes shot up to look directly into his. "Me. How am I supposed to do that? I have no idea who they are or where to even begin to find out."

"Destiny will unfold as it is supposed to," he said calmly. "It is the one constant in any universe."

Shifting her weight back and forth in frustration she seized on another question. "Well then tell me more about them, about their ancestry, the other five bloodlines."

"The Arcanists carry the blood of the six races that inhabited the Five Realms. You and I belong to the realm of witches; the other realms were home to elves, fae, mermaids, dragon gypsies, and celestials."

"Celestials?"

"I believe mortals refer to their kind as angels."

"Of course," she nodded. That made perfect sense considering the Guardian was surrounded by winged protectors. "So, the Guardian of Deities was a celestial?"

"Yes, but unlike all the others. Much more powerful. The celestials are a unique race." Sebastian said, his voice softening as he remembered the powerful entities sacrifice.

"How so?"

"The Thanissia races are governed by the elements, they are the foundation of our powers and our life force. Each race is ruled by one specific element, which provides us with the magic our powers need, and a balance within our world. The celestials are not ruled by an element, they are born from one—*spirit.* The ether is their life force, they are innately linked to its essence and cannot exist without its power. While it provides them with unlimited power and links them to all the other elements, it is also their greatest weakness. Unlike the rest of the races, they cannot exist outside our universe."

"Why only five realms if there are six races?"

"The elves and fae have always existed on one realm. Their magic is similar, both ruled by the element Air, but it was not a peaceful existence. They were once very different, and those differences made them mortal enemies for many millennia. Originally, the fae lived on a different plane of existence among the ether that surrounded the world of the elves. The magic of their individual planes was connected, which often caused malcontent between the races as each claimed supremacy over the element that ruled their shared world. They were also very different entities. Fae could be mischievous and spiteful while the elves more gracious and disciplined, differences that kept them constantly in turmoil. Eventually, a war broke out between the two races. Many lives were lost, and their realm was badly damaged as the magic essence infusing both their powers was abused. The Warlicians managed the situation as best they could but our honor code does not allow us to use warrior magic on like-kind."

"Like-kind?"

"Others in our universe, other magical entities," he explained. "The Guardian eventually intervened, after the war damaged the fairy plane leaving the entire race of fae homeless. He made them see reason, showed them they could live in one world in peace and solidarity while retaining their magical differences. The fae and elves signed a peace doctrine, allowing them to cohabit their realm within the same plane. Over time their races became strong allies, which in turn made both their peoples more powerful."

"In union, the magic they fought over became stronger."

"Precisely," Sebastian stated. "The air realm is one of the most beautiful realms of our universe. The races used the magic of the same element differently, but their opposing essences eventually bonded, creating a unique essence that both races had the ability to manipulate. That essence not only enhanced their magical abilities and all the energy that existed in their realm but infused in every part of their world—it is definitely something to see."

She noticed the sadness in his eyes when he spoke of the worlds that lay in a distant universe, forgotten.

"Do the ancient realms have anything to do with the prophecy?"

"They have everything to do with it, the prophecy cannot be realized without the essence of the ether. The magic of the Thanissia Universe is powerful and must be harnessed if the ancient dark is to be defeated in this world. The ether can only be restored if the magic of all five realms is re-energized."

"How?" She snapped.

Sebastian, seeming to ignore her tone, motioning for Dane to follow as he headed back toward the old contorted tree from which he had emerged.

"This is the entrance to the other realms," he said, patting the massive trunk affectionately. "The portals to each are contained within. It is the only connection between this world and the Five Realms."

"An old tree is a portal to another universe." Her voice was tight with sarcasm, and she winced when she heard it echo back at her.

"This is not just an old tree Dane, this is an Elder Oak, a species that resides only in the realm of the fae and elves, and it is not the portals themselves, but a vessel that holds them. It has magical properties where time and space do not exist, which provides a sacred place where the volatile magic required to make portals finds stability. This Elder Oak holds the gateway to our past and unlocks the knowledge required for the future. It is essentially the giver of destiny."

"Why is it here if the realms are dead? Why keep a portal open to the other worlds?"

"The realms are not dead my dear they are in a magical stasis. A form of unconsciousness, like a deep unending sleep. The Thanissia Universe cannot die, it is a magical entity, a creation of the ether from which all things are connected. Like its inhabitants, in its own way it too is immortal. Its essence is still there but exists inconspicuously. Once we discovered that the magic contained within the realms was feeding the ancient dark and enhancing its power, it became imperative to deactivate the realms. Culling the magic was the only way to defeat it, unfortunately, it also meant the end for our kind."

A haunting sadness crossed his face and when he spoke again, his voice was thick with longing.

"The portals were created so that only an Arcanist can invoke its power to return to their ancestral worlds, awaken the magic, and claim their birthright. It is the only way to defend against the Second Rising."

"So, then I can return to the realms and awaken the ancient magic."

Sebastian shook his head, "It is not that simple. Only the one that carries the blood of their ancestors can unlock that specific realm's portal. All those whose destinies intertwine must be found."

"But how? I have no idea who these others are, how am I going to find them?" She asked, the scope of her task becoming larger by the minute.

"Patience, you must first unlock your own powers by accepting your birthright, then the others born of the prophecy will be revealed."

She looked hard at Sebastian, irritated that he spoke in riddles and revealed very little of any help.

"Will the portals open for us? Mortals I mean." The magic in her veins began to pulse at the idea of her presence in an ancient and magical realm.

"A mortal yes, but the blood of your ancestors flows through you. The portals contain magic that will only come forth from the tree when summoned by one who is born from the ancients."

"And when I get to our realm, what then? Are you coming or is there another like you waiting to guide me on the other side?"

"Unfortunately, I am not able to pass through the portal yet. I was given the power of light transfer, the ability to alter my physical form and become light, so that I may exist on this world indefinitely, but it has left me tethered to the Elder Oak. My ability to leave its protection is diminished until I am released by the celestial. I too need an Arcanists help."

"So, there is no one to help."

Sebastian shook his head sadly, "There were only a few of us that survived the Great War but there was one tasked with staying on our world, to guard the Book of Realms, but I am not sure he will be of much help."

"The Book of Realms?" Dane asked.

"It is a sacred and ancient tome, a combined grimoire representing all the magical races. The pages contain a record of our history, the lineages of each race, detailed information about the Thanissia Universe, the races, and the individual realms. The book is a doctrine of our magic. Spells, incantations, enchantments, and curses from every race are contained within its pages. The Book of Realms holds the secrets of elemental magic and the power of the ether and is a vital part of our birthright and our survival for it connects the entire universe, all the races, and the magical properties. It will be imperative that it is retrieved from where it was hidden."

"And where is that?"

"I do not know only the Warlician tasked with keeping it safe, is trusted with that knowledge.

Dane signed; her frustration obvious to Sebastian.

"We each have our own destiny Dane, some are linked to one another for a greater purpose, and others traverse their path alone, but all have meaning and direction and require patience. I realize it is difficult, what is being asked of you, even more so when much of your destiny still lies unanswered. There will be a time when all is revealed that I can promise you."

CHAPTER 16

DANE WALKED AROUND THE CIRCUMFERENCE of the tree, her fingers sliding over the rough bark as she went. "How do they open, the portals?"

"The portals only respond to a magical key known as a portal stone and the stones will only respond to those who are born from the specific bloodline of its realms inhabitants. Only those that possess the ancient blood can evoke the power of the corresponding portal stone and use it to open the portal to their ancestor's homeland."

"And I suppose you are going to tell me where to find these portal stones," she said, assuming this was going to be another task she would have to figure out on her own.

"I do not need to, you already know where they are," he responded motioning to the ground at the base of the tree where the Irish Guardian moss still flourished.

She walked over to the spot where she had found the buried stone the other day, bending down she brushed off the dirt and leaves. The stone with the strange double pentacle symbol was still there, waiting. Looking back up at Sebastian she asked. "This is a portal stone?"

"No, it is a vessel. The stones are contained within." He answered. "You must open it to access them."

Turning her attention back to the stone, she slowly removed the soil from around the edges, digging down until she could just get her fingers underneath. The stone box was heavy and embedded in the dirt. Wiggling it back and forth she managed to get more fingers underneath until she had the grip to pull the box from its hiding spot. Dusting off the remaining soil she searched the surfaces for a way to open the box. There was no definite lid, no hinges, no cracks or crevices just a small keyhole on the left side.

"The key," she whispered, standing up and walking over to her backpack where it lay in the middle of the clearing. Pulling her grandfather's medallion from the side pocket she opened the back and pulled the small key from its interior.

With Sebastian's eyes following her, she walked back to the tree, picked up the stone box and inserted the key into the hole. There was a slight resistance and then a loud click. She heard a whirring sound coming from inside the stone box as unseen tumblers spun and clicked into place. The rock face began to rise, revealing five small gray stones laying insignificantly on a black velvet cushion. Engraved on the inside of the lid was an inscription:

*The door to destiny will open to those who possess
the blood of the ancients.*

Each stone had a colored symbol painted on its surface which she recognized immediately for they matched the five glyphs that encircled the double pentacle on the stone box. She guessed by their coloring and her newfound knowledge of the ancient realms that each glyph probably symbolized one of the elements—earth, water, air, fire, and spirit. Picking up the earth stone she held it gently in her palm. Its surface was cool but as it lay there, she could feel a tingling warmth begin to emanate from its surface. A slight vibration kindling within its core.

Suddenly, Sebastian's voice echoed in the air behind her. "Warlician warriors, like this world's modern witches, are governed by the earth element. Our powers derive from the energy found in the natural environment. The earth's energy is within you. Your bloodline is pure, and the stone recognizes it. If there was any doubt as to your true destiny, there lies your answer."

He pointed at the stone she held in her palm, nodding his approval as the rune began to glow.

She stared, mesmerized by the glowing green stone barely aware of the stinging warmth that sprung from its surface. The other stones lay silent in the box oblivious to her presence, only this stone acknowledged her existence, only this stone would lead her to her families' true origins.

Carefully she placed the stone back in the box with the others where it immediately stopped glowing and went cold.

"Dywen," Sebastian said unexpectedly.

"Excuse me?"

A smile appeared briefly on his face. "It is the name of your ancestral realm, my home."

She nodded, saying the name over and over in her head. It sounded like it was born from the earth, a word that belonged in another time and place.

"You must keep the stones safe until their time has come." He stared at her with piercing green eyes, the importance of these stones emphasized by his tone.

He shivered slightly, his physical presence weakening. "I am unable to stay in this form much longer and I have given you all I can, for now. You must go home and prepare immediately for your journey to Dywen, for time is no longer on our side. The first portal must be opened under the light of a full moon. You must open the portal to Dywen tomorrow night."

"Tomorrow!" She exclaimed.

Everything was happening so quickly she barely had time to process one thing before another was revealed. "How long will I be gone? I have a job, people who will miss me, commitments and responsibilities. I can't just take off indefinitely."

He looked at her and smiled knowingly. "Time passes more quickly in the realms than it does here on earth. You should have plenty of time to find your way before anyone that matters here misses you."

"How quickly does time pass?" She asked hesitantly, not sure if she really wanted to know the answer.

Sebastian thought for a minute before answering. "Time is irrelevant in the Thanissia Universe. It happens but its passing does not affect the lives of individuals. Here every aspect of mortal life is affected by time. Mortals feel the passing of time more acutely than immortals, because for us time holds no end, therefore it is of little importance."

He stopped speaking when he noticed her confused and anxious face.

"To put it proportionately in mortal terms, weeks can

pass in Thanissia but only a few days will have expired here."

"Then, I guess disappearing for a weekend will do," she said making a mental note to rearrange her schedule to free her up for the next five days.

"Dane, you cannot speak of this to anyone, do you understand?

"Why?"

"This journey must be taken without any interference from this world," he said firmly.

"Not even my parents, they are already involved in much of what has been going on. They are both witches. My father is of the Callan, I mean Callathian bloodline. It is his ancestors that I descend from." She argued, sure that telling her parents would be alright.

"Not even them. I am sorry, but this must be your journey and yours alone. There will be a time when all is revealed, and this world will know of its fate, but for now, your path must be kept secret from everyone. Do you understand?"

She stubbornly nodded in acknowledgment.

"There is one more thing you must be aware of," he said looking at her with grave concern. "As I mentioned, the people of the Thanissia Universe were immortals, your ancestors were immortals. When you make the journey and claim your birthright the result will be the same. You will be sacrificing your mortality."

Her eyes widened as the realization of what Sebastian was saying hit her. "I will become immortal?"

"Yes," he said. "It is the only way. If your destiny is fulfilled and you and the others can achieve victory over the ancient dark, you will outlive all that you love. You must understand and accept the sacrifices. It is a heavy burden for one who was born into a mortal life, but one that you must carry, nonetheless."

A heavy sadness wrapped around her heart as she thought about living through the loss of her family and friends.

But at least they will have a life, she thought, the images of the dead from Sebastian's memories once again floated through her mind.

Silently, she walked to her backpack, tucking the stone box into it and turning to face him.

"Will you be here when I get back Sebastian?" Dane asked, unsure if his destiny had now been fulfilled.

"I will," he acknowledged. "My task is far from over and my destiny is not yet complete, but for now I am fading, alas I must return to my other self."

His voice was growing weak and his form began to ebb. Suddenly, white light sprang from the tree, creeping across the cold ground to encase him in its brilliance.

As the light and Sebastian receded back into the tree, she heard his voice in her mind, *"Make haste, there is much to do. We will speak again upon your return."*

As the sound of his voice dissipated the clearing once again fell silent, shadows lengthening as nightfall neared.

Whistling for Tyson she hurried out of the clearing, moving down the trail quickly trying to outrun the sinking sun. As she reached the familiarity of the Wrangler a single thought crossed her mind *why was all of this not affecting her more?* A man from a tree had appeared and told her of the existence of ancient magical realms and mythical races. He confirmed her destiny as one of the Arcanists—the saviors of mankind and told her she must give up her mortality.

She was a witch in a modern world so normal was not in her vocabulary but to not even question the validity of his claims. Was she willing to give up everything she had ever known for an age-old prophecy that may not even be true? To journey alone into a magical realm, frozen in another time, without forethought.

She stood quietly in the darkening parking lot, a peaceful calm falling over her. She already knew why she was taking such a risky leap of faith—because somewhere deep inside she had always known her destiny was not yet complete.

Dane tossed and turned, sweat beads forming on her upper lip, as she moaned softly in her sleep. Tyson watched her intently, his head resting protectively on her stomach as she wrestled with whatever dream was actively engaging her subconscious.

The half-moon hung high in the night sky filtering ghostly light down across her townhome, encasing it in an eerie silvery glow. There was an unnatural silence that hung over her neighborhood as the late hours ticked by unnoticed. She struggled with the dream that had invaded her mind as the unusual quiet, which hung heavy outside, entered her room in a slithering whisper.

Tyson growled a low guttural sound that escaped the skin surrounding his throat. His body tensed as he detected the change in the room's atmosphere. He did not move from his protective position determined to guard his master as she continued to be assaulted by her unconscious mind.

The mist was thick, and it left a damp film on her skin

as she tried to find her way through the gray dawn. There wasn't a sound, nothing familiar, nothing to guide her through the fog that clogged her breath and stifled her movement. She stopped walking, as she gasped for breath, but the fog was suffocating, its heaviness pushing down on her, sinking into her skin and saturating her entire being. Exhaustion overtook her senses. She dropped to the ground, her knees sinking into the wet soil. She was tired, she just wanted to lay down, to sleep.

Closing her eyes, she felt a twinge in the back of her mind, as an image began to surface. Through her fatigue, she forced herself not to ignore the vision. She concentrated, willing her mind to focus, blocking out the cold, the damp, and the exhaustion that threatened to take over. It was a Celtic cross; the points of the cross emulated the spearheaded finials of a wrought-iron fence. Constructed of elaborate knotwork the ring had ends that curved out in arced points. The surface of the cross was cracked in places and the black lines resembled faded ink.

It hung in her mind willing her to take notice as the fog surrounded her in its cold damp embrace, pulling her down until only blackness prevailed.

She woke suddenly, the feel of the clammy fog still covering her skin. Sweat trickled down her face and chest as she struggled to adjust her eyesight to the soft moonlight that filtered through the dark room.

Tyson lay quietly staring at her, his brow furrowed in worry. She smiled, reassuring him she was OK, his tail thumping in response. Gingerly he crawled up toward the top part of the bed, nudging her chin gently and laying his large head on her chest. She kissed his nose and turned slightly, so she could see the bedside clock. Its glowing red numbers showed her it was almost three in the morning. Cuddling back under the warm duvet, she thought about the dream.

It was different from the others, she had felt lost in the fog, alone, directionless until the cross had appeared. Seeing it had made her feel safe, secure, no longer afraid of the suffocating fog that held her in its grip. The cross had been a comforting sight, but she had no idea why. As her mind tried to decipher the strange dream she finally drifted into a deep, exhausted and undisturbed sleep.

CHAPTER 17

DANE WOKE FEELING TIRED AND anxious—*probably not a good way to start off her new life as the savior of mankind,* she thought, squinting against the glare of the bulbs above her vanity.

Showering quickly, she dried her hair and packed a few essentials into her small make-up bag. Since she had no idea what to expect on Dywen, she didn't know how to dress. Did it have seasons? Would it be cold or warm? Deciding to be optimistic but cautious, she dressed in jeans, knee-high black boots, a beige long sleeve scoop neck t-shirt, and a light brown canvas safari jacket. She packed an extra pair of jeans, some underwear and socks, a few extra short and long-sleeve t-shirts, a light sweater, and a light waterproof jacket.

On the outside of her right boot, she strapped a leather sheath containing a hunting knife her grandfather had given her for her eighteenth birthday. A compass was in one of her jacket pockets along with a book of waterproof matches and her cell phone and in her back jeans pocket, she put a small utility knife.

Grabbing her backpack, she walked to the front door, hesitating briefly to pull on a slouchy thin wool hat and wrap a gauzy scarf around her neck. Checking for the third time that her grandfather's medallion was around her neck she grabbed her leather gloves and headed out the door.

Other than the medallion the only jewelry she wore was a watch, and the wood and leather bracelet that Kai's father had made for her birthday—to remind her of home. She rechecked the essentials in her backpack before putting it in the back of the Jeep—water, food, a few toiletries, a flashlight, extra batteries, and some magical items. Everything a girl might need on a trip to a distant realm.

The early morning sun lit up the tips of the ice-covered trees that hung low over Stevie's driveway as she pulled in fifteen minutes later. Snow-heavy branches grazed the top of her Jeep as she pulled up and parked beside Stevie's old Land Rover. More snow had fallen last night, and it coated the town with a beautiful white blanket.

She felt a twinge of uncertainty as she exited the Wrangler and climbed the steps, knocking on Stevie's front door. She hoped Stevie would not ask too many questions about her plans because the lies were now getting bigger and harder to keep track of. Getting no response, she used her key and entered the house.

Tyson scampered around the living room and kitchen before she could even announce their arrival, finally disappearing down the hallway determined to find Diego. An excited commotion alerted her that he had found what he was looking for. A few minutes later Stevie stumbled out of her bedroom and down the hallway her red-rimmed eyes begging for quiet.

"Rough night?" Dane asked heading into the kitchen to start the coffee.

"Not rough, just long," she responded heading into the bathroom to splash cold water on her face and brush her teeth.

"What happened?"

"Gabby had another rough night."

"More dreams?"

She took two mugs out of the cupboard placing Stevie's under the coffee machine spout as she pressed the brew button, watching as the brown liquid poured into the cup, its steam rising lazily into the air. The kitchen filled with the enticing aroma.

Stevie shivered as she took a sip from the cup Dane handed her.

"It was the same as the others, visions of landscapes and then you and me walking through a foggy forest, as shadows surrounded us."

Dane thought about the dream she had last night, the fog, the feeling of familiarity and comfort she felt at seeing the Celtic cross. It was all so strange. "Thanks for looking after Tyson while I'm gone."

"Of course, where did you say you are going again."

"Catskills," she lied.

Dane concocted a story about meeting a prospective client in the Catskills, a remote location for photographing wildlife. She wanted to make sure her friends understood she couldn't be contacted as she was sure her cell phone wouldn't work in a distant universe. She had also sent her parents a quick text this morning telling them the same thing. Dane hated lying to them and texting instead of calling made it a little easier. Her mother had sent back a long response, saying they were still looking into the situation and reiterating the need to talk about her second awakening and new powers when she got home. If they only knew how different she was going to be, when she got back. Her new telepathic ability may seem insignificant compared to her pending immortality.

Her mom had also asked about the redhead, but Dane hadn't seen her since the night of her birthday dinner. Although she had wanted to return to the old flour mill, she hadn't had the time and now, with things getting extremely complicated, it would have to wait until she returned.

After a few more minutes chatting with Stevie, she said goodbye and headed toward the train station. She had arranged for a rental car, a Chevrolet Trax so that her Jeep would stay in the station parking lot where it belonged. Leaving her vehicle at the trailhead was too much of a risk; the Trax would go unnoticed if any of her friends decided to hike while she was away.

After filling out the rental car paperwork, and doing a few last-minute errands, it was after three when she pulled into the trailhead parking lot. Sunset was approximately 4:45, which should give her enough time to hike to the clearing before then. Grabbing her backpack and locking the car she headed into the woods stopping suddenly when the irony of the journey she was about to take hit her—*more secrets and lies in a life filled with secrets and lies, and now more alone than ever.* She felt a slight constriction in her chest as the walls that she had erected so many years ago, closed even tighter around her heart.

Hiking toward the clearing, she thought about her friends and how often over the years she had yearned to be normal like them. They would never know the truth, especially now as her new destiny would most likely take her further away from them, her pending immortality making it impossible to stay with anyone for very long. Tears stung her eyes as she felt that familiar hollow ache wrap itself around her heart. Her truth was a world full of hidden magic, her friend's truth was ignorant bliss. The small gap that existed between those truths was about to expand, possibly destroying the relationships she had with her mortal friends.

She felt the magic pulsing through her veins as she entered the clearing. The sun was sinking below the horizon casting shadows across the forest floor, but a pale white glow seeped warmly from the trunk of the Elder Oak. Sebastian stood waiting by the tree, his black cape sweeping the forest floor as he came toward her. "Are you ready to begin your journey?"

"I think so," she responded, quick to cover up the nervous energy that had been building as she had come up the trail.

"And you are willing to accept your destiny and all its responsibilities."

"Yes," she whispered her heart pounding so hard she was sure Sebastian could hear it.

"This is going to send you on an entirely new path Dane, and there will be sacrifices to be made."

"I understand Sebastian. I have lived with a secret most of my life, hiding who I am from the entire world and building relationships on half-truths. This is just more of the same." She lifted an eyebrow and smirked. "Anyway, it's not like I can refuse."

He looked at her affectionately understanding what she meant. "Our destiny does not always give us a choice that is true, but there is always a way for us to find peace with our fate."

She nodded, knowing deep down that the choice she was making was indeed the correct one and that her destiny would unfold the way it was intended. She had accepted her role in this prophecy and was determined to see it through, at whatever cost. "I am fine and ready. I won't let you down, Sebastian."

He squeezed her shoulder and gave her a reassuring smile. "The moon is out and will be reaching its apex in a few hours. We must prepare."

She followed his gaze. The full moon's ghostly glow was visible behind the farthest branches of the treetops.

Sebastian pointed at a large root, motioning for her to sit down. Flinging his cape up behind him as he sat, he looked at her, his brow furrowed and an intense seriousness in his eyes.

"There are things you must know and remember before you enter the portal."

His tone was somber as he looked intensely at her. "As I told you before our world is in what we call stasis; a magical dormancy. While your presence may rouse the magic from this dormancy, only reigniting the Druidstone can power and strengthen that magic fully. The Druidstone is essential to the magic of the realm and is also where you will be given your birthright. It is located at the top of the highest mountain on Dywen, residing in a sacred place called the Temple of Earth. It will not be an easy journey. You must go to the ancient city first. The location of the Temple of Earth and how to navigate the perils of the mountain can be found in the Great Hall of the Warlician Barracks, inside the city walls.

A shadow passed over Sebastian's features.

"I am not sure where the portal will open on the other side, so you must be vigilant. Without a direct link in the ancient realm to stabilize it the portal may be erratic, and you could emerge anywhere. Dywen is the largest of the realms and not easy to navigate as it has a multitude of varying landscapes, some harsher than others. For guidance, look to the sky and head directly toward the two moons. They are visible constantly during the day and night and will guide you to *Arcadium*, the ancient city of Dywen for they hang directly over it."

Sebastian placed his hands firmly on her shoulders, looking deep into her eyes. "Besides activating the Druidstone you must locate and return with the *Book of Realms* and the *Essence of Ether*, as both these items are essential to what is coming. This will not be an easy task as both these items have been magically hidden. Dywen's magic will strengthen after the Druidstone has been reactivated and your birthright fulfilled. Harness the ancient magic of your ancestors Dane it will guide you through your tasks and help you find what you desire. Rely on your instincts, they will not fail you."

"What about the other Warlician? The one tasked with looking after the book. Will he not help?" She asked not understanding why this other warrior was not involved in making her arrival in Dywen an easier transition.

"You must be wary of him for he has been in a deep sleep for billions of centuries. He will know nothing of the time that has passed or the world beyond his own. His instinct for survival will be stronger than his memory of the past, his need to protect the book his only priority. He will be unreliable at best. He will not know you, nor trust you and he will not hesitate to harm if he deems you a threat, so you must proceed with caution."

Reaching into his pocket, he handed her a large silver coin. On one side was engraved a tree its trunk an inverted sword, the other a dagger piercing a sphere.

"What is it?"

"It will ensure your protection."

"How is an old coin going to do that?"

"One side is your family crest," he said pointing to the side with the tree, "the other is the mark of The Order, one he knows well. When he finds you, and he will, show him this and he'll know that you are one of us."

She turned the coin over and over in her hand inspecting the dented pewter surface and the ancient etchings before storing it safely inside the front zippered pocket of her jacket.

Sebastian turned, gesturing for her to follow him to the base of the tree. His green eyes softening as he stared deep into hers.

"Remember Dane, listen to your instincts they will guide you and never second guess your intuition it will rarely be misleading." He paused briefly before continuing a heavy sadness coating his voice as he spoke, "You carry a heavy burden my dear but accept your destiny and you will prevail."

Gracing her with a knowing smile he stood and faced the trunk, the full moon's glow casting it in a soft ethereal light.

Lifting his hand, he placed it on the flat part of the scar, light springing from his fingertips. Closing his eyes, he recited something in a tongue she did not recognize. Suddenly the smooth bark beneath his hand disappeared and in its place, was a flat panel with five corresponding holes, each a different color.

He took a few steps back, gesturing for Dane to proceed.

Quickly, she removed from her backpack the leather bag where she had stored the portal stone. Its glow ignited the moment it touched her skin. She carefully placed it in the corresponding green hole in the panel. The stone glowed for a moment longer and then began to throb, a hum that pulsated through the dark clearing as the full moon's light bathed the old Elder Oak in an enchanted silver glow.

She took a few steps back as a green light began to seep from the portal stone down the trunk of the tree, over the ground and upward, forming an arched doorway of rotating green light. She stared in awe at the portal, the brilliance of its green glow was stunning, a shimmering gateway to a land lost in time.

Smiling she turned to Sebastian. "Thank you," she said squeezing his hand gently. "I will miss you."

"I will never be far," he replied, as small white sparks began to emanate from his body and his physical form once again transformed to light.

She watched until the last of his light receded into the tree before turning to face the portal, its haunting hum beckoning her. Clasping the medallion that hung around her neck she took a deep breath, shifting the weight of her backpack and taking a step toward the portal. Suddenly, she heard Sebastian's voice in her head—*go now and uncover your past.*

With his words echoing in her mind Dane walked through the portal, unsure as to what she would find on the other side. As the portal's green light encircled her body, carrying her into the unknown, she readied herself to meet her true destiny.

CHAPTER 18

D ANE STOOD ON THE PRECIPICE of a magnificent
waterfall, its mist gently caressing her face. The
rumble of its cascading flow silenced any other
sounds evident in this world as it thundered powerfully to
the river hundreds of feet below.

From her position atop the waterfall, she had an
unspoiled view of the breathtaking landscape that stretched
before her. The massive green forest was the color of emer-
alds, its expanse cut in half by the waterfall's river that
wound through it like an aqua green snake, sparkling
vibrantly as it basked in the day's golden hue. In the
distance hung two moons, their silver surfaces shimmering
in the sunlight. The first was enormous as it hovered low to
the ground, allowing her to make out the slight imperfections on its surface. The three rings encircling its perimeter
reflected the sun's rays, casting a colorful prism of light
outward. A second much smaller moon sat just to its left. It
too shimmered in the sunlight but its surface was smooth as
glass and void of any blemishes.

She could see for miles in every direction, the magnificent beauty of this land taking her breath away as she turned, slowly scanning the different horizons. A mountain range towered up in the distance, gray rock peaks reaching gracefully into the cloud bank that hovered over their tips. Behind her stretched an expanse of dusty flatland, large rock formations scattered across its vastness. The barren land seemed to fall off the edge of the distant horizon as heat waves shimmered on its surface.

The surreal beauty of this realm was haunting. She smiled, this was the world she had seen in her visions, her ancestor's homeland.

Luckily, the portal had opened at the top of a waterfall making it easy to get her bearings and see where she needed to go. She had emerged from the portal feeling slightly hazy and a little nauseous, but it had passed quickly as she stood gazing out over the realm of her ancestors.

As she scanned the landscapes in awe a glint exploded in her peripheral vision, and she turned quickly to see what had caused it. Off in the distance, directly below the moons, she could make out a structure rising from the edge of the thick forest.

She removed the binoculars from her backpack, training the lenses in its direction. Tall stone turrets reached silently upward from the lush green forest, their silver-tipped spires piercing the blue sky. Beyond the stone castle and the city walls, snuggled quaintly into a pristine vale, she could see a village; smaller stone and wood structures nestled together on empty dirt streets.

Arcadium, she thought her eyes straining as she looked for movement even though she knew she would find none.

She could feel the deafening silence of this world as it wound around her.

A gentle breeze ruffled her hair, whispering as it blew by, its wisps tainted with the scent of unknown flowers. She closed her eyes letting the warm breeze caress her skin. Suddenly, she felt a slight tug on her magic as her existence in this world began to awaken a pulse that had been lost long ago. A Callathian had returned home and Dywen knew it.

She glanced at her watch the hands firmly set at 8:15. She had been in the portal for less than two minutes.

Taking out her compass she noted the direction of the village. She would need to go southeast from the other side of the waterfall to reach the city. She looked around for a path or any indication of how to get down, but none was visible from where she stood. Walking slowly, she circled the top of the waterfall looking over the edge, the pounding water hurtling to the canyon floor below. Making her way to the backside she found no way down there either, only a rope ladder that hung precariously down the cliff and ended on a small ledge about twenty feet below. She could see nothing beyond the ledge as the vegetation was too thick, so with no other options, she began to descend carefully down the rickety ladder.

Near the bottom, she saw the cliff jutted in and hidden beneath its ledge was an opening. Taking the flashlight from her backpack she pointed the beam into the darkness. Dusty stone stairs descended the inside of the waterfall where she could hear the faint rumble of the water echoing far below.

"This must be the way down," she said softly, hoping

that she would not drop hundreds of feet to her death because ancient stairs gave way beneath her.

Carefully, she began to descend, slowly testing the ability of each to hold her weight before she continued to the next. The stairs spiraled downward into the dark, and she lost sight of them as they left the reach of her flashlight's beam. Hopeful that they would hold. She descended quicker allowing the beam to race ahead of her, confirming there were no obstacles waiting.

Eventually, she reached the bottom of the staircase, the rumble of the waterfall much louder now. Daylight lit up the far wall. She headed in that direction, finding a small opening in the thick rock, that led outside.

As she exited, she could feel the spray from the waterfall pounding ferociously only feet away, a deafening roar that drowned out every other sound around it. She realized quickly that she was on the opposite side of the waterfall. Checking the compass again she confirmed that southeast was now on the backside of the waterfall. Unable to see the spires or the moons from where she stood she searched the area for a trail or a way through the thick forest. Skirting the river's edge, she found a break in the foliage about a hundred feet down. A worn stone path led into the trees, and she followed it in hopes that it would circle back and take her in the correct direction. Otherwise, she may be getting hopelessly lost in a dense and unknown forest.

She trekked through the thick, shadowy woods for what seemed like hours, the slowness of her watch reminding her, this world was not her own. She stopped occasionally to check her direction and drink water but kept moving at a consistent pace hoping to emerge from the forest before Dywen's day ended, whenever that might be.

The similar appearance of Dywen to earth was uncanny making Dane feel more comfortable and at home with her surroundings. The differences between the two were evident only in Dywen's visual intensity. The green of the foliage was surreal, vibrant and bright as each leaf shone like it was covered in shimmering dew. There was an abundance of large colorful flowers that seemed to thrive in this shadowy environment, each showcasing brilliant unique colors not found back home. Thick root-like vines hung in loops from large trees coiling around the trunks and swaying lazily in the light breeze; a warm soothing gust that consistently carried the delicate scent of unfamiliar flowers.

She could feel the life pulsing through every part of the forest. It was alive with a renewed sense of purpose, an essence that beckoned to her as she passed.

Stopping at a small stream, she bent down and dangled her fingers in the cool water, a tingle creeping up her arm as the water flowed by her fingertips. She could sense the water's direction, felt it ebb and flow as it moved around rocks and through the thick reeds that dotted its surface. The sand at its bottom was soft but determined as it fought the pull of the current. The sweetness of the clean water flowed over her senses, immersing her in its life force. All her senses were electrified by the energy that ran through this world. She had never been so in tune with the natural environment or experienced such intensity—it was exhilarating.

The light was beginning to fade as she made her way into a small clearing near a rock cut jutting out from the side of a small knoll. Satiny green moss clung desperately to the knoll's stone surface, cascading gently down its side and onto the forest floor. She quickly took stock of her surroundings deciding this would be a good place to camp for the night.

Placing her backpack against the tree she took the knife from the sheath strapped to her calf and went in search of firewood. Finding some, she gathered a few rocks and placed them in a circle around the wood, building a small fire pit. Once the fire was lit, she took out the small thin blanket she had brought from home and laid it on the soft mossy ground using her backpack as a backrest. She ate her sandwich and an apple, listening to the crackle of the fire and thinking about all the wonders of this new world that were immersing her senses in its strange magical essence.

As the light faded into night and the forest went dark, Dane began to feel a heaviness pressing down on her heart, a loneliness quite unexpected. She reached into the side pocket of her backpack and took out a crinkled photograph. Staring back at her were the faces of her mother, father, and her five best friends. The ache in her heart expanded until she couldn't bear to look at the photo any longer. Tucking it carefully back in the pocket she concentrated instead on the task that loomed ahead of her.

Tomorrow she must reach the city and find the way to the Druidstone. *Always keep the moons in front of you*, he had told her, and you will find what you seek. Great advice if she could see the moons through the dense canopy of the forest. Currently, she was relying on intuition and luck.

The fire died down and the surrounding area fell into shadows. Without the bright light of the sun blocking them, she could see the two moons shining like silver orbs in the night sky their shimmering light filtering down through the small breaks in the forest canopy. They were much larger than they were from the top of the waterfall, so she was thankfully heading in the right direction.

Settling back onto her blanket, she propped her head comfortably on her backpack, as the dark sky peeked down at her. The canopy seemed to open at night. Branches recoiling slightly letting the moonlight seep unobstructed to the forest floor. As the sky darkened, thousands of stars appeared twinkling erratically against the inky backdrop. The stars were different here, there were no constellations that she recognized, and the stars seemed closer to the ground. There was a faint green-tinged haze that encircled each star adding to the brilliance of its glow. Layer upon layers of stars, one in front of the other, twinkled in a subtle pattern. The night sky was alive, she could feel the magic pulsing through the air as the breeze carried the moonlight across the land. The energy encapsulated in this world was comforting and it made her feel safe. She closed her eyes letting the rustle of the overhead leaves lull her to sleep.

She was awakened the next morning by the sun as it rose over the horizon and pierced the small knoll with its blinding golden rays. The temperature had risen, and it was humid and sticky in the forest. She changed into a cotton tank and tied her jacket onto the loop of her backpack. Quickly, eating a bagel and drinking some water, she doused the still warm fire with sand ensuring that all the embers were completely out before leaving.

Pulling out her father's compass she checked her bearings and then headed south toward where she had seen the moons hovering in the sky last night. She had no sense of time as her watch still ticked unnaturally slow only minutes passing through the entire night. It was extremely unnerving, so she made the decision to take it off, tucking it away in one of the pockets of her jacket. She needed to exist in Dywen's time and truly immerse herself in this new environment, hopefully, it would reset her internal clock and force her to coexist with her natural instincts and awareness.

As she made her way through the thick forest, she took in all the smells, sights, and sounds, reveling in their vitality and their ability to intoxicate the senses. Her fingertips experienced subtle vibrations as they touched petals, leaves, and bark. She could feel the essence of this world pumping through her blood. Her senses were on fire as they were stretched to the brink by the ever-growing energy that seeped endlessly out of the surrounding environment, curiously aware of her presence.

As she continued down the small path, she heard a faint sound echoing in the distance. Stopping, she waited and listened. The noise seemed to be coming from above the treetops. Moving quickly through the lush growth, she reached a spot where the sky was visible. The strange sound was closer now, and she could make it out; a deep, powerful, musical bellow that combined with a steady flapping. It grew in intensity as it neared the spot where she stood. Shielding her eyes from the bright sun she scanned the sky for the source.

Suddenly, a dark shadow came into view sailing gracefully through the sky above her. As it flew past, she could see that it was indeed a bird; a large black bird. The powerful bird dipped and curled through the bright blue sky, its grace and power on full display. The sheen of its sleek black feathers reflecting the sunlight causing a strange kaleidoscope of greens to arc out from the tips. The sound it made was also unique; it was not the typical frantic cawing of a seagull or crow but a calm, strong, and confident musical bellow.

She watched as the bird patrolled the sky dipping close to the ground and then soaring upward, its impressive wingspan adding grace to the bird's movements. Eventually, the bird flew out of sight, the peace of the forest no longer disrupted by the bird's vocalization. As she turned to continue down the forest path, she wondered about its sudden appearance. Since arriving on Dywen, she had noticed that there didn't seem to be any living entities, at least none that she had seen. There were no insects or wildlife, making the appearance of this magnificent bird extremely unexpected, especially in a world that had apparently been void of all life forms for billions of centuries.

Finally, the dense forest began to thin. The large trees became smaller and the mossy carpet that spread across the forest floor morphed into a carpet of thick green grass, its dewy tips glistening in the late morning sunlight. The edge of the forest was just ahead and the two moons that hung in the sky were even larger and closer.

Cautiously, she emerged from the thick woods, feeling a curious stirring in the landscape around her as her energy invaded yet another part of this realm, arousing the primordial magic from its profound sleep.

CHAPTER 19

WARM SCENTED AIR CARESSED HER skin as she stood looking at the pure white crushed stone pathway that lay in front of her, winding its way toward the heart of the city. The stone sparkled in the midday sunshine; its purity flanked on either side by lush green lawns. The dazzling white of the stone path was a stark contrast to the harshness of the dark, aged metal of the city gates that it led to.

Dane could see the heavy gates not far from where she had emerged—*a world of contradictions*—she thought, acknowledging how powerful yet serene Dywen's landscapes and atmosphere could be.

The city was surrounded by a high stone wall that seemingly went on indefinitely in both directions. Large trees lined the path on either side, their weeping foliage and whimsical limbs reaching gracefully for the ground below. Flowers sprung from the grassy green carpet creating a medley of bright colors and hues that dotted the terrain— the colors of Dywen unnaturally perfect.

An intoxicating aroma drifted past where she stood, making her senses tingle as a faint whisper rustled through the tree branches. Even with the distracting sounds of nature, she could still feel the eerie silence that emanated from inside the stone walls surrounding the abandoned city. This world had existed only for itself for centuries, its life force had disappeared long ago and thus its essence had dwindled, eventually becoming a solitary entity devoid of purpose. The longer she was in this world the stronger its pulse was getting, a delicate tug that pulled on her inner magic and rippled through her blood. The ancient magic encased in this world's energy seemed curious about her yet hesitant, as it slowly observed this new presence that had unexpectedly appeared in its long-forgotten realm.

She moved cautiously onto the path and followed it toward the city gates. With each step, the whispering in the trees intensified and their limbs seemed to awaken, frantically stroking the ground, the breeze lifting their leaves in response.

The spires of the city buildings loomed high above the stone wall, the bright sun casting their shadows outward like long silent fingers. The heavy metal gate loomed just ahead; its dark iron creaked as she approached. She stopped when she reached the gate, feeling the strength of the dark metal pushing toward her. Two large doors stood menacingly in front of her, their cold thick iron temporarily stopping her progress. Lifting her hand, she placed it gently on the cool metal's surface, studying the exterior with renewed interest. There were delicate carvings embedded in the iron facing, symbols, and lines that followed the grain of the metal. She recognized one—the Callan, or Callathian, family crest. She wondered if the etchings represented the families of those that resided in Dywen, a silent shrine, a memory of the past.

Removing her hand from the gate's cool metal surface she reached for the large handle, pushing down firmly against ancient metal that had been unused for centuries. The handle resisted at first but eventually gave way to her pressure, groaning as it begrudgingly lifted the latch on the other side. She pushed on the right side of the gate struggling to move its massive bulk as it grated on its ancient hinges in resistance. It groaned awkwardly as she continued to push it open revealing Arcadium—the ancient, forgotten city of Dywen.

The moment she passed through the gates the whispering in the trees stopped, the city was silent, nothing stirred inside these walls. She gazed across the expansive courtyard that stretched before her feeling the weight of the eerie silence as it pressed down.

The centuries of neglect were apparent in the courtyard —grass had sprung up between the cracks of the cobblestones and the small saplings that encircled the courtyard wall sagged pathetically. A large fountain stood silently in the middle, its ancient stone pillars cracked and disintegrating with age. The water had dried up long ago and the copper taps were rusted and corroded covered in a flaky green patina. The stone buildings that surrounded the courtyard stood silently, their windows staring vacantly, long forgetting any memory of their past inhabitants. Some doors to the buildings were ajar, many were bolted shut, large ancient locks rusted and crumbling. She stood quietly, breathing in the stale air that lay heavy in the immediate area. She could not feel the pulse of Dywen inside these walls. Not even an echo of its past existed inside the city; it was as if this part of the world had extinguished long ago.

She moved across the courtyard toward a stone archway at the far end. It seemed to be the only way out of the circular courtyard other than the large gates she had entered through. The archway was connected to a large structure that resembled a church, its towering steeple extending proudly into the sky. As she reached the courtyard fountain, she saw hundreds of coins lying forgotten at the bottom of its basin—wishes of long-departed inhabitants perhaps. The coins were large, much bigger than anything in the mortal world. She bent down to pick one up, careful not to disturb the silence that engulfed the village square. Flipping the coin from one side to the other she examined the piece carefully. The metal was discolored, tarnished from centuries of exposure to the elements, its surfaces dented, and edges chipped. The coin was thin and void of design on one side, the other displaying a small symbol—a cross emblazoned with a moon and intersecting a scythe. She placed the coin back on the fountain floor careful not to disturb the others.

Continuing toward the stoned archway she slowed as she passed the aging storefronts. Each had a small wooden sign hanging from a wrought iron post above the door. Her eyes scanned her surroundings, sure that she was in the heart of the city, a town square or market, perhaps. There was a magical herb shop, an apothecary that once sold tonics and potions, a blacksmith and weapon guild, an alchemist, and many other businesses that catered to the witches and warlocks that at one time inhabited this realm. The merchandise still displayed in the windows was covered with a thick layer of dust and cobwebs. Damp moss clung to the underside of the roof's overhangs as unimpeded ivy crept haphazardly up many of the building's exterior walls. She imagined that the inside of these small shops would be just as vacant and aged as their exteriors—a haunting indication of a lost past.

As she reached the massive stone archway, she felt a small tingle crawl up her spine and her skin prickled as she felt unseen eyes boring into the back of her head. In their gaze, she could sense curiosity and interest. Hesitating briefly, she slowly turned back around to the courtyard, scanning the area for any sign of someone watching her. As her eyes moved past the fountain, she saw it—the large black bird that she had seen patrolling the sky earlier. It was perched atop the middle pillar of the fountain, its brilliant green eyes trained on her unblinking, its head cocked curiously to the side. It stared for a few more seconds and then opened its large wings and flew gracefully upward, circling the courtyard once before disappearing into the distance. She watched the bird fly away, slightly unsettled by the way it had looked at her, seemingly sizing her up for unknown reasons.

Shaking off the eerie feeling she moved back to the stone archway.

The stone used to make the archway was different from the other stone located throughout the courtyard. It was a dull gray, marbled with black and white crystallized veins that cut unrefined patterns through its surface. The stone glistened in the sunlight as the tiny embedded fragments caught its rays. The top of the arch was carved with ancient symbols and runes, one of which Dane recognized as the mark of The Order—the dagger through the sphere. The opening lead into a shadowy tunnel that stretched away from the courtyard and toward, she assumed, the area where the Warlician barracks were located.

The tunnel was cooler than the village square and a dank stench assaulted her nostrils as she entered, increasing in intensity the further from the tunnel opening she got. She had just enough natural light to make out the walls and the direction of the tunnel but decided to take out the flashlight before venturing in further. The beam flickered momentarily before illuminating the stone walls in a bright yellow glow. Water trickled slowly down the tunnel walls providing nourishment to the thick moss that clung to the stone. Cobwebs hung from the ceiling of the tunnel, swaying gently in what little breeze found its way into this dark corridor. She hurried through the tunnel, her footsteps echoing somewhere in the distance.

About a hundred feet in she came upon a small wrought iron gate blocking further access to the tunnel. It stood ajar, one of the metal anchors holding the left post was aged and rusted and had pulled slightly from the wall. A massive iron lock hung from one of the horizontal rails and it clanged against the metal as she pushed on the gate, opening it without too much resistance from the creaking metal hinges.

As she continued through the rest of the tunnel, she noticed the air was becoming less suffocating and the musty smell was receding. The walls were dry and there was no moss clinging desperately to their surfaces. Iron torch holders lined both sides of the tunnel walls here and as she moved passed them each magically lit, startling her. The flames from the torches cast a bright orange glow through the dark shadowy passageway, its light dancing merrily on the stone walls, adding much-needed warmth to the damp, dim space.

She grazed her fingertips along the wall stopping as she felt a vibration ripple through the cool stones. The world here was not silent like in the courtyard, the energy trapped within these stone walls was alive and curiously taking notice of her presence.

The end of the tunnel finally came into view as bright sunlight spilled into the dark space ahead. Squinting as she exited the tunnel, she stood for a moment allowing her eyes to adjust to the glare before surveying her surroundings.

The tunnel had opened into another courtyard, this one much larger than the town square. There were no trees, or decorative monuments, just an expansive stone patio that fronted a metal and stone fence. Located at intervals throughout the courtyard were iron and stone pits, in each a fire burned. At the back of the courtyard, the metal and stone fence flanked a series of wide steps and landings that led up to a huge stone building surrounded by square guard towers—a military-style encampment. Knowing she had found the barracks she crossed the courtyard, quickly ascending the stone stairs to the first landing, where a small stone outbuilding stood vacant. Hurrying past she continued upward toward the barracks.

Halfway up the second set of steps, she slowed as a warning ignited chills across her skin. Her senses reacting to a strange energy invading the space directly behind her. Recognizing a possible danger, she stopped, allowing her senses to engage with whatever it was that now stood feet away. The energy behind her was different from anything she had felt before. It was strong, balanced, and calm, yet she could feel how it pulsed with anticipation and curiosity. There was something distinct about it, a raw intensity born from power and confidence. She took a deep breath, calming her nerves and preparing herself to face whatever it was that had snuck up behind her.

CHAPTER 20

TURNING SLOWLY, DANE WAS SURPRISED to find the tip of a long thick blade pointing directly at her. The blade, held steady by its possessor, was inches from her throat, the razor-sharp edge shone menacingly in the sunlight. She took another deep breath before she allowed her eyes to travel slowly down the length of the glinting steel.

The blade was etched through its center with a row of Celtic trinity knots. The hilt was solid metal, the guard intricately carved, the grip wrapped with thick black leather, and held steadfast by a strong tanned hand. She steadied her breathing before lifting her eyes to the face of the man that held the blade's tip precariously to her throat.

There, standing a few steps below her was the most striking individual she had ever seen. His tanned face was smooth, his square jaw covered with a faint shadow of stubble. His flashing green eyes held an intensity that made her shiver as he stared directly at her, his eyes never wavering from her own. He was dressed all in black—a sleeveless shirt the only item on his torso other than the breastplate. It was adorned with a silver medallion displaying the symbol of The Order worn by the Warlician warriors. Unlike Sebastian, he wore no cloak and his attire was dusty and worn. The belt that encircled his waist and held his sword's sheath was a thick black leather, adorned with small metal pieces. His black pants were tucked into tall leather boots that were scuffed and faded. Another black sheath was strapped to his thigh where the hilt of a silver knife wrapped with braided black leather was visible. His strong muscular arms were tattooed in multiple places, intricately detailed artwork dissecting his tanned skin.

Her heart jumped as her eyes fell on a tattoo located on the inside of his forearm. She had seen that tattoo before, it was in her dream last night. It was the Celtic cross!

Stunned, her eyes moved back up to meet his unwavering gaze, his green eyes flashing from intensity to interest as he held the stare of the stranger that stood before him. She could feel his confused energy at her presence, but his face did not betray him, his strong jaw remained clenched with determination, the sword never wavering as he held the tip firmly against her skin.

A slight breeze moved past where they stood, ruffling his dark hair. The small braids woven at his temples swayed slightly, the black leather that tied their ends colliding into one another as they did.

Minutes passed as she waited for the man to say something as he stood quietly holding the sword steady, its sharp blade trained on her throat. Unsure of whether to speak she decided to smile instead. As she pulled her face into an awkward grin, the man's grip tightened on the sword, shifting his weight onto his back leg as his brow furrowed into a scowl.

"My name is Dane," she blurted out causing the stranger to press the tip of his sword firmly into the flesh of her neck, the cold steel digging into her skin. She winced at the stinging pressure, growing anxious as her instincts intensified their warning of danger. Slowly, she lifted her hands in surrender and to show him she meant him no harm. He pulled back the blade slightly, careful not to take his eyes from hers.

Taking her left hand, she indicated that she was going to put it in her pocket. He watched her carefully but did not react to her slow careful movements. She reached into her jacket pocket where she had put the coin that Sebastian had given her. Pulling it out, she held it between her thumb and forefinger, showing it to him over the edge of the blade he still held steady at her throat. She could see a memory cross his eyes as he stared at the metal piece in her hand. His face softening slightly as his grip on the sword relaxed.

"Who gave you that?" He asked catching her by surprise at this sudden unexpected verbal interaction.

His voice was deep, cloaked with a husky tone that indicated an extended period of silence. *Sexy,* she thought, groaning outwardly at the absurdity of where her mind had just gone. The stranger cocked his head at the sound and once again tightened his grip on the sword.

"Sebastian," she replied softly, watching as a spark of recognition crossed his face. He continued to stare into her eyes for a few more seconds, an awkward silence surrounding them as she shifted her weight uncomfortably. "He said you would understand."

Lowering his sword, he placed it back into the sheath

that hung from his left hip. He climbed the steps toward where she stood until his brilliant green eyes were level with hers.

"You are a Callathian?" He asked although she was sure he already knew the answer. "From the new realm?"

"Yes," she responded shyly, aware of the sensations his proximity ignited in her. "But it's Callan now."

He seemed to ignore her last statement. "Then you are also an Arcanist."

"Apparently, that is correct as well," she confirmed, still not use to the new title that she now found herself being referred to as.

The warrior nodded, his brow furrowing in concentration as he began to connect his past life to the things that were happening at this moment. She could see him shaking off the centuries of sleep that had claimed him, his thoughts racing as they linked the past to the present.

He moved up to stand on the same step, his body inches from hers, his bright green eyes burrowing deep into her own. Her breath caught in her chest as his gaze intensified penetrating what little defenses she possessed. As his energy mingled with her own, she shifted uncomfortably realizing that the man standing inches from her was causing her heart to beat a little faster.

Breaking his gaze, she looked down at her own boots, the toes now covered in dust. She took a deep breath, steadying herself and her unabashed thoughts before slowly raising her eyes back to his. A slight smirk played mischievously at the corners of his full lips making her even more uncomfortable in his presence. This time she was unable to look away, mesmerized by the perfect shape of his jawline, the way his nose was slightly crooked at the bridge, and the long scar that ran from the outside corner of his left eye, intersecting his eyebrow and separating it into two sections. His dark lashes framed his light green eyes perfectly and his long thick hair curled gently at his shoulders.

This man and his imperfections were beautiful.

The warrior leaned in closer, reaching into her energy with his own. His head cocked slightly as the playful smirk intensified, his eyes flashing with something too quick for her to recognize.

As her heart pounded in her chest and her will to block him from entering her private domain weakened, he suddenly pulled back, moved around her, and began walking up the remaining stone steps.

Inhaling deeply as a shudder ran through her core, she turned and followed him with her gaze until he had reached the top. He looked down at her and smiled, a small dimple appearing on his left cheek and in his deep, husky voice said, "You may call me Rafe."

Embarrassed and confused by the effect that Rafe's proximity had on her she was unable to move up the stairs after him, paralyzed by the feelings that were conflicting with one another inside her. Tingling warmth had crept over her as she stared deeply into his green eyes and for a brief second, she had felt powerless. He had mesmerized her, making her feel out of control, a sensation that she did not enjoy. Control was something she had mastered a long time ago. She did not relinquish it easily. He, however, had managed to bypass her defenses effortlessly, his energy rushing through her, sending her into a tailspin. Her pounding heart betraying her as she shamelessly allowed herself to be distracted by him.

Shaking her head, she glanced up at the man who now stood staring down at her from the pinnacle of the wide staircase, waiting. Tentatively, she climbed the remaining stairs, joining him at the top.

Fully aware of his presence beside her, she surveyed the lush grounds that lay before them. The grass was a stunning deep green, the silver dew sparkled on its surface creating an illusion that the landscape was swaying methodically back and forth. The stone building with the guard towers she had seen from the bottom loomed majestically in front of them, perched on a hill not far from where they stood. She could see ivy, covered in large purple flowers, twisting and climbing its way up the sides of the turrets. Flags still waved proudly at their metal tips, the passing of time visible in their faded colors and tattered ends. The moat that surrounded the barracks was filled with brilliant aqua-hued water, and she could easily see the sandy bottom through its crystal-clear depth as they crossed the bridge leading to the barrack's large iron doors.

From the corner of her eye, she noticed something coming toward them in the sky. At first, it was only a speck. An insignificant mar on the pale blue perfection of the morning sky, but as it drew closer, she recognized the shape. It was the large black bird she had seen in the city market earlier, and it was making its way toward them at an impressive speed, its wings pushing hard against the air currents as it propelled its large frame forward.

Before she could open her mouth to warn Rafe, the large bird swooped in, landing gently on his shoulder, its large knowing eyes trained suspiciously on her.

"Ah, I wondered where you had gotten to my friend," he said, raising his leather-bound forearm, the large bird moving down off his shoulder, his eyes never straying from Dane.

"This bird belongs to you?" She asked realizing that this must have been the reason that Rafe knew she had invaded his world and could so easily sneak up on her.

"He does," he answered looking at the bird with pride. "His name is Farrimore.

"He is extraordinary. I've never seen anything like it."

"I suspect you haven't no. He is an ancient Hawkitete, a rare bird that hails from the farthest regions of this world. They are a remarkable breed," he said stroking Farrimore under his beak. "They have a keen sense of sight and smell, are strong, agile fliers, able to fly for long periods of time without resting. Their powerful beaks can easily rip through a man's skin. Hawkitetes are extremely intelligent, vigilant, fiercely loyal and are known for their protection skills, making them a popular familiar for warriors in battle."

Farrimore ruffled his feathers as if he recognized Rafe praising him.

"He seems extremely attached to you," she commented, noticing how the bird kept nudging Rafe's shoulder with his head.

"We have been through a lot together; he is a very faithful companion."

She nodded noticing the softness in his tone, an indication of the deep affection he had for his magnificent feathered friend.

Following him up to the large iron doors of the barracks, she smirked as she caught Farrimore glancing over his shoulder, eyeing her with mistrust. His loyalty to his master was certainly not in question.

As they came to the entrance, she noticed there were no

handles visible on this side of the iron doors. She watched curiously as he placed his hand on a large metal plate embedded into the stone on the right-hand side, muttering something to himself under his breath. Slowly, the heavy doors began to shudder and groan, swinging inward, ancient hinges grinding as they opened. Turning to face her he said. "You will find that many doors in the Warlician barracks are magically closed, only warriors and specific incantations can open them."

Nodding, she realized how lucky she was that Rafe had found her and would be able to lead her to the items she needed without any obstacles that could cause her time and grief. She was beginning to wonder how Sebastian could put so much faith in her knowing she was going to be so far out of her realm, literally. She shook her head in frustration as she walked through the massive iron doors, her ire at Sebastian forgotten as she entered the home of her warrior ancestors.

They stood in what seemed to be the training grounds, an impressive arena space surrounded on the far side by coliseum-style seating. A massive combat pit claimed most of the center of the arena, the area encircling it filled with equipment and gear. Ancient weapons hung in racks from the stone walls, their sharp edges glinting in the sunlight. An area containing targets and fighting dummies, besieged with the scars of training, was to the left of the pit. Another filled with contraptions she assumed was used for strength and conditioning, to the right and a special area dedicated to the crafting of a warrior's magical abilities lay in the shadows of the back corner.

Following Rafe through the arena toward a door located under the seating area, she sensed a change in the energy that sizzled through the surrounding air. She could feel a calming strength rising inside her as the ground beneath her became more familiar, her own energy recognizing the path of her ancestors. There was a familiarity implanted in her surroundings, an ancient echo from the past that encased her in a comforting embrace. She could sense traces of an age-old magic, its essence floating aimlessly. Feeling its curiosity as it recognized her blood, her own magic throbbed through her veins in response, heightened by the foreign essence that seeped around her. Her blood ached to meld with the ancient magic, her own magic feeding off the essence of old. She could feel the power of her ancestors in this place, a forgotten shadow of the past. Relaxing she allowed the ancient magic to penetrate her skin, flowing into her unimpeded.

Suddenly, an uneasiness passed through her. A cold unyielding sensation that crept under her skin. There was something beyond the sensation; a presence in her mind. At first, it was fleeting. A wisp of a memory that tugged at the shadowy recesses. But as the ancient magic of her ancestors mingled with her own essence she could feel it grow; a dark menacing shadow that forced its way further into her mind.

She tried to block the unfamiliar energy from invading her thoughts, but its presence remained—growing stronger as the magic in this world took notice. An explosion of pain rattled through her head as she tried to call out to Rafe, blackness obscuring her vision. A dark energy wrapped itself around her mind, pushing itself deeper into her consciousness. It was saturated by a heavy smell of rot and decay, a putrid stench that overwhelmed her senses. She fought to regain control, as she felt herself slipping into a dark abyss, her body collapsing to the ground. There was something evil in her mind, an unforgiving, unfeeling presence burrowing into the deepest recesses and flooding her with its memories.

A shadowy smoke hurtled through the universe, an entity older than time, a chilling cold surrounding it, evil dripping from its depths. It was fueled by an unsated hunger, a primeval yearning to feed, to destroy, to survive. An empty hollowness was left in its wake as it was drawn to its destination by the scent of magic. This universe was full of magic, ancient and powerful, a feeding ground perfect for its kind, a place where thirst, hunger, and death combined. It careened through time and space, a shadowy predator racing toward an unsuspecting prey. The horror and fear that its presence would incite and the destruction it would unleash would be unimaginable.

The magic of the universe beckoned, pulling it forward through the magical barrier surrounding the unsuspecting realms. A strong scent of blood, flesh, and death surround it. Nothing would survive. Its evil cut mercilessly through the realms feeding off the magic. Carnage followed as it rid the lands of the vermin, their blood turning the countryside red. It fed and killed, repeating the cycle as each realm fell under its reign of terror. It relished how the puny inhabitants tried to fight back. Their valiant efforts were squashed under its rampage as their horror became a stench that fueled its rage.

As its power grew, theirs diminished. This universe was now its domain and it would wipe clean the existence of the magical beings that wrongly thought it theirs.

CHAPTER 21

THE HEADACHE EXPLODING IN A kaleidoscope of colors behind her eyelids caused her to wince in pain. Nausea rolled in waves over her body, its intensity causing her stomach to clench. As the last of the disturbing memory faded from her mind and the dark energy's grip released her, she felt a twinge in her consciousness and then nothing. She tried to open her eyes, but she was too exhausted, so she remained in the blackness.

Somewhere in the back of her mind, she heard a voice calling her name over and over. It was faint, a hollow, whisper that echoed in her mind. She wanted to answer but she couldn't. The dark energy had exhausted her. She could feel the film of sweat that covered her skin, prickling in the heat. Her heart pounded erratically in her chest, and she was finding it difficult to breathe.

The voice was getting louder, the throbbing in her head no longer drowning it out.

"DANE," the voice said again, its tone vibrating off the inside of her skull. "Can you hear me?"

She wanted it all to stop. *Quiet,* she begged.

"DANE!" The voice said again, this time with more force and less patience.

She could feel strong hands grasp her shoulders shaking them roughly. The indent the fingers made on her bare skin tingled as a strange raw sensation ran through her. An unknown magical essence was seeping through her pores its energy making her feel safe, its power comforting as it provided her with a renewed sense of awareness. The headache diminished and the malaise that tortured her body began to calm. Slowly, she opened her eyes, allowing them to adjust to the light before focusing on the face that stared down at her.

I know you, she thought as she recognized that perfect jawline, the scar in the eyebrow, and the sexy laugh lines that framed brilliant green eyes.

His brow was furrowed, and his perfect lips were drawn tight. She could not tell whether Rafe was concerned or irritated by her lack of response. She smiled up at him seeing his face soften as he waited for her to gain control. As her mind once again became her own, she realized that the strong hands encircling her shoulders belonged to him, as did the unknown calming energy that she could still feel pulsating through her veins.

Struggling, she managed to push herself into a sitting position, shaking the remaining cobwebs of the vision from her mind. "Sorry," she muttered feeling the strange tingle on her skin where his hands still touched her.

"How do you feel?"

"Better, thanks."

"What did you see?" he asked casually.

"What do you mean?"

"You had a vision, didn't you?"

"Why would you think that?" She asked trying not to show surprise at his uncanny perception.

"I have been around a very long time, Callathian. I understand the magic of this world, a magic that has been suddenly thrust upon you. Telepathic connections are part of a Warlician's power it is a way we communicate with one another. All Warlicians have this ability but only a few are blessed with the capacity to connect minds with another kind. Your ancestors are what we call Timestoppers, they were gifted with the ability to enter another's mind and see their thoughts and memories. It is a rare gift but one I assume you possess, although currently, it seems you are unable to control it."

"My father is a Timestopper. He was the only one left in my world until my second awakening," she whispered. "But I wasn't trying to see anything, not willingly anyway. Something entered my mind flooding me with its memories."

"Has anything like this ever happened to you before?" He asked, the concern showing on his face.

"Once," she replied thinking back to the time she touched Lilith's arm in the alleyway.

He nodded helping her to her feet, wrapping his strong arm around her waist to steady her as she wobbled slightly. He gazed deeply into her eyes, the intensity of his stare making her feel uncomfortable. Pulling her in toward him he leaned closer, the tingle on her skin escalating as their bodies touched. She could feel his hot breath as it grazed her cheek his lips moving to within inches of her ear. "You must learn to control this power Callathian, or it will control you."

Releasing her, he took a step back. "What exactly did you see?"

Taking a deep breath, she relayed her vision as best she could, her mind slightly blurred by the residual pain. He listened intently, his eyes flashing with hatred as she described this world's past—*his past*. The pain of the memories evident in the way he clenched his jaw as she spoke.

"It knows who you are Dane. It can feel you through Dywen's magic."

"What does?"

"The ancient dark."

"The entity that you banished? The one that destroyed these realms?" She asked, surprise heightening her voice.

He nodded. "This is what the Guardian of Deities feared, that awakening the magic in these realms would, in turn, rouse the ancient dark from its slumber. It has recognized that Dywen is waking and the ancient magic is drawn to you. If it figures out who you are, it will try to control you before you have a chance to gain your ancestral powers, before you become a threat. You are extremely vulnerable without the full power of your ancestor's magic. If it attempts to assail you again, you must try to resist, don't let it enter your mind. Once the Druidstone has been reactivated, and you have received your birthright, your telepathy should be manageable."

Turning he extended his arm to Farrimore who gracefully flew down from the wall and perched on it.

"Come Callathian," he said as he strode toward the iron door at the far end of the outer sanctum. "We won't have much time. The Second Rising will be set in motion soon enough. It is time for you to accept your destiny, to become who you truly are."

The inside of the barracks was reminiscent of the castles and knight's quarters of medieval times. They were so reflective of that culture that she half expected to see a round table and a sword in a stone. The room the outside door led to was large. Its stone walls reached up twenty feet to vaulted wood beam ceilings. Iron torch holders dotted the walls and large tapestries, draped over iron bars, hung high above the room. Sun filtered through small arched windows piercing the shadows that hid in the corners, its soft light adding unexpected warmth to the barracks gloom. Warlician family crests hung proudly on the stone walls, each a reminder of the sacrifice that these men made to defend and keep peace in the realms.

There was a large stone table that sat prominently at the back of the room on a large raised platform. It was surrounded by heavy wood and leather chairs their tall wood backs carved with intricate detail, their black leather worn and faded. A heavy layer of dust covered the table's surface, particles caught in the ray's cast by the midday sun, floated helplessly.

Ceiling-high bookcases surrounded two sides of the space, their shelves littered with leather bound books and parchment scrolls. The room echoed of a haunting past— one that breathed of pride, glory, confidence, duty, and loyalty. She could feel its essence floating in the dusty air. The longer she stood inside these hallowed walls the more a feeling of power grew within her.

"We will rest here for the night but in the morning, we must begin our journey," Rafe said motioning for Dane to follow him down a long wide hallway, just off the great room.

They passed numerous closed doors as they walked

down the hall, those that stood open revealed a kitchen, a small pantry, and a bathing chamber.

Exiting the building through the east side, they emerged into a quiet, peaceful garden ripe with blossoms, color, and fragrance. In the middle of the garden was a large tree its gnarled and crooked limbs reached both up toward the sky and sweeping down toward the earth. Moss clung heavy to its branches and swayed gently back and forth in the early evening breeze. The tree was a smaller version of the Elder Oak that lived deep in Braemore Woods. She wondered if this was the anchor portal on this side.

She continued walking toward it, the setting sun washing the tree in a bright orange haze, its leaves set afire by the waning glow. The entire visual was stunning, the beauty and tranquility of this land overwhelming but no more so than here at this very moment as the fiery sun exploded in a kaleidoscope of oranges across this peaceful garden.

Rafe noticed the look on her face as the beauty of the sun-filled garden captivated her. Silently, he came up behind her leaning in toward her left ear.

"The beauty that is Dywen is magical even for us, but for you, seeing it for the first time, it must be unimaginable."

She tensed as she felt his body brush gently up against hers. Her skin tingled at the touch, his voice sending shivers up her spine as it whispered softly in her ear. She closed her eyes feeling his energy reaching into her own, caressing, exploring, intertwining. As his shallow breath caressed her cheek, she felt her body ache with anticipation. She wanted him to touch her, she wanted to feel his skin against her own, to breathe in his scent, to know how he tasted.

Suddenly, his energy was gone. She quickly opened her eyes and turned in time to see him walking away, his hand clenching and unclenching. The bare skin of his arms glistened with a sheer film of sweat and his muscles were taut under his tanned tattooed skin. She watched breathlessly as his retreating form headed toward an open doorway, yet wary of the overwhelming desire she just felt for this man— a man who, only a few hours earlier, was a stranger. She'd never felt this out of control of her emotions, this consumed by her senses. Her body was reacting to him of its own free will. It was both freeing and frustrating. She would have to figure out how to control her fluctuating chemical reactions to his energy or completing her task could become increasingly more difficult.

Rafe could very well be an enticing distraction.

On the other side of the garden were the sleeping quarters. He showed her to one of the rooms; a small square chamber that looked out onto the garden. The room contained a wooden bunk, a wash bowl, and a high-backed wooden chair. A wool blanket and pillow were placed neatly at the end of the bed and a small woven rug graced the middle of the stone floor. Gauze curtains hung from the window and blew gracefully inward as the breeze from the garden found its way through the opening. There was a small closet at one end of the room and a narrow door that led to a small bathroom at the other. Above the bed was a large crest which she recognized immediately.

Rafe noticed the recognition that passed over her face as she admired the crest. "This room belonged to your ancestor, Claaven Callathian, my mentor, and friend," he said softly, a look of sadness flashed briefly across his face as he leaned casually in the doorway. "I am across the hall if you need anything."

She thanked him as he walked out.

Alone in the small room, her thoughts turned briefly to home, her friends, family, Tyson. She took the crumbled picture from her backpack and leaned it against the candle that stood on the bedside table, wondering what they were all doing at this moment.

She spent the next few minutes washing up and trying to get the dust and dirt out of her clothes. Putting on a pair of gray sweats and an old worn blue college sweatshirt she pulled her hair into a ponytail and washed her face.

The room was darkening. She lit the candle, dousing the room in a warm flickering glow. She yawned, stretching her aching muscles as she crawled into bed, pulling the wool blanket up to her chin.

Closing her eyes, she thought about Rafe and the unexpected and rather uncontrollable reflective reaction her body had when he was near. The tension was palpable, and she hoped that he was not aware of her internal longings.

Trouble, she thought as sleep engulfed her tired mind.

CHAPTER 22

DANE WOKE TO FARRIMORE SITTING in her open window staring suspiciously at her. She was unsure as to why this bird was still so wary of her presence, especially since his master seemed at ease with her. Maybe Farrimore needed more time because he sensed that she was not from this world or maybe he was just over-protective of Rafe because they had been alone in this realm for so long.

"Well good morning to you Farrimore," she said sweetly, refusing to give the bird any satisfaction. Farrimore's feathers ruffled at the sound of her voice. His head cocked as he shuffled uncomfortably on the windowsill. Giving her another beady stare, he spread his vast wings and flew into the garden.

She smiled feeling slightly giddy at her perceived victory.

Stretching out the remaining visages of sleep she climbed out of bed and headed to the bathroom to clean up. There was no shower or bath, so she made do with the large washbasin and the toiletry items she had brought from home. After washing her hair and doing her best with a quick sponge bath, she pulled out a clean pale blue t-shirt from her bag, pairing it with the jeans and boots she'd dusted off last night. Her long dark hair hung in damp waves around her tanned face, and she subconsciously ran her fingers through it as her mind wandered.

Packing up her backpack and strapping her knife to her ankle she placed her aviator sunglasses on top of her head and headed out the bedroom door in search of Rafe.

Timidly, she knocked on the door across the hall listening for any sign of his presence. There was a slight noise on the other side of the door and then it quickly swung open, startling her momentarily. He stood framed in the doorway, a slight scowl on his handsome face.

Her gaze immediately dropped to his shirtless chest, studying all the tattoos that were carved into his muscular skin. Some were intricate, others simple but one drew her attention away from the others. It was on the right side of his stomach, just above his waistband. The outer edge resembled Celtic knotwork; intricate black lines that wove in and out of one another creating a circle on his skin. Contained within the circle were a series of intersecting curved lines that formed a tribal-style triquetra. For some unexplained reason, she was drawn to this tattoo, its power and beauty stirring something deep inside of her.

Slowly, she reached out her hand. She could feel his gaze on her, but she was unable to stop herself, her fingers stretching toward his stomach until they grazed the stunning tattoo. As her fingers connected with his skin, he abruptly pulled away.

"Sorry," she said weakly, embarrassed by what she had just done.

He stared at her, curiously amused and bewildered by this strange, beautiful woman standing in front of him, but unaccustomed to feeling another's touch. Her fingers were soft and cool on his skin, and he had felt a slight tingle in his tattoo where she brushed her fingertips across it.

"You are a curious woman Callathian," he said, grabbing his shirt and heading out the door past her.

She stood in the doorway embarrassed and astonished at the way she had acted. Although she wasn't known for her shyness, this undeniable and uncontrollable attraction she felt for him was unlike anything she had ever experienced. The more she was around him the more she felt unrestricted by all the walls and distance she had built up around herself, over the years. She did not instinctively pull away from him, instead, she wanted to get closer, to experience all these new feelings that were cascading over her. Finally, she felt like she did not have to hide who she truly was. Newfound freedom in a strange and uninhabited land.

Still, it was making her act irrational. She needed to remain calm and in control. There was too much at stake for her to lose focus. Gaining back her wits, she walked down the hallway to find him.

Sitting at the table she tried desperately to avoid his eyes. Putting her head down she began devouring the food he placed in front of her. She had not realized how hungry she was as she quickly ate the bowl of broth and the chunk of crusty bread.

"I'm sorry, it is not much, but it is all I have for now," he said breaking the awkward silence as he got up and rinsed off his dish. "Would you like more?"

"No thanks, that was perfect," she responded still not daring to look at him.

"Did you sleep well?" He inquired casually, taking her empty bowl and rinsing it in the large bucket of hot water.

"Yes."

"That is good, for you will need your strength to awaken this world."

She raised her eyes, staring into his piercing green ones, a slight flutter drifting through her stomach. "I thought this world was already awakening with my presence here. I can feel its magic and life force getting stronger."

"Dywen knows you are here; it recognizes your energy. It is curious, but it is not yet awake—only re-energizing the Druidstone can fulfill that."

"Sebastian told me a little about this stone but what exactly is it?" She asked, beginning to feel slightly more comfortable looking him in the eye again.

"All the magic contained within the Thanissia Universe comes from the elements. Each race is ruled by one of the foundation elements—water, air, earth, fire, and spirit, and each realm has a Druidstone; an alter that is the power source for the world's magic. The stones connect a specific element with its people and their environment and in turn, magic is generated and harnessed for use. Dywen is an earth element. We are a nature-based race, our magic is grounded by the elements of the earth, and we can use the elemental power to create and distribute our magic. For you and me to gain our magic you must re-activate the Druid-stone so that it can once again power the earth magic embedded in this world."

"So, you no longer have powers?" She asked curiously.

"My powers, like this world are in dormancy. I still have

them but there is not enough magical energy in the environment to harness, what little magic is left is fused to the doors to the barracks allowing them to open and lock. As I said, our powers are dependent on the strength of this world's magic, we are nothing without the magical essence of our ancestral realm."

Dane sat for a moment and let his words sink in. She had been feeling the environment ever since she had arrived on Dywen, sensing the ancient magic as it explored her own. She had been confusing knowledge of her presence, with the world awakening. If the strength and power she had felt in the ancient magic while in dormancy was any indicator, she was sure she would be in awe of the explosiveness of that power when fully awake.

"What do we need to do first?" she asked.

"We will travel to the Temple of Earth at the top of *Ardrin Gorm*. This is where Dywen's Druidstone is located." He hesitated before continuing, "I must warn you; this is not an easy journey. The temple is as old as this world and the path up Ardrin Gorm is perilous. Without my magic to help us, it will be even more so."

She stood up and grabbed her backpack. "We better get going then!" She was beginning to understand that this foreign world was never going to be an easy conquest even with Rafe by her side.

"We must make one stop on the way out."

Reaching for his sword that was lying on a nearby table, he strapped it effortlessly to his side. Picking up a large backpack he glanced at her. "Come."

They walked side-by-side through the dank hallways of the barracks, Farrimore sailing easily through the air ahead of them. As they reached the great hall he slowed, turning to face her, a slight shadow passing over his handsome features. "Your ancestor, Claaven Callathian, was the most powerful Warlician that ever lived. Many of us benefited greatly from his tutelage and many of us lived through the Great War because of his tenacity when training us. Sebastian and I were two of those lucky enough to have called him a friend as well as a mentor. After his death, I felt a great loss, his presence haunted my sleep for many a night. He was a great warrior and a great man. When I was tasked with staying on Dywen after the Great War and guarding the Book of Realms, I kept something of his here with me so that I could be sure that it would always be in the hands of a Callathian. I knew that one day his ancestor would rise, and his legacy would live on in them."

He turned and walked purposefully to the bookcases scanning the shelves until he found what he was looking for. Slowly, he pulled out specific books until there was a subtle click and a puff of dust blew lazily up into the air. The bookcase began to shudder its girth sliding clumsily to the left revealing a dark passageway hidden behind its depth.

"Come," Rafe said as he reached for the lit torch on the wall. "It is time to pass on his legacy."

CHAPTER 23

THE AIR WAS MUSTY AND stale in the shadowy stone passage, the cramped quarters giving Dane a moment of uncertainty as the walls seemed to close in around her. He must have felt her hesitation because he unexpectedly squeezed her hand before moving quickly forward into the dark. As she entered behind him, the light from his torch provided a touch of warmth to the chill that saturated the air. The passageway was long. Winding its way downward, leading somewhere underground.

Eventually, they exited the stuffy corridor emerging into a small space. To her left was a simple wooden door, straight ahead was a large barred gate, reminiscent of the doors on an old prison cell. The room behind the bars was cloaked in shadows, an aching silence seeping from its depths.

Rafe walked over to the bars and whispered an incantation as he rested his hand on the metal plate bolted to its center. Like all the other locked doors it opened without hesitation, and he entered the room, his torchlight scattering the shadows. She followed, unsure as to what she was going to see but strangely excited, nonetheless.

The chamber was small. Its stone walls covered with dark purple, velvet tapestries, all of which were draped upward by thick iron hooks. A shield bearing the image of the Callathian crest hung on the back wall, its gleaming metal reflecting the glow of light from his torch. There was nothing else in the chamber except for a tall stone slab standing majestically in the middle of the room.

Laying at its center, on a plush piece of purple velvet, was the most beautiful sword she had ever seen. The blade was thick and gleamed brilliantly in the torchlight, a slight silvery aura pulsed around its metal. There looked to be an inscription carved delicately into the metal blade but at this distance, she could not make out what it said.

Respectfully, she approached the stone slab, careful not to disturb the energy in the air that she could feel sizzling around the sword. As she drew near she sensed a slight vibrating hum coming from the sword, feeling a strange familiarity with its energy. The blade seemed to glow in anticipation, its gleaming silver reaching out toward her. Atop the pommel was a pentacle, each point gleaming with a precious stone of differing colors. The grip was solid metal, tightly wrapped in black leather, the strips intricately woven around and through one another. In the middle of the guard was carved a tree; its roots and leaves stretching out to each side making up the length.

The tree of life—she thought immediately recognizing the important symbol.

The inscription on the blade was now clearly visible, written in an old-world Celtic script.

"The fate of the realms lies in the shadow of one," she whispered, her voice reverberating off the stone walls breaking the venerable silence that encased the room.

"What does it mean?" she asked, turning to face Rafe.

"I am not entirely sure. It appeared on the blade after the Great War after Claaven perished. I believe it is a message, part of the prophecy. I assume it is referring to your destiny."

"But the prophecy says that there are other Arcanists, how can I be the only one to dictate the realms fate?"

"There is much you need to learn about our past Dane," he said understanding her frustration. "There is also much we need to understand with respect to the prophecy and how it relates to the future. I, unfortunately, do not have all the answers. The prophecy came to us during the Great War when most of the races were immersed in battle with the ancient dark. We had heard that the Druid seers had succumbed to visions of the future, distant lands, and individuals not yet born but the story changed depending on who did the telling and to whom they were speaking. As the war raged on, there were different versions of the prophecy that found their way through our lands. If there is a singular prophecy its truth will be recorded in the Book of Realms. The Druids would have documented their visions in its pages. Any information that will help guide you and the other Arcanists will be in that book. If the prophecy comes to light, the knowledge contained in the Book of Realms could be invaluable."

"So, you have seen the Book of Realms. You know where to find it?"

"I know where it is hidden but no I have never seen it. It has only ever been in the possession of the Guardian of

Deities. To my knowledge, no supernatural has ever laid eyes on it other than a very small select group of race elders. The book is extremely powerful which is why it was hidden, waiting for someone of great destiny to wield it."

"And let me guess, that person is me—*the shadowy one.*" She said sarcastically assuming the inscription in the sword referred to the one powerful enough to wield the magic of this sacred tome.

"I believe so," he answered slightly confused by the unfamiliar tone of her voice.

"I was being sarcastic," she said noting the confusion on his face.

"I do not understand this sarcastic."

"Sarcasm," she corrected. Confronted with his furrowed brow she contemplated how to explain it in a way that a billion centuries-old warrior would understand. "Mockery? Ridicule?"

"This I understand, but the fight between good and evil is nothing to mock," he said casting her a strange look.

"Sorry," she replied, realizing the vast differences between her present world and Rafe's antiquated one.

He nodded and then gestured toward the sword. "It is yours now, it belongs with you."

She turned back to the stunning blade that sat gleaming against the purple velvet backdrop, the vibrating hum once again catching her attention. The sheen of the blade ebbed and swelled under her gaze. She reached out and lowered her hand toward the grip feeling a slight throbbing as she entered the space surrounding it. The sword's energy flicked and sizzled, her hand tingling as she gripped the handle, lifting the blade from its resting place. The sword was surprisingly light for its size, the grip fitting perfectly in her palm, and the length seemed just right for her height. It was if the blade were made specifically for her.

Turning toward Rafe, she noted the slight smile that had appeared on his face.

"What?" She asked holding the blade at a forty-five-degree angle in front of her.

"It recognizes a Callathian," he answered, nodding toward the sword. "It has morphed its form to fit you."

She looked again at the sword. Watching as a green light pulsed from the top of the pommel to the tip of the blade, continuing to ebb and flow over the sword's length for a few more seconds before disappearing.

He walked toward her with his hand outstretched. "Hand me the sword."

Dropping the tip of the blade toward the ground she flipped the sword in her hand, clutching the blade below the guard, the handle now facing him. He grabbed the hilt and immediately dropped the sword to the ground, clutching his hand in pain. Rushing to his side, she inspected his hand—a festering raw scar ran across the inside of his palm.

"What can I do?"

"Nothing," he responded grimacing slightly. "I will be fine in a moment."

She held his hand gently, watching as the garish redness of the burn slowly faded and the pus filled skin returned to a healthy normal.

"What was that all about?" She inquired when his hand no longer showed any signs of the burn.

"The sword has become one with your energy. Only you can wield it. It is your weapon now and yours alone. Callathian blades are unique that way, the magic embedded in their steel responds only to the Callathian bloodlines magical energy. Anyone else who touches the metal is quickly rejected."

"I wouldn't exactly call burning your hand being rejected!"

"That was nothing, it knows I am Warlician, if I was not, the damage would have been far worse."

He walked to the stone slab and retrieved the sword's sheath that still lay on the plush velvet. Handing the black leather casing to her, she tied it around her waist. The thick leather hung perfectly down her side, and she was amazed at the beautiful detailing that decorated its length. The body of the sheath was adorned with small braided straps each end clasped to the next with a silver metal band. A large metal pentacle was attached to the outer side of the casing about two inches from the top. Just below, burnt into the supple leather was the outline of her family's crest. The bottom of the sheath was covered with a solid metal tip, its surface delicately carved with more Celtic knotwork.

She picked the sword from the ground where Rafe had dropped it, sliding it comfortably into the casing, surprised at how familiar it felt hanging at her side. Motioning for her to follow, they left the small room and headed across the open space toward the simple wooden door.

He slowed as he reached the faded wood, his body slumping slightly as he turned to look at her.

She could see a deep sadness in his eyes, which had her wondering what was behind this door.

"There is something you must understand before we enter," he said, his demeanor suddenly changing as he tried to explain. "A few of the remaining Warlician warriors were caught in different realms during stasis, trapped as the portals shut and the magic decreased. Some were wounded and most likely perished, but others may still be in dormancy waiting until the realms magic can awaken them. I tell you this because, although I am supposed to be here on Dywen alone, I am not."

He opened the door to reveal another small room but this time, instead of a stone slab and a sword, she saw a glass coffin containing a female.

Glancing back to Rafe, she noticed his eyes were locked on the female in the coffin, a hint of sadness swirling around him.

"Who is she?"

He entered the small room without answering, placing his hand affectionately on the coffin's clear top. He paused briefly, his deep sadness filling the small space. "She is my sister."

She moved in beside him gazing down at the girl in the glass coffin. Her face was peaceful but pale. A smattering of freckles noticeable across the bridge of her nose. Long, black hair lay in soft curls around her face and like her brother she was dressed head to toe in black. The long sleeves of her shirt were slightly tattered at the cuffs, her leather vest was worn and tied up the middle with a fine braided cord. Thick leggings were tucked into knee-high leather boots and a leather and metal belt wrapped multiple times around her waist. She had a small moon-shaped tattoo on her neck and wore a thick silver ring, an insignia engraved on its face.

Inside the coffin, laying to her left was a bow and a large knife, both of which she assumed, were her weapons.

She looked so young that it made it difficult for Dane to picture her in combat. As she continued to stand silently beside him, something dawned on her. "I didn't think there were any other female Warlicians."

"There is not. You are the only one. My sister is not a Warlician—she is just head-strong and does not do as she is told."

She noticed a faint smile cross his lips as he affectionately described his sister. A slight twinge of sadness tugged at her heart. "I'm sorry."

"Sorry for what?" He asked meeting her gaze, his green eyes locking onto hers with a sudden intensity.

"For the loss of your sister," she stammered, her body reacting again to the way he looked at her.

He laughed suddenly, startling her. She looked at him with a confused frown as he continued to fill the small room with his snickering.

"I am sorry Dane; I did not explain properly before I showed you this room. My sister, *Tauria*, is not dead. She is in stasis similar to this realm. Unlike me, she cannot stay vigilant in this world, she does not possess that kind of power, nor does she belong here anymore. Therefore, her body cannot function the way it would if our realm's magic was at its strength. As our world fell into dormancy so did my sister, it's her magic's way of protecting her."

"So, she will wake up?" She asked somewhat relieved to know that his sister wasn't dead.

"She will," he said softly. "But not until the magic of Dywen is re-energized and even then, it will take some time."

She hesitated before asking her next question as she did not want to seem like she was prying. "If she is not meant to be here then, why is she?"

A scowl crossed his features. "Tauria is willful and does

not listen to what she is told. Both my father and brother were Warlician warriors and my mother a powerful healer. My father had always thought it best that the women in our family know how to fight, and both my sister and mother were very skilled in combat. When the Great War started many of our race were called upon to battle, fighting alongside the Warlician warriors. Our father and mother were killed in the Great War, our brother along with them."

He stopped for a moment, shoulders sagging under the memory of all the war had cost him. "I was all that Tauria had left and when I was tasked with staying on Dywen and guarding the book, it meant that she had to go with the other remaining survivors to the new world—your earth. She was not happy about my decision, but she reluctantly went with the final group—or, so I thought. It was not until all the portals had closed did I discover that she had remained here on Dywen."

He turned to look at her, his eyes full of conflicting emotions. "My sister is stubborn and defiant, but she is all that I have left. I could not stay angry at her for long as we did not have much time before her life-force would recede into dormancy along with our world. I quickly retrieved a preservation chamber from our healing center and transported it here so that she would be safe until the prophecy came to pass. It did not take long for Dywen to go into stasis and with it, so did Tauria. I placed her in the preservation chamber just days before my life-force and magic began to diminish."

She felt his angst as he recalled the final days he had with his sister who now lay silent before them. Absently, she reached out and gently touched his back feeling him tense slightly under her touch.

"We must go now," he said his voice stronger and more in control as he gestured toward the open door. As they reached it, he paused briefly to look one last time at his sleeping sister before closing the door tightly behind him.

She felt a sudden rush of emotion as her heart ached for all that he had gone through, for all that he had lost and still must endure. She could sense a sadness and vulnerability that weighed heavy on his energy.

Feeling her eyes upon him he turned to look at her, bright green eyes boring deep into her own. A sudden flash of desire sizzled between them. His chest heaved as he tightened his hand on the grip of his sword. Without a word or acknowledging the intensity that had materialized between them Rafe broke their gaze and headed into the shadows of the passage leaving her standing alone in a breathless silence.

CHAPTER 24

FTER EXITING THE BARRACKS RAFE led her quickly through the outer sanctum, stopping briefly to retrieve the 'Essence of Ether' from its lock box in the armory, before heading directly into the thick forest. The small vial was tucked safely in her coat pocket. She still had no idea why it was important. He had not elaborated only saying it was a purified and blessed liquid from the sacred underground springs on Etheriem, the spirit realm of the celestials.

"If Sebastian requires it, there must be a good reason." He responded when she had inquired. Dane had surmised that sharing information did not seem to be a high priority for Warlician warriors.

As they moved quickly through the forest toward the mountain range in the distance, she listened to the leaves rustling softly as they passed. It was a calm and soothing sound that revitalized her energy as she quickened her pace to keep up. The forest foliage thickened as they moved further away from the city, and she could feel an unknown sensation running through her body the deeper they went into the untouched natural beauty of Dywen.

Rafe moved expertly through the underbrush, and she followed as best she could, ducking under low hanging vines, and sidestepping fallen tree branches.

She heard Farrimore's cry in the distance and the sound of running water just up ahead where the tree line thinned. Sunlight penetrated the diminishing foliage casting a gentle, golden glow across the forest floor. There was a warm breeze blowing through the trees, and she detected a hint of salt in its wisps as it gently caressed her face.

He disappeared around a large tree, and she followed squinting at the intensity of the bright morning light as she exited the tree line.

They had emerged from the forest near a small crystal blue lake, its entire circumference surrounded by stones and large flat rocks. At the far end, a small waterfall cascaded down the smooth face of a tall stone ridge, splashing off large boulders and into the lake below in a torrent of foamy spray. The lake seemed shallow; the white sand bottom easily seen through the clear blue water as it glimmered below. The sunlight reflected off the water's ripples, sending sparkling light dancing across its surface. They were closer to the mountain range, and she could see the gray rocky tips peeking majestically over the green canopy of the forest.

The smell of salt was stronger here, its tangy scent engaging her nose. Crouching at the water's edge, she submerged her hand, feeling the wet coolness on her fingertips. Scooping the water into her palm she lifted it to her nose—*saltwater*—she thought her eyes scanning the shining surface. That must be the reason for the pure white bottom.

"It is, what you would call an anomaly," Rafe said, his voice suddenly behind her. "A salted lake. All the bodies of water across the Thanissia Universe are freshwater except for this one. The lake bed produces the salt through a seeping process. The waterfall is fed by an underground cavern that connects to this lake, so it too is salted. This lake was very sacred to our people as it has undeniable healing powers and provides Dywen with an important magical element that cannot be found anywhere else in the universe. As I'm sure you know, salt has powerful protective qualities which made this lake integral to our people's magic."

She nodded, as she did understand how essential salt was to magic. It was still very much a part of modern protection spells, in addition to purification and blessing rituals. She drew her hand once more through the cool liquid, intrigued even more by this body of water because of its uniqueness and haunting beauty.

"Dane, we must continue if we are to get to the bottom of the mountain by nightfall," he said pointing to the largest of the mountains that rose imposingly in the distance.

She stood, her gaze following the direction he was pointing. Wiping her wet hands on her jeans she watched him walk off, headed for a small sand path near the far end of the lake. Glancing one last time at the quiet ethereal beauty of the salted lake she picked up her backpack and followed.

Halfway around the lake, the sand path narrowed as they came upon a wide opening cut into the surrounding vegetation. The opening was flanked on either side by small stone pillars etched with unfamiliar symbols. Small iron cauldrons, containing a flame that burned a soft purple, sat atop each pillar. She could smell sage and a scent that she did not recognize; an earthy sweet smell with a hint of mint. He must have seen her trying to figure out the odd aroma because he quickly told her it was Balor Root, a rare herb that can only be found in the forests of Dywen and was used in barrier spells. It was this that made the cauldron flames burn purple.

He dug into the small pouch strapped to his belt and took out a white chalky powder which he carefully threw into each of the flames.

Suddenly, the flames hissed and turned a deep orange. Grabbing her hand, he quickly dragged her through the pillars and onto the stone path on the other side. Within seconds the flames in each cauldron reverted to their purple tint.

"What did you do?" She asked as he moved up the path away from her.

"The powder blocks the barrier spell for a very short time, it is the only way to pass the sacred fires and reach Ardrin Gorm. The entrance has been magically blocked for centuries allowing no one to pass who does not possess the powder," he explained.

She shook her head in amazement and frustration— why Sebastian believed her instincts were enough to get her through all the magical traps and safeguards that were clearly still very much active in this realm, was truly baffling.

Thankfully, she had Rafe.

He turned toward her as if he had heard her thinking his name, bright green eyes piercing her own and causing her breath to catch in her chest. His tanned skin glistened as small beads of perspiration formed on his forehead. She shifted from one foot to the other as she became increasingly uncomfortable under his penetrating stare. The roar of her blood was deafening as it raced past her ears. She dropped her eyes trying to avoid his intense gaze, but she could still feel his eyes upon her—*why was he staring at her?*

Slowly lifting her eyes, she was surprised to see him walking quickly back toward her. He grabbed both her hands and held them in his own, pulling her in closer until she was within inches of him. His perfect jaw clenched as he held her gaze. Startled by the sudden contact she held her breath, tensing slightly, her skin began to tingle under his grasp. She could feel his energy mingle with her own, curiously exploring its deepest corners. A slight crackling sputtered in the air around them as he moved in even closer, his lips grazing her cheek and continuing up to her ear.

She could feel his breath on her neck and the pulse of his life force as it wound deeply into her very core. Closing her eyes, she relaxed into the rhythm of his pulse, listening intently as he whispered the same three words over and over into her ear—*Breha, Salya, Veroneh.*

Slowly he pulled back, dropping her hands and gently brushing away a strand of hair that had blown across her cheek.

"You have been blessed and will not be seen as a threat as we pass down the sacred path to the base of the mountain," he said his breath quick and unsteady. "There are many traps that lay in wait for intruders who may accidentally find their way onto this path. The blessing I just performed identifies you as Warlician, your aura has been cleansed and my energy will camouflage your own for now. Once we have activated the Druidstone, your aura will change permanently as it fuses with your ancestral home-land and reveals your true identity. Dywen will then see you for what you actually are—not just a mere curiosity but as one of its own."

Her pulse was racing, a small bead of sweat slid down her back. She could still feel the tingle in her skin where his hands had grasped hers. His closeness was intoxicating and unnerving, but she continued to stare into his eyes acutely aware that the surrounding air was still crackling.

He leaned in close again, his lips inches from her own, his green eyes full of desire. She tried desperately to catch her breath and gain her composure but the air that surrounded them was ignited with energy, pulling them closer. His eyes penetrated hers for a moment longer and then suddenly he closed them, his body tensing, his jaw clenching.

Without a word, he turned and walked up the path leaving her once again, bewildered.

The path was surprisingly well maintained for a world that had been vacant of life and magic for billions of centuries. None of the vegetation that grew on either side had invaded the path's space. The stones, while worn, were still very much visible in the distance and the path was well lit by the natural light that filtered through the trees.

They walked quickly as the sun began its descent behind the mountains neither one saying a word acknowledging the tension building between them.

The canopy above them opened, and she stopped to look up at the two moons that hung in the distance, their large silver spheres marking the location of the city. Rafe had stopped up ahead and as she joined him he handed her his canteen waiting patiently as she greedily drank the cool water.

"The path is going to start to incline now for a few miles, there are points at which it gets a little rocky and more difficult to navigate. Are you OK?" He asked, a slight look of concern visible on his face.

"I am fine," she replied, a slight tinge of annoyance making her response a little sharper than she would have liked.

"I am sorry if I offended."

"You didn't," she said, forcing a smile in reassurance. His brow furrowed even more, but he nodded, accepting her reply.

They reached the base of the mountain shortly before the sun set completely. Rafe hurried to find a notch in the mountain base that he could use as a shelter. He erected a small tarp, built a campfire, and laid out two sets of blankets while she went to fetch water from the mountain stream. He cooked a quick meal of rice mixed with large white beans and chicken, passing her a thick slice of bread, they ate in exhausted silence.

The night sky emerged overhead, stars exploding in the darkness as the two moons shined luminously, their silver glow casting strands of moonlight across the small campsite. There were no other sounds in the night sky just a slight rustle of the forest leaves and the gurgling of the mountain stream. Farrimore had perched on a branch that overhung the stream, his head tucked tightly under his wing as he slept. She lay her head on her backpack, staring at the stars and listening to the odd silence that surrounded them. Soon her eyes began to droop as the warmth of the fire lulled her into a deep and peaceful sleep.

He lay awake, staring at the sleeping face of the woman who was destined to not only save this world but her own. The firelight flickered across her face, and he reached out to touch her but quickly withdrew his hand. He was confused by the unbridled desire he felt for her, this beautiful stranger who had appeared suddenly in this forgotten land. Inexplicably drawn to her in a way he could not control nor understand.

He shifted uncomfortably trying to ignore the longing as old memories flooded through his mind. The things he had seen, heard, and knew were almost unbearable but his own destiny would not allow him to be weakened by the past. He thought about the prophecy that had been whispered between survivors of the Great War, the reality of it now sleeping next to him. The Second Rising was destined to be far worse, and she and the others were their only hope. There was much to do, and he worried that they did not have the time, especially now that the ancient dark was aware of her presence.

His body tensed as he thought about the coming war. He had been tasked with protecting the realms and their magic and now he must protect Dane and the others as well. As the fire cast its last flickering light across her sleeping face, one thought passed through his mind—*he could not fail her.*

CHAPTER 25

THE MORNING AIR WAS CRISP, its bite waking Dane. Sluggishly she opened her eyes. Her back was to Rafe, but she could hear him breathing softly close behind her. His arm was casually draped over her torso, and she gently lifted it, sliding quietly away from him. She looked around the clearing. The fire was out but the embers still glowed a deep red and the morning dew that blanketed the ground was sparkling in the early sunlight. On a rock jutting out from the side of the mountain, Farrimore sat quietly eyeing her suspiciously.

Ignoring him she grabbed her backpack and headed down to the stream to wash up. She was just pulling on a clean shirt when she heard the snap of a twig behind her. Whirling around she came face to face with Rafe, who looked just as sexy in the early morning sun as he did by firelight. She swallowed hard, holding her breath as he sauntered toward her closing the distance between them.

"Sorry I startled you," he said his voice slightly huskier than normal as his eyes traveled over her torso. "I thought I would find you down here when I woke up and saw you were missing."

"Not missing," she noted, quickly pulling down the hem of her shirt, "Just freshening up."

He gave her a coy smile before walking past her and filling up his canteen. He peeled off his shirt and crouched at the stream's edge, splashing water on his face and using the canteen to douse his head.

She watched silently as he finished, her eyes wandering over the taut, muscular surface of his back.

"Dane?"

The unexpected sound of his voice brought her out of her daze. Her eyes flying up to his face, which was now turned looking at her over his shoulder.

"I said, we can have breakfast before we leave, but we must be on our way soon as the trek to the top of Ardrin Gorm will take us two sun cycles. Are you OK?"

"Sorry, yes fine."

The smirk appeared on his lips once again and he stood. Water streamed down his torso as his green eyes pierced her own. "We can camp at *Moonladen Fall* tonight and continue to the Temple of Earth tomorrow. Once there, you will reactivate the Druidstone and accept your birthright. Doing so will complete your transformation and begin the process of awakening Dywen's magic from stasis. I am not sure how long this process will take but once Dywen's magic is again at full power, our magic will be as well."

He pulled on his shirt, slung the canteen across his body and headed back to camp, giving her a knowing look as he did.

She could feel the heat rise in her face as he passed by

inches from where she stood. His hand gently grazed hers, as their shoulders touched, igniting a subtle tingle in her skin as their energy collided.

After he disappeared down the path, she sat for a moment at the edge of the stream, listening to the gurgling of the clear cool mountain water as it flowed lazily by.

She jumped up suddenly as a thought exploded in her mind, *her magic!*

She had been so overwhelmed since arriving in Dywen that she had not even thought to try to use her own magic in this realm. Unlike the races of the Thanissia Universe who required the magic of the realms to power their own elemental magic, her magic was a part of her being, only using nature's natural energy to amplify it.

She took a deep breath, concentrating on the magic she could feel flowing through her veins. Lifting her right hand, she focused on the toothbrush that lay on top of her backpack willing it to move upward—*nothing*. She turned in the direction of the campsite and opened her mind, actively seeking Rafe's essence with her empathic ability—again nothing.

Why do my powers not work here? she thought.

Was it because she was in another time, or in a dimension where she did not belong? At least not as the witch she was in the modern world. Without her natural powers, she was as helpless as Rafe, which made her even more curious as to what would happen once Dywen's magic was reactivated.

Feeling anxious once again, by the lack of control she had in this new world, she quickly gathered up her things and headed back to camp.

Within the hour, they were trekking up the mountain

following a small stone and dirt path that led to the first peak of Ardrin Gorm; a flat area that he had referred to as Moonladen Fall. She walked closely behind him, her heart pounding in anticipation the higher up the mountainside they climbed. She had no expectations about what they would find at the top, but his vagueness had been frustrating. When she pressed him on the Druidstone at breakfast, he had simply responded that she would know what to do when she got there. Unfortunately, she was not sure that she 'knew' any of the things that he and Sebastian were sure that she would or should. A doubt that was beginning to make her question her instincts and the faith they both had in her.

Lost in her self-reflection she did not realize how far up the mountain they had climbed until she heard his voice announce their arrival.

She stopped abruptly as she reached the first peak, awed by the stunning view that lay in front of her. This area of the mountain was flat and surrounded on three sides by Ardrin Gorm's larger peak. The lush emerald green grass was thick and dewy and the tall vegetation that bordered its circumference was dotted with huge orange flowers their petals open wide to the sun. In the center of all this vibrancy was a waterfall cascading in powerful sheets from the middle of the mountainside splashing soundlessly into a large base pool below. Moonladen Fall was a hidden mountain oasis.

The air on the peak was fresh and clean, and she breathed in deeply enjoying the coolness that filled her lungs and tickled her nose. The sun was beginning to sink in the sky and as the mountain cast large shadows over the area, she noticed the water begin to glow. As the sky darkened, the waterfall and base pool shimmered with tiny specks of light. It reminded her of the thousands of fireflies that used to take over her parent's backyard on hot summer nights.

It was breathtaking.

"It's beautiful," she exclaimed, mesmerized by the twinkling that flitted across the water's surface.

"It is," he agreed moving closer to the far side of the mountain where stone steps connected this area with the path that led up to the top. She followed, finding it difficult to take her eyes off the water as the sky darkened and the twinkling radiance intensified.

"What makes the water shine like that?"

"No one knows."

He put their gear down in the open grassy area yards from the water's edge. "Some say it is Dywen's magic; others say there is something in the mountain that affects the water. No one has been able to confirm why the water shimmers the way it does in the dark, we have just learned to accept and enjoy it."

The darkening sky made the water shine even brighter and a soft silvery glow reflected off the mountain's walls, bouncing back to cast a subtle luminosity on the surrounding area. As Rafe busied himself getting their bedding out and building a fire, she walked the perimeter of the base pool taking in every inch of this tranquil place.

The water was shallow and a brilliant aqua, the sand surrounding its edge, pure white and as fine as powder. She bent down, picking up a handful of sand and letting it sift through her fingertips, the warmth of the day's sun still apparent in its grains. The waterfall was strangely quiet where it hit the base pool and the spray it cast was minimal.

There was hardly any breeze in the oasis as it was protected on three sides by the towering mountain, its rock face shooting straight up into the dark clouds above. She walked over to the mountain, running her fingertips across its grainy smoothness, feeling the coolness that emanated from the rock. The vegetation that grew at its base was just as awe-inspiring, dark green large-leaf bushes supporting enormous orange flowers with equally large petals. Inside each petal were pale blues and purples and the soft fragrance they released ignited a calming effect when she breathed in deeply. The remaining area was a thick carpet of lush green grass, not a weed or blemish marring its perfect surface.

Slowly, she made her way back to the base pool where Rafe had set up camp, the last of the sunlight disappearing below the horizon. The area was awash in the shimmering glow of the twinkling water and both the waterfall and the base pool glowed from within—Moonladen Fall was the perfect name.

He was sitting on a blanket at the edge of the sandy beach near where a small campfire burned. The smell of cooking meat wafted through the night air, and she saw a large copper pot sitting directly on the bright red embers. She sat down beside him, sensing him tense as her shoulder grazed his.

"Are you hungry?" He asked, his smoky voice igniting her insides.

"Starving," she replied quickly, desperately trying to ignore the effect he had on her. "It smells delicious. What is it?"

"It was my mother's recipe, a Celtic stew. It has been in

my family for generations," he said proudly. "I hope you like lamb."

She smiled and nodded, a slight tug on her heart reminding her of how much she missed her parents and her friends. He scooped out two large bowls of steaming hot stew, handing one to her. They sat close to one another on the blanket, quietly eating and watching the water sparkle enchantingly under the star-filled night sky. After dinner, he brought out a leather flask and poured a tin tumbler full of a dark red liquid and handed it to her.

"Another family recipe?" She asked taking a large sip of the strong bold-flavored wine.

"No, this is all mine," he grinned, raising his own glass to his lips. "Eddinberry wine. I make it from berries that can only be found in the lush grow lands of the Fae. The berry is tart but mixed with the right herbs and spices and a touch of honey, I have managed to create a very tasty wine."

"It is very good," she admitted allowing him to pour more into her tumbler, "And, I assume, very well-aged considering how long the portals to the other realms have been closed." She giggled, enjoying the taste of the rich, bold flavor of the berries on her lips.

He nodded, a knowing smile crossing his handsome face. "Perfectly aged some would say."

They sat in silence for a few more minutes, taking in the ethereal beauty the mountain offered. The double moons glowed brightly in the night sky casting a pale silvery radiance over the forest below. The stars that littered the sky were so close that she felt like they were falling to the ground.

Soon, she began noticing the wines affects, the soothing

influence it had on her body as the alcohol coursed through her bloodstream.

"Let's go swimming," she blurted out before her foggy mind had a chance to comprehend the idea properly.

He looked at her curiously but before he could utter a word in response she was up and walking to the water's edge, peeling off one piece of clothing after another. He observed silently as the last of her clothing hit the sand, and she dove into the sparkling base pool. She surfaced in the middle of the pool, her long dark hair dripping with water and her hands crossed modestly over her chest.

"Are you coming in?" she said coyly, her green eyes flashing and her cheeks flush with the effects of the wine.

He smiled, enjoying the boldness of this woman yet unsure about the emotions that stirred in him when he looked at her. Getting to his feet, he sauntered down to the edge of the water, his breathing quickening as he realized what he was about to do. The lights of the base pool glowed around her as she stood chest deep in the water watching him—she was beautiful.

"It's warm," she stated, one eyebrow lifting as she winked playfully at him. "Come in. I won't look, and I don't bite."

Giggling, she turned around so that her back was to him. She had submerged herself up to her neck and her dark hair floated gently around her. He hesitated, trying to regain control of the fledgling emotions that were running through him but as he continued to watch her a strong desire stirred inside. He fumbled with his clothes, his eyes never leaving her as he succumbed to the longing. As the cool night air hit his bare skin, he dove into the warm water, swimming out to the middle to join her.

She smiled as she heard the splash, turning toward him just as he reached her. Their eyes locked, and the air sizzled. He stared at her; his eyes full of lust as his hands reached around her waist pulling her into him.

She gasped as her skin touched his, a jolt of desire running through her body. Her hand reached up, gently caressing the scar on his eyebrow. Her finger tracing the pale skin down through his eyelid and across his sculpted cheekbone. Reaching behind his head she dug her fingers into his long, wet hair, pushing through the thick strands until her hand cupped the back of his neck. She did not say a word, she just stared into his eyes the power of their combined energies flooding them both with a craving that could not be ignored.

She was inches from his face, her eyes begging him to kiss her. His hands tightened around her waist in response bringing her lower body closer to him. She watched a single droplet of water run down his tanned face as he leaned in, his lips gently brushing hers. Her body tensed, exploding with sensations as her hand clasped his neck, and she pressed her mouth harder against his. His tongue pushed through her lips exploring the inside of her mouth, tantalizing her with the erotic movement. Her mind filled with passion as her entire body tingled with anticipation, an unquenchable desire pleading for his touch.

Releasing her mouth Rafe lifted her onto him. She wrapped her legs tightly around his back as he drove himself deep inside of her. A passionate hunger rolled through her as he thrust himself deeper and deeper, his mouth hungrily tasting her neck, her mouth, her breasts. They made passionate love in the water, and then he carried her to the sand where they made love again, this time slowly, the intensity of their first encounter diminished by their need to understand this extreme attraction.

He explored every inch of her, taking his time as he drove her to new heights of arousal and release. Her entire body was ignited by his energy, she could feel his need for her, his desire. She experienced every moment that he did, their lovemaking intensified by the innate connection that seemed to draw the two of them together. Her skin tingled in every place that his fingers touched; her mouth could not get enough of his. She could not think of anything but him, her longing, and how her body ached for his touch. It was surreal and intoxicating.

As he entered her for the third time, she felt a peculiar sensation on her pelvic bone, a slight prickle that ignited her already hot skin. Too aroused to care she ignored the strange sensation concentrating instead on his mouth as it found hers, and she was once again completely lost in him.

CHAPTER 26

THERE WAS SOMETHING SURREAL ABOUT Dywen's night sky and the way the stars throbbed against the dark backdrop as if they were alive—a heartbeat in an endless black void. The two moons hung extremely low, making Dywen seem a bit smaller from this vantage point.

It was late in the evening and Dane's body was still humming from their lovemaking as she lay quietly beside Rafe, her head on his chest, her legs intertwined with his. She looked away from the twinkling canvas and up at his face, the light from the dying campfire highlighting his rugged features, with its fading orange glow. Pulling herself up, she gently kissed the side of his jawline, her fingers sliding provocatively across his chest to play with the metal rune that hung from a leather string around his neck.

He winked at her, a knowing smile crossing his lips.

"We need to get some sleep," he said, pulling her in tighter as desire grew in his eyes.

"I know," she responded coyly, playfully tracing his mouth with her fingertip.

He pressed his lips to the top of her forehead, his husky voice whispering her name as his mouth began to travel down the length of her face. He lingered briefly, kissing her eyes and nose before his lips found their way to hers. She could feel the heat rising inside her as his kiss deepened; his hands exploring her body, caressing her skin and setting it afire.

She felt the intensity build inside him as it fueled his movement, the desire that overtook his senses flooded through her. It was a strange sensation, feeling his emotions. Intuitive like her empath abilities yet much more intimate. As if she was experiencing, how every fiber of his body reacted to her.

Rafe's kisses traveled down her neck, lingering briefly on her breasts before his soft tongue traced a path down the center of her stomach. The strange sensations intensified but her attention was diverted as her body reacted to the heat swelling inside her. He kissed her belly button gently as his mouth moved to the left side of her stomach. Her skin ached under the softness of his warm mouth and her body arched upward in response.

Suddenly, the caressing stopped, and the air became heavy with an uncomfortable silence. She sensed the shock that rifled through him, a slight panic saturating his skin as his confusion pulsed around them.

A small gasp escaped Rafe's lips and suddenly the fevered moment of passion was gone.

"Dane," he whispered moving his body away from hers and into a sitting position.

She saw the color drain from his face as his eyes stayed

locked on her stomach. A bewildered expression clouded his tanned features and his body stiffened. Slowly, he reached out a trembling hand. His finger touched the area on her pelvic bone where earlier she had felt the odd prickling sensation.

Unnerved by the sudden change in his behavior she quickly glanced down at her stomach, her eyes searching the spot where his finger lay. There on the skin, where an hour before had been void of any blemishes, was a black inked tattoo. It was difficult to make out in the subtle glow of the firelight, but she felt like she had seen the image before.

"It's my tattoo," he stammered, absently touching his pelvis with his other hand.

She looked closely at the artwork that covered much of his torso, her eyes scanning each tattoo for similarities. Drifting downward, her eyes stopped on the tattoo visible just above his waistband—the one she had been so drawn to the day before. The breath caught in her throat as her eyes traced the intricate black lines that wove through his skin. It was identical to the one that had magically appeared on her pelvic bone!

Her eyes flew to his face, her heart pounding in her chest as she suddenly found it extremely difficult to breathe. She watched him intently, confusion etched on her features as a new kind of panic began to swell inside.

"It is so rare," he whispered to himself, shaking his head.

"What is?" She asked her voice squeaking out the question as she tried to quell the alarm that threatened to stifle her breathing.

His eyes met hers, confusion and disbelief, a raging

clutter of his emotions suffocating her as they overtook her senses.

"Binding," he whispered.

Binding! The word screamed in her head. *What the hell is that?!*

As if reading her mind, he began to explain. "Binding is when two supernaturals become emotionally connected to one another. Their senses are intertwined. They feel everything the other does. It is an extremely intense and intimate experience and extremely rare. A binding can occur only if two individuals share a similar destiny and normally that destiny is of great consequence."

"But I am not a supernatural. I am mortal." She responded. Her skin was clammy and there was a sharp pain in her chest.

"That is why this binding is even more obscure, it seems to have recognized your destiny before it has even started."

She stared dumbfounded at him, not sure what to say. Her head was spinning. She felt nauseous. "Have you ever known of another binding?"

"Only one—your ancestor Claaven Callathian and his wife, Seri."

He took a deep breath as the anxiousness that drenched her emotions slammed into him.

"But how do you know this binding occurred to us?" The concept of being bound to another person, magically or otherwise, was overwhelming, especially when she did not have a say in the matter. "I don't feel any different."

"This tattoo," he said pointing to his own. "This is my identity marking, every male supernatural has one. When a binding occurs, the identity marking is transferred to his mate. It appears in the exact same spot on the body as his and is identical in every way. The only difference is that it is a mirror image of the original identity marking—a reverse tattoo.

She held her breath and looked down at the tattoo, then back to the one on his pelvic bone. It was an identical version, a mirror image of his. She grabbed the blanket and jumped to her feet, wrapping herself in the heavy cloth.

"What does this mean?" She said, her mind whirling, her hands shaking. She was very attracted to Rafe and obviously, she enjoyed his company, but binding, that sounded so permanent.

She didn't do permanent!

Her breath began to quicken as the panic began to claim her rationality.

"Dane, calm down," he said firmly, grasping her by the bare shoulders and pulling her toward him, using his own energy to slow her erratic breathing.

Tears welled up in her eyes and their emotions intertwined, intensifying their sensitive connection. His hand lifted her chin, his gaze penetrating her fear and calming her wayward nerves. As she began to relax under his intense stare, she saw something in his eyes that she'd never seen before—*herself.* Not just a mirrored reflection, but her entire being, every intimate part of her, all the deepest, darkest, hidden spaces in her soul were now visible in his eyes.

A sudden feeling of euphoria caressed her skin as her mind began to expand. Her hands trembled in his as small beads of perspiration pushed to the surface. She sank deeper into the warm cocoon of his energy as it wrapped itself gently around her, intertwining with her own as his emotions surrendered themselves to their connection. She could feel his desire to protect her, to keep her safe, as he continued to hold her tightly against him. There was a strength inside of him, but she could also feel a vulnerability hidden deep within. The walls inside her crumbled as his emotions flooded through her. The parts of herself that lay hidden for so long revealed themselves to him. All the fear and angst that had built up over the years drained away. She felt strong, confident, safely wrapped in this man's energy. Even though she had no control over the depths that he could see, quite frankly, for once, she didn't care. There was no longer a need to hide or for secrets. Her breathing evened, allowing the emotional connection to take over her body, her mind, and her senses as it coursed unrestricted through her veins.

Continuing to stare into his eyes, she heard the rhythmic thump of a beating heart. It was faint at first but then as their connection deepened it grew, its rhythm altering to match her own. For the first time in her life, she did not feel alone. She did not feel like she had to hide who she truly was or be ashamed of it. The link between them was raw and exposed and much more intense than any of the empathic connections she had experienced in the past. Her energy was completely wrapped up in his and as their hearts synchronized, they began to breathe as one.

Rafe held her shoulders tightly until he sensed her relax and accept their shared destiny, at which time, he stopped resisting the massive flow of emotions and energy that were desperately trying to join with hers. He watched with curious abandon as she felt what he felt, succumbing to the fate that not only brought them together but made them one. As the binding process continued, he experienced an onslaught of raw emotions, long contained inside a woman who carried a heavy burden. Their destinies collided, inter-twining as he felt his heart explode with love for the woman who stood vulnerable before him. He had never experienced feelings this intense nor experienced something so raw and natural. As their heartbeats and breathing combined in unison, he knew things would never be the same. They were one now and she would be a part of him forever.

The magical exchange lasted only moments but when he let go of her shoulders and stepped away, he felt exhausted.

Dane collapsed to the sand the blanket still wrapped tightly around her naked body, staring silently at the water as it sparkled brilliantly in the dark night, a look of disbelief on her pale face.

He lowered himself into a sitting position beside her, his eyes never leaving her face. Gently, he wrapped her in his arms, pulling her close, his instinct to protect her taking over.

"What are you thinking?" He asked softly, feeling the confusion and frustration resurface inside her.

She hesitated before turning to face him. "I was trying to figure out how this will work exactly, I mean how we are going to be together. We are from two different worlds, and you are, well much older than me."

A small smirk played on her lips, her sarcasm a feeble attempt at hiding her anxious energy.

He smiled and kissed her forehead, worried that this ancient magical pact, a shared destiny, may be too daunting for a woman so immersed in her own independence.

"It is true I am much older than you, but I am immortal. I don't age and once you claim your birthright neither will you so that is quite frankly a non-issue. As far as us being from two different dimensions, well that is not really a problem either. Since the earth was created by the life force and magic of the Thanissia Universe, the two are forever tethered."

"So, you can go to earth without any consequences?" She asked slightly relieved that she would not have to go back home alone.

"Well yes and no," he answered noticing the concern that flashed across her face. "I am able to travel through the sphere of the Thanissia realms without consequences, but your realm is slightly different. It is born of ancient magic but is not sustained by it, so my presence there would be like a ripple in the fabric of time. There is a possibility that my energy will cause unforeseen effects, of which, I am uncertain. Further, unlike you, I was not born on earth. My life force is not anchored to that dimension. Although I can exist on earth for a short time by staying tethered to this world, my immortality is vulnerable. I am a supernatural being on a mortal plane, so I will begin to age, and I suspect will be easier to kill."

"Kill?" She yelped, "I thought you were immortal!"

"Immortal, yes, but invincible I am not." He smirked, at the lack of knowledge she had of her ancestors and their capabilities. "Immortals can die, Dane, it is just very difficult. Although we live for a very long time, sooner or later every supernaturals' life force extinguishes."

"But Sebastian has been on earth for billions of years," she replied, searching his eyes for answers.

"Yes, but his life force was manipulated by the Guardian of Deities into a special form of light stasis so that he would be able to exist in the mortal world indefinitely. Sebastian is in his own unique form of stasis, he does not age, nor can his life force be extinguished, but he is unable to exist like you or me. As you know he can take multiple forms, but he is unable to wander from the portal opening that tethers him to this universe. This is the only way for us to exist in your world indefinitely, but it too comes at a cost."

She looked at him, a sadness causing her eyes to shine with tears.

"There is nothing for you to worry about, even with my vulnerabilities, I am still much more than a mortal," he said kissing the top of her head.

She nodded and leaned into him, her head resting heavy on his shoulder as she grappled with the enormity of her destiny—*their destiny*.

"Let's get some sleep," he said, gently guiding her backward onto the blanket and pulling her in tight toward him. "Tomorrow is going to be trying, a day of sacrifice that will change your life and who you are forever, putting you on a path toward a destiny that cannot be stopped once it begins."

She closed her eyes, happy to be nestled into the crook of his strong arms. The scent of his musky skin calmed her as she listened to the metrical beating of their hearts. The soft rustle of leaves and the gentle hiss of the waterfall were seductive. She began to relax succumbing to her emotional exhaustion. With his arms wrapped tightly around her, she felt safe and unencumbered by her past, not afraid to journey into the vast unknown of her future.

Unfortunately, she knew this tranquility was a temporary facade—a false euphoria that would eventually be shattered by a looming violent reality, embedded in the history of a long-forgotten past.

CHAPTER 27

THEY REACHED THE TOP OF Ardrin Gorm by mid-morning. The sun blazing high in the sky caused small beads of sweat to trickle down Dane's back as she pulled herself up the final ledge and stood exhausted beside Rafe.

The view from the pinnacle was breathtaking, the overwhelming beauty of Dywen on full display. She scanned the countryside as it stretched out for miles in each direction. From this vantage point every vale, river, and forest was visible—an immaculate canvas of nature, a kaleidoscope of vivid colors. A multitude of differing landscapes meticulously contributing to this realms power and stunning ambiance.

To the south, the metal spires of the city reached majestically out of the lush green forest that surrounded it. To the southwest, the waterfall where she had come into this world could be seen throwing its thunderous mist in every direction. The east and west were claimed by the thick forest that stretched as far as the eye could see the only disturbance to its expanse, the brilliant blue hue of the river that ran proudly through it. Off in the distance, on the other side of the waterfall near the western horizon, a simmering dusty haze was hovering just above the ground.

"What is that?" She asked pointing toward the odd dust clouds that rose in the distance.

He followed her gaze across the vast green expanses of the forest to the edge of the horizon. "The Dead Lands," he said, offering no further explanation.

"Sounds ominous," she replied, shooting him a curious look.

"Not really."

Turning without another word he walked toward a big pile of rocks that lay toward the back of the mountaintop.

She raised an eyebrow at his retreating back, her exasperation a reminder that she was dealing with an ancient warrior, not a talented conversationalist. Getting information from him was never going to be easy.

The pinnacle of Ardrin Gorm was vastly different from its first peak where they had spent last night. It was a crag of hard rock and stones with little to no vegetation or green space. There didn't seem to be much living up here besides a few wispy, dry stalks of tall brown grass that rustled in the wind as it swirled in squalls over the mountain's tip. The temperature on the higher plateau was much cooler causing a slight chill to sting her nostrils as she breathed in deeply. Winds blew in swirling gusts, and she noticed a slight hint of lavender scenting its wisps.

The thinner air made it harder to catch her breath as she hurried her pace, following Rafe as he reached the large rock formation situated at the back of the pinnacle. As she neared the boulders, she could see a small opening cut into the rocks. He did not hesitate when he reached the opening, walking right through and disappearing behind the rock face. She followed cautiously, picking her way through the large boulders until she came to a gravel path.

The path was lined on either side by six-foot rock walls. Its surface was peculiar. It was smooth and stratified like shale but contained crystallized flecks throughout its thin layers. The stone was a pale gray with ribbons of blues and greens embedded into its surface, the effect was beautiful and another reminder of Dywen's exceptional diversity. The walls were cool to the touch, yet she felt a warm spark under her fingertips as she ran them over the smooth stone.

Farther up the path, she noticed small rivers of water running down portions of the wall, trickling from thin cracks in the surface and creating small pools on the ground. Other than Rafe's footsteps echoing somewhere up ahead, the gentle trickle of the water was the only sound evident on the shadowy path.

She moved in silently behind him as he led her a few hundred yards up the rock path. He never spoke or turned back to make sure she was still behind him because he knew, like she did, where she was, their energy forever inter-twined. After her initial reaction to their binding, she had calmed down and accepted their fate, the surreal intimacy of their connection both disconcerting and comforting. Being so emotionally vulnerable to someone was going to take some getting used to.

After a few more minutes of hiking up the narrow path, he stopped and turned toward her, his eyes searching hers. A hint of concern knotted his brow as he moved closer. His hand caressed her cheek as his lips brushed against hers. A strange mindfulness pulsating around them.

"I can't go any further," he said taking a step back. "This is your journey, your destiny, and you must continue to the Temple of Earth alone."

She could sense his conflicting emotions, the need to protect her conflicting with the respect he had for what she needed to do.

"But I thought our destinies were joined now?" She stated, uncertain if she wanted to continue without him.

He smiled and gently took her hands. "We have a shared destiny, this is true, but your destiny as it was written long ago, is still your own."

Nodding, her heart pounding loudly in her chest, she released his hand and stepped by him, walking a few feet past him before she felt his conflicted emotions rearing up inside her. She felt his energy exploding as he moved quickly toward her grabbing her hand and pulling her into him.

"Please, be careful," he said gently as he leaned in and brushed his lips across hers again. Her head spun as his heady scent filled her senses and the arm that encircled her waist tightened. She smiled at him and took a deep breath trying to calm the shaking in her hands. She placed her hand on the side of his face and looked deeply into his eyes, the bright green of his irises flickering with emotion.

"I'll be fine." She murmured, pulling back her shoulders and untangling herself from his strong grip.

She didn't look back as she walked away because she didn't want to see the worry etched on his face, the apprehension she could feel following her down the path was enough. Although she wished she didn't have to continue without him, she understood how destinies worked, each designed for one specific person, which often meant walking one's journey alone.

She thought back to the beginning when this new destiny had been revealed to her and how unfazed she had been. It was almost like somewhere deep in her subconscious she had always known there was something more. A place with someone where she wouldn't feel alone, isolated by who she was. Now in a distant realm, the home of her immortal ancestors, she was discovering her true self for the first time, uncovering her magical heritage and the destiny she was meant for.

Unfortunately, becoming her true self meant she had the fate of mankind in her hands and an ancient evil entity in her head. Maybe her initial bravado toward her unexpected new destiny was somewhat misplaced.

As she ventured further down the path, it began to widen and the stone walls that flanked it became even taller, stretching upward twenty feet. The high walls blocked the afternoon sun and the path soon became immersed in cool shadows, causing her to shiver as goosebumps formed on her skin.

She reached a sharp corner in the path, noticing an ancient glyph carved into the stone wall. It was the same one engraved on the lock plate of her grandfather's chest— an ancient symbol for earth. She turned the corner and was confronted with a large wooden door, its iron hinges and round handle rusted with time. At its center, emblazoned on a large metal disc was the same glyph.

The Temple of Earth, she thought, the sanctity of this place not lost on her as she stood dwarfed by the massive door.

Hesitantly, she pulled on the rusty handle surprised when the door did not resist. Hinges groaning, it begrudgingly opened revealing the temple's inner sanctum.

The temple was serene, a small bright green grassy area surrounded by a circular stone wall. It was empty except for a pale gray stone slab at its center. The slab was about four feet thick with wide stone steps leading up to its top. In the middle of the slab sat a white-stone altar its surface glistening in the late afternoon sunlight.

Her eyes surveyed the surrounding wall, its interior surface displaying five glyphs carved into its rock at specific intervals. Small stone steps were located beneath each of them. She walked gingerly toward the stone slab unsure of what her presence in this sacred place may do. A slight breeze entered the clearing from the open door, the smell of jasmine on its wisps. Her hair blew haphazardly around her face as the breeze circled around the area. Brushing the chaotic strands away from her eyes, she ascended the altar's stairs.

As she reached the top, she could see that the glistening white altar was made from Calcite, a protecting, grounding, and centering stone that is known for increasing and amplifying energy. Calcite would be the perfect stone for an altar that powered or funneled magic. She walked around the altar impressed by the beautifully carved piece of stone; its corners polished to a smooth finish.

At its center stood what she guessed was the Druidstone, a small column, also made of Calcite, its base buried in a gray stone cauldron filled with dry, cracked earth. She was surprised by the simplicity of the Druidstone, its ordinariness not echoing the importance of its power. It wasn't very big, maybe a foot tall, and its sides were smooth except for the back where a large green gem was embedded. Besides the gem, the only thing that marred the surface of the Druidstone was a round indentation in its top. At the bottom of the indentation was the familiar carving of the ancient glyph, representing earth.

The breeze in the clearing calmed suddenly and an eerie silence once again emanated from the walls. The sun was beginning to descend, and the entire altar was draped in long-reaching shadows.

Carefully, she touched the Druidstone, its surface warming under her skin. A slight vibration quivered in the stone tickling her fingertips. Taking a step back she waited for something to happen, for the Druidstone to recognize her energy but the stone lay quiet, its initial reaction to her touch ineffective. She lowered her hand looking around the clearing for a clue as to how to activate the Druidstone.

Sebastian had said she would instinctively know but standing here in the middle of the temple without a clue, she felt he may have been somewhat misguided in his wisdom.

"Think," she said aloud, her voice echoing in the clearing as her eyes scanned the surrounding walls. As she stared at the glyphs, an idea came to her. She hurried down from the altar, heading to the outer wall and the glyph carved into it directly in front of the altar. She recognized the familiar series of lines and dots immediately; it was a moon glyph and it represented earth.

Circling the stone wall, she studied the other four glyphs, each one a moon glyph representing one of the other elements—fire, air, water, and spirit. There was a straight line carved into the stone between each, a continuous mark that encircled the entire wall and connected the glyphs to one other.

A circle, she thought, climbing the steps under the water glyph until it was at eye level. The lines of the glyph were carved deep into the stone, but its dots were raised. Carefully, she pushed on the first dot. It began to sink into the wall under the weight of her finger; she kept pushing it deeper until she heard a slight click. Smiling, she did the same to the second dot until it too clicked into place. Sure, she was on to something she hurried around the clearing, pushing in the dots on all the glyphs until the last one clicked into place.

She waited with excitement for something to happen but the stillness in the clearing continued. Confused, she walked back up to the altar and examined the Druidstone again, her eyes resting on the indentation in its top, the glyph at its bottom catching the midday sun.

Why would there be an indentation? Why not just carve the earth glyph right onto the flat surface? She thought, her hand absently playing with her grandfather's medallion that hung on its thick chain around her neck.

Somewhere in the back of her mind, a hunch surfaced. Taking the medallion from around her neck she placed it in the indentation located on the top of the Druidstone, allowing the thick chain to hang down the side, resting on the dry cracked earth below. Suddenly, the green gem in the middle of the medallion began to glow and a slight hum echoed from the Druidstone. The medallion was an amulet as well as a key!

The hum intensified as the green gem implanted in the back of the Druidstone also began to glow, becoming more vibrant as a small beam of light shot out across the clearing toward the earth glyph on the far wall. The green beam penetrated the glyph, filling the carved lines with its light. It continued to spread through the adjoining lines in the stone walls, filling each of the remaining glyphs with the same green light. Once the final glyph ignited the green beams began to cross the clearing diagonally, beams of light stretching across from one glyph to another until a pattern began to develop.

As the final beam ignited, the one that joined the Druidstone with the earth glyph extinguished and the humming ceased. She stood in the middle of the altar as the beams of light, crisscrossing the clearing crackled and sizzled around her.

She turned slowly in a circle the early twilight making the beams shape more vivid—*she was standing at the center of a pentacle.*

Dane could feel the magic of the temple flickering around her as the atmosphere inside the walls ignited. Turning back to the Druidstone she noticed that the dried earth in the cauldron at its base was now a rich, thick, dark soil. The crystallization in the Calcite reflected the green light pulsating through the temple, illuminating an etching on one side of the Druidstone that had been unseen before.

She looked closer at the writing—*Moongre fol Sentra Tailae ben.* Reading the incantation out loud, she struggled to pronounce the ancient language, repeating the incantation over and over until suddenly English words formed in her head—*Moonbeams will ignite the magic within.*

The Druidstone must be powered by the moon.

Ancient magic sizzled around her as she continued to read the archaic words aloud. Soon, she began to sense a stirring in the clearing as the beams of moonlight crisscrossing the altar began to pulsate, their glow ebbing and surging in rhythm with her voice. She could feel the temple respond, its ancient magic waking from its long slumber as the reactivated Druidstone drenched it with power.

Continuing to chant the incantation in her ancestor's native tongue, the green beams grew to a blinding glow, pulsating as each word echoed against the stone walls. Slowly, the beams of the pentacle bent toward the altar, wrapping themselves around her, caressing her in their warm radiance. Her body felt weightless as ancient energy from the Druidstone seeped into her veins dousing her with a magic long forgotten. She felt the power of her ancestors coursing through her, their strength, pain, and death, all marking her blood as her birthright flooded into her. The magic coursing through every fiber of her being as she struggled to not succumb to the overwhelming primal power.

The beams continued to tighten around her body as her heart began to slow. A strange feeling manifesting deep within her chest, her pulse diminishing until she could barely feel or hear the beat of her heart. A tingling coolness washed over her skin, briefly masking the searing pain that followed closely behind. Her primal scream ripped through the clearing as a penetrating burning scorched her insides. Pain wracked her body. Her breathing became labored as her vision faded, her mind numbed, and her body went limp. The only thing she could do before she collapsed unconscious on the stone slab was listen as her human heart took its *final beat.*

Rafe heard the scream as he stood pacing just outside the temple's large wood door. Its anguish pierced the darkening sky causing his heart to ache and his skin to crawl.

His instincts wanted him to run to her, but he knew he could not. The temple was a sacred place. It was forbidden to enter without purpose. He knew by the shift in the energy that surrounded the temple that her transformation was almost complete. She would soon emerge from it different from when she went in.

He leaned against the cool stone wall as her conflicting emotions saturated him, the pain and confusion ransacking her body, left him weak and disoriented. His skin was drenched in perspiration as he struggled not to falter under the weight of her turmoil as he experienced her emotions simultaneously. He could feel her fading as the transformation took her human life force, the air above the clearing echoing a deadly silence.

The sun disappeared behind the distant horizon as the silvery glow of the two moons intensified, casting their beams across the land. The energy in the surrounding air began to change. He sensed the ancient magic as it found its way back to the surface, its archaic energy gaining strength, as the Druidstone powered the realm's core. She had succeeded in her quest and now Dywen was awakening from its eternal slumber. Soon elemental earth magic would ignite the ancient energy in every corner of these lands. The realm would regain its power and in return, it would provide them both with theirs.

The deadly silence continued, and he eventually stopped pacing, watching instead, the evening sky above the clearing for any signs that she would emerge from the Temple of Earth soon.

Green beams arced skyward, their glow crackling and hissing as they stretched higher into the sky before exploding in a dazzling shower of green light, cascading across the multiple landscapes of Dywen.

It is done, he thought, as the last of the green light faded into the twilight and the air began to hum with the ancient essence—*she was now one of them.*

CHAPTER 28

THE MOUNTAIN RANGE RAN AS far as the eye could see, its white-tipped peaks glistening under the silver sun that shone in the crystal clear blue sky. The vale that sat nestled in the side of the mountain was breathtakingly surreal, its landscape picturesque. Large white and purple flowers dotted the lush carpet of green grass that swayed in the summer breeze. A tiny stream trickled through its center; the water so clear she could easily see the river rock covered bottom. Tiny colorful fish darted back and forth, enjoying the warmth of the sun as it sparkled on the stream's surface. A warm breeze blew across the vale, the scent of lavender and gardenia exploding in its wake. Across the stream was a large Elder Oak, its massive green canopy a stunning contrast to the dark backdrop of the mountains. In its shadow sat a small cottage, its worn wood boards and burnished tin roof adding to its welcoming and comforting appeal.

Her gaze was drawn up toward the top of the mountains, where a haze tinged the edges of the vale, a strange blur distorting whatever existed beyond its boundaries. She looked around at the idyllic setting, its perfection disconcerting. She felt a strange tug at her senses, a warning, alerting her to the fact that something was not quite right about this place. The vale seemed to be shrouded in an eerie silence; a suffocating denseness hid just beyond its perimeter. Something unseen seeping slowly into the vale through its perimeter. Her eyes were drawn back to the strange blur, its appearance in the perfectly serene vale seemed oddly out of place.

Shifting her attention, she gazed back at the cottage. She was instinctively drawn to the lonely structure as if somewhere deep inside she knew that the cottage held answers. She walked toward the small bridge, her movements fluid and precise. The rickety boards creaked out their displeasure as she crossed. The silence engulfing the vale grew in its intensity, and she could feel the hollowness that permeated its path as it crept closer.

There was a small stone kiln at the edge of the property and as she passed it, she noticed the embers were still warm from recent use. Suddenly, the creak of rusty hinges broke the odd silence that cloaked the vale and the front door of the cottage opened.

She was stunned by the sudden appearance and engaging beauty of the woman who emerged. The stranger walked toward her, long blonde hair hanging in a glistening sheen down her back, small wisps fluttering behind her as she moved. The sides were pulled back into small braids revealing a dark streak that ran defiantly through her blond hair, behind her right ear. Her pale skin was flawless, her eyes, a light gold with flecks of silver and violet highlighting the irises making them glisten as she emerged from the shadows of the Elder Oak. She wore a simple outfit of thin black pants, knee-high leather boots, a white gauzy blouse and a tan leather vest. Hanging from her neck was a glass and silver orb, tied to a long thin black leather string. Inside the orb was a small crystal, its edges sparkling erratically as it too caught the sunlight.

"We have been waiting for you," the woman said hugging her warmly. She stiffened slightly under the unfamiliar and unexpected embrace.

"Quickly Claaven we don't have much time," the woman called over her shoulder as a man emerged from the cottage. His gentle eyes were the color of fresh sage, his tanned face was etched with scars, some hidden by the unshaven scruff that covered the lower part. Sections of his long white hair were braided at the temples, small beads hanging at their ends. He was dressed all in black and his leather boots were dusty and worn. Around his neck was a silver medallion which bore markings that she was sure she had seen before.

She studied him as he approached, the name the woman had called him still echoing in her ears.

"Have we met before?" She asked as he came to stand beside the woman. She felt an odd type of kinship with this stranger. Desperately she searched her memory for clues, but its recesses were clouded by a thick fog.

His smile was genuine and comforting as he shook his head. "I'm afraid not." His deep voice was soothing and emitted a quiet power that relayed a sense of importance and stature.

"Where am I?" She asked

"Somewhere of your making," he responded his eyes never leaving her face.

Confused by his response she looked around for anything familiar. "Why am I here?"

"You have begun your journey," the woman answered. "You have come to the place where we are born and where we return to."

"Am I dead?" She asked calmly.

"No," said the woman, grasping her hand. "Quite the opposite. You have come here to begin your journey not to end it."

"Your true destiny has begun," the man said holding out his hand. "Now that the magic has been reborn you must claim your birthright."

She reached out slowly, taking his hand. She did not understand the meaning of his words but instinctively she knew she was meant to be here, to be with them.

The man began muttering something under his breath as the three of them stood in a circle, hands interlocked. The air in the vale began to swirl making the Elder Oak groan in response, its low hanging limbs swinging back and forth. She could feel a shift in the energy around her as his incantation awakened the ancient magic that lay dormant within him and the woman. She watched as a soft golden light seeped from her, a green one from him, the energy surrounding their bodies.

Slowly, the light moved away from them manifesting into a singular orb at the center of the circle. The orb hovered momentarily before beginning to spin, its speed increasing as sparks began to spit out from its center. Unexpectedly, the ball of light flew directly into her, flooding her with a warm glow, a choir of whispers exploding in her head. A kaleidoscope of images passed through her mind as an electric tingle surged through the couple's hands into her own. Suddenly, she was aware of the past, the present, and the uncertain future; her ancestor's knowledge passed through generations was now her own. Her birthright had been fulfilled.

The whispering and images ceased as the last of the ancient magic they possessed were transferred to her. The vale became quiet once again as the man released her hand and looked her directly in the eye.

"You have all you need my child; your destiny is now your own." Squeezing her shoulder, he smiled and then turned and walked away.

"Come Seri," he called over his shoulder as he retreated toward the cottage, "our time here is no more."

The woman nodded at him in acknowledgment.

Smiling warmly and with a light twinkling in the depths of her beautiful eyes, she said calmly. "We will always be with you now. Do not fear what is to come for you will never be alone."

Releasing her hand, she too turned and walked away, glancing back only once before the two of them faded away in a shimmering golden light.

The sky above the vale began to darken, and the air cooled. The vivid green of the grass faded, and the majestic mountains began to disappear as the hazy blur hovering beyond their edges descended. The beauty of this place was slowly disappearing as a black shadow seeped from the blur swallowing everything in its path until the vale was nothing more than the spot where she stood.

As the shadow drew near, she thought she heard a familiar voice hidden in its depths calling her name. It was faint at first but grew in strength as the black shadow crept its way toward her. As the thick dark ink washed through her mind, she heard the strange tick of a clock off in the distance, its haunting sound echoing through the darkness as the hand of unconsciousness pulled her down toward that familiar voice.

CHAPTER 29

R AFE RAN TOWARD DANE, CALLING her name as he
sprinted up the altar steps. He had heard her
speaking as he stood waiting beyond the temple
door and then felt a presence surrounding her. He was not
concerned for her well-being as he could feel she was not
afraid, it was the energy of the presence that made him
disobey the forbidden and enter the sacred sanctuary, for it
was familiar to him.

To his surprise, he found her standing on the altar her
eyes closed and her mouth uttering incoherent words. She
was doused with a subtle white light as the familiar sparks
of ancient energy flared around her. He watched in awe as
pure white light swirled in a ball in front of her and then
disappeared inside her. The presence he felt surrounding
her retreated and disappeared leaving only a fragmented
whisper of the past and a haunting sadness. Her eyes flew
open, glazed eyes staring at something in the distance,
curiosity, and confusion contorting her beautiful features

before she lost consciousness and collapsed onto the stone altar.

He could hear a hollow ticktock somewhere in the distance as he held her limp body, the low incessant rhythm echoing through the quiet night. Gently he whispered her name over and over until finally, her eyes fluttered open. He saw a strange shadow cloud them before the confusion cleared, and she focused on his face.

"Hi," she said, her hand reaching up to touch his face.

"How do you feel," he asked, trying not to reveal his concern.

"I'm OK."

She struggled to sit up in her weakened state, leaning on him for support. Her mind was still foggy. Carefully shook her head trying to release the last of the cobwebs.

Looking at him tentatively she whispered, "I saw them."

He helped her to her feet. "Saw who?"

"Claaven and Seri," she said without hesitation, her clear mind now able to make the connection. He continued to stare, his green eyes blank, her words apparently not eliciting any type of outward reaction.

"Where?" He asked, the feeling of familiarity the strange energy had provoked now making sense.

"I'm not sure where we were. Seri said it was a place of my making."

Surprise showed on his face and his stare hardened momentarily causing a cold chill to run up her spine.

He hesitated before he whispered, *"The Gilded Lands."*

"What are the Gilded Lands?" She asked, "Or do I not want to know."

He took a deep breath, a cloud of concern passing over his handsome features. "The Gilded Lands is the place where my people, our people," he corrected, "begin their life cycle and where they return to when it ends."

"That is what Seri said," she whispered. "Where is this place?"

"It is in the ethereal plane, a place of peace, tranquility and rest. A place where people go but do not return. It is the destination of a supernaturals' life force, its final journey." He hesitated momentarily, his face wrinkling at the brow as if he were trying to come to terms with her statement. "What happened when you were there?"

She shook her head trying to recall all the details of this place. "It was a beautiful place, tranquil but there was something lurking beyond its edges, something that felt empty and dark, waiting. They appeared to me, Seri and Claaven, but I did not know who they were, even when she spoke his name. There was a memory hovering at the edges of my mind, but I could not grasp it. My memories seemed stifled somehow as if I was only supposed to function in that moment. Anyway, they took my hand and Claaven began an incantation and suddenly their magic passed to me. I could feel their past, I understood their world, and the magic gave me knowledge and power—*an ancient knowing*. Then they disappeared, and a black shadow began to fall over the vale. It did not belong there; its energy was malevolent. It entered the vale seeping from its seams, swallowing up the surrounding tranquility until it swallowed me too."

She looked deep into his eyes as her hands reached up to rest on either side of his face. "The voice I heard, calling to me in the darkness, it was you, you led me back."

Rafe hugged her tightly, the feelings he had for this woman were overwhelming. The mere thought of her entering the Gilded Lands was too much to bear, but that she had returned was even more inconceivable, especially since he was sure the black shadow in there with her was the ancient dark. It had somehow connected with her subconscious mind and was able to manifest its presence within it.

Releasing her, he turned and walked slowly around the stone altar, he needed to think, his mind trying desperately to process the information she had provided.

"I have never known anyone to inherit magic. The people of the Thanissia Universe are all born with it. It is who we are, magical beings from birth, harnessing the magic of the elements that we are born from. How that magic was to be transferred to each of the Arcanists has always been the great mystery surrounding the ancient prophecy. I believe I now understand. The ancient magic must be encapsulated in your bloodline even though our magic ceased to exist in your world. Magical races never truly die unless the bloodline ends. The prophecy declares that the Arcanists are all born from the six ancient blood-lines, so the magic from this world must reside within you, all of you, waiting. That is why the Druidstones in each realm must be reactivated. None of you can regain your powers without the help of your ancestors who have passed on."

Rafe's pacing picked up speed as he thought out loud. "You see, the ethereal plane lays in stasis just like the realms, therefore, only re-awakening the ancient magic will allow it to be transferred. It must be why you were chosen first to receive your birthright. Your heritage is unique Dane for you are the daughter of two sacred bloodlines because of the binding of Claaven and Seri. You have the blood magic of both the Warlician and the Celestial flowing through you. You are born of the earth but marked by spirit. It must be the reason they were the ones to pass the ancient magic on to you. In our world, it is extremely rare that couplings happen outside of one's own race. The fact that your ancestors and your birthright are a mixture of two powerful races means that the ancient magic you have just inherited is extremely rare. How that will manifest in you is unknown especially since you possess magic from your own world."

"Do you feel any different?" He asked coming back to her side.

"No," she said wondering why she didn't.

"Well, in time the magic will reveal itself to you and you will learn about your new powers and how to wield them. But for now, we must go. The realm is waking, and we will soon be able to use magic to find the Book of Realms."

He gathered up their gear and led her back through the stone-walled path, the moon's glow the only guiding light.

Emerging onto the dusty crag he stopped.

"We will go down the backside of the mountain. It is quicker but unfortunately a more difficult way to traverse the peak." Taking her hand, he looked deep into her eyes. "Remember you are immortal now, trust your instincts, and allow the magic to guide you."

She nodded. Looking past him, her eyes searched the top of the mountain. There was something different about the barren landscape now, it seemed more alive, vibrant. Small swirls of dust sparkled in the moonlight; their flecks caught in the moon's beams. The dry grass blew gracefully back and forth in the night breeze, the rustling melodic. She listened intently, her senses far acuter, immersing her in the hidden energy that sprang from this realm and bringing back Sebastian's words—*your being will become one with the environment.*

As they descended, the magic began opening around her, seeping into every corner and space. The tall grasses waved gently back and forth, and the trees stretched their limbs. There was a multitude of smells in the air, drifting past her nose, and tickling her mind. Vibrant colors claimed the landscape as Dywen burst into a kaleidoscope of color. The realm was being re-energized by the Druidstone, and she could feel it breathe as new life pumped into its tired ancient bones. Everything around her hummed; a beautiful chorus of nature singing as it fed off the ancient magic that flowed unseen across the landscape.

Her focus narrowed as she followed Rafe down the mountain trail, the path running precariously close to the edge. Twice she lost her footing on some loose stones causing her to stumble toward the cliff side. Shifting her weight, she had easily maneuvered a correction and continued down the hazardous trail without losing a beat.

She felt stronger, more certain of herself, as her movements became acutely precise. Allowing her instincts to guide her, she ran faster, jumping over fallen logs and easily traversing through thick foliage. Her breathing calmed as it matched her pace. The further down the mountain they descended the more intense the magical energy became. Adrenaline pounded through her veins, her eyes taking in every minuscule aspect of the surrounding landscape. She ran with ease finding a grace in her movement, which allowed her to skim over the ground effortlessly. Her skin was covered with a thin sheen of sweat that glistened with magical energy in the emerging dawn's subtle light. Slowly, she became one with her ancestral world. Her senses heightened as her surroundings intensified and became vivid.

The cracks in the bark of the trees were visible as she ran by them, their edges carved by years of exposure to the sun and wind. The early morning dew drops clung desperately to the leaves, their movement shimmering as they ran slowly down their hosts. She could taste their salty, earthy tang on her tongue as she ran by.

The trees groaned overhead whispering their good mornings as she and Rafe made their way through the thickening forest at the base of the mountain. The scents that wafted by on the morning breeze tickled her nose as the rising sun broke radiantly over the distant horizon, bathing the landscape in its early morning warmth.

She slowed her pace and closed her eyes allowing her instincts to guide her. This newfound feeling of control that seeped from every pore was exhilarating, intoxicating, and powerful. Opening her eyes again, she saw Rafe slowing his pace as he exited the edge of the forest up ahead.

The dawn broke, its elusive light penetrating the trees as she emerged to see him standing at the edge of a small cliff, a black silhouette highlighted by the early morning glare. She walked forward standing quietly beside him, surveying the landscape that stretched endlessly before them.

"The Dead Lands," he said a somber look on his face as he gestured to the wide expanse of barren land present in the canyon below.

"The Dead Lands," she repeated, as she scanned the dirt landscape, shocked by its stark opposition to the natural beauty of the rest of Dywen. The floor of the canyon was parched, its cracked muted color palette void of any vitality. Large aging rock formations protruded up toward the sky, their dark exteriors battered by years of exposure, were dusty and crumbling. Small dust clouds churned in the ravine below and the air wafting upward was stale and heavy, a lifeless blanket that wrapped itself silently around her. There were no signs of any vegetation or water, and she could see no life of any kind roaming the scarred, dry lands below. She did not feel the same energy awakening here as she had in other parts of Dywen, everything here was unpleasantly stagnant.

"The Dead Lands is a blemish on this beautiful world," he said as if reading her thoughts. "They exist as a stark reminder that the element earth has many and often opposing sides. Nothing grows here, nothing exists, nothing ever has but its presence is needed to provide balance to our magic."

She stared at the parched wasteland below as it stretched unyielding across this part of the realm. Silently, she acknowledged the power that opposites had when combined. Although each could exist separately, they were balanced when together and similarly, so was this world. For all Dywen's vibrant beauty, its dark side was just as important to its overall existence.

The raw strength that pulsated from this bleak landscape was unexpected but undeniable, and she could feel its tug, an opposing energy that lay lifeless on her skin.

Shifting her thoughts away from the unappealing landscape, she focused back on why they were here.

"This is where the Book of Realms is hidden?" She asked her eyes scanning the vast expanse looking for a clue.

"It is, I can feel it," he responded, a dark shadow passing over his eyes. "It is also the place my parents and brother perished."

Her breath caught in her chest as her blood chilled. Turning to him she put her hand gently on his back continuing to experience the haunting pain that coursed through his body at the memory of his family. She was not sure she would ever get used to this transference of emotions that she and Rafe now shared. She waited silently until the last of the painful memories subsided, and he took a deep breath.

"We must head inland toward the dry sea," he said, pointing toward a massive rock formation that towered ominously in the distance. "The book has been hidden just east of it in the underground caverns."

She nodded, adjusting her backpack as she followed him along the edge of the cliff to a small path that would lead them down into the suffocating wasteland below.

CHAPTER 30

D ANE PULLED HER SCARF OVER the lower half of her face attempting to stop the dust from entering her mouth. The trek across the Dead Lands was exhausting as the barren landscape continued to sap her energy and strength. Rafe stopped on multiple occasions to have her drink water and rest, but the strange fatigue continued to weave itself through the air. She dragged her feet along the cracked ground struggling to move forward, her body aching, her limbs almost too heavy to move.

The sun pounded down on them as the heat in this unbearable dust bowl scorched her skin. She had already removed her jacket and shirt and now trekked through the wastelands in just a tank top. Rafe seemed less affected by the sudden shift in the environment, but his skin too glistened with sweat as he walked ahead of her.

"Stop fighting the process, Dane," he snapped, turning to watch her as she struggled to keep up. "We are children of the earth and we must adapt to all its forms."

Taking her by the shoulders he looked deeply into her eyes. "Let it in, it will not harm you," he murmured.

She felt the peculiar tug as the dead energy tried to enter her, but this time instead of willing it away she allowed it entry. Its energy was dense and stifling, a thick fog that traveled through her veins and up into her mind. Its long dusty fingers dragging themselves up her skin as it fused with the ancient magic already pulsing through her body.

Suddenly, she felt a sharp sting that made her gasp for breath as her legs gave out underneath her. He held her steady, keeping her upright with his strong muscular hands. Her head spun as the dust began to settle on her skin its suffocating density dispersing through her being. It seemed like forever before the feeling came back into her legs, and she could stand on her own. She was embarrassed by how weak and fragile she must look to him.

He released her and took a step back, allowing her to amalgamate to her new surroundings.

"Better?" he asked, a tinge of concern making his voice crack.

She nodded, still finding it difficult to take a breath as the energy of the Dead Lands finished fusing with her own. She began to feel better. The different magical essences contained in the varying landscapes of Dywen left her with an uneasy sense of contrast and balance.

The sun had peaked, blazing a path across the clear blue sky as they reached the enormous rock formation that marked the proximity of the caverns. It stood in the center of a dry seabed; its surface ravaged by water that had dried up long ago. A dark ring still encircled the rock face, an eerie reminder of the sea that once claimed this part of the land.

She surveyed the landscape to the east, heat waves distorting her view as she searched the cracked earth for the opening to the caverns.

"Almost there," he acknowledged taking out the canteen one more time and handing it to her.

Sliding her back down the large rock, she sat in its cool shadow, thankful to be out of the blazing sun. Quickly, she removed her scarf from her face, rinsing it in water before putting it back over her mouth. They rested for a few more moments allowing her to assimilate to the Dead Lands before continuing to the underground caverns.

As they reached their destination, she could see the opening was created by a series of long slate ledges leading down into an even larger crater, hidden beneath the surface. The ledges narrowed as they went deeper into the earth, eventually disappearing into the shadows below. Carved into one side were stone steps, an iron railing leading the way down into the darkness. They circled the crater's opening and descended the first few steps stopping only to retrieve a torch from a small crevice near the top of the staircase. She trailed behind him following the light of his torch, tentatively testing the stairs and the rusty railing as she walked further down into the cool shadows below. The midday heat lessened the further they descended into the dark and in its place, a musty dampness emerged to assault her nostrils. It was a putrid smell that reminded her of decaying plants.

He waited for her at the bottom, the torchlight highlighting the frown on his face, his body language betraying his agitation long before she felt the uneasiness that heightened his energy. As she reached him, he turned and hastily walked down a small corridor cut into the cavern wall before she could ask him what was wrong.

Following the glow of the torchlight, she hurried after him, snaking her way carefully through the long damp stone corridor, emerging into a large round room. The walls were slightly damp from the coolness, the dirt floor dry and dusty. The room was barren except for Rafe who stood at its center, waiting.

"The book has been hidden by an ancient concealment spell," he said removing his pack and searching inside for a small vial of powder. "We will need to release the spell and allow the book to call to you."

"Why would the book call to me?" She asked confused by his assertion.

"The book can only be retrieved by an elder, and since you are of the elder bloodline, a daughter of Seri, the book should reveal its whereabouts to you." He retorted, an edge to his voice that made her shudder unexpectedly.

Removing a vine that crept up the cavern wall, he stripped the wooden root of leaves. Using the split tip like a pencil he drew a large rune in the dirt at the room's center.

"Dywen's magic is strong enough now for me to reverse the concealment spell."

Tossing the root to the side he removed the cork from the vial and dusted the runes outline with the yellow powder, reciting an ancient incantation in the language of his ancestors as he walked. The powder hit the edges of the rune, sparking and sizzling as it ignited the ancient symbol in a bright orange fire.

As the rune burned, images suddenly began to appear on the cavern walls, flaming in the same crackling fire. The images revealed themselves one at a time as a cold creeping chill began inching its way down her spine. The walls were engulfed by burning runes, the singeing fire burning for a few minutes longer before fizzling out in a whispering hiss, leaving nothing behind but the smell of scorched ash floating in the air.

Suddenly, she felt a shift in the energy that swirled around her, its essence exploding as an onslaught of emotions engulfed her—surprise, anxiety, fear, hate, confusion, all radiating from Rafe as he stood in the middle of the room. He turned slowly, gaping at the remnants of the singed runes that had unexpectedly appeared on the cavern walls.

Without warning, he turned and bolted back through the corridor, passing her so quickly she barely felt the emotional war that raged inside of him.

His unexpected reaction to the fiery runes caused her to hesitate briefly as she stared after him, stunned by his sudden exit. Regaining her senses, she darted through the dark corridor emerging into the cavern just as he was about to ascend the stairs.

"STOP!" She yelled, her voice sounding more demanding than she had intended as it echoed loudly off the cavern walls.

He reacted abruptly, turning on his heel, and striding angrily back toward her. His sudden advancement was so unexpected that she involuntarily retreated backward until her movement was stopped by the cavern wall behind her.

His eyes were ablaze as he halted inches from where she stood, his breath ragged, a small gleam of sweat shimmering on his brow. He stood silent like a predator assessing his prey before striking, his intense gaze making her squirm with discomfort. He continued to stare at her, his brow furrowed, his eyes darkening with anger.

She fidgeted as her heart raced and her entire body involuntarily reacted to the shifting and pulsating energy. He smelled of sweat and sandalwood. A manly scent that wafted seductively around him. It was both intoxicating and frightening, which caused her to forget momentarily the penetrating fury that she felt seeping from his pores. Her mind numbed as their chemistry erupted, its multifaceted surfaces reflecting the passion they had enjoyed only a day earlier. As she stood helplessly caught in his powerful energy, she sensed a change in him, something dark that simmered just below the surface.

Something he didn't want her to see.

He leaned in closer, reaching up and placing his left hand on the cavern wall above her ear. Dane could feel his breath hot on her cheek as his dark stare pierced through her. She was caught in between fear and desire, trapped unwittingly by a man who both confused and excited her. Shifting her weight as his angry energy crushed down on her their eyes locked, but neither spoke as the air sizzled around them.

Dane reeled from the conflicting energy that battled deep inside her—being bound to a man so tortured was exhausting. Deepening her stare, she felt her defiance surface. Pushing up her shoulders she stood taller so that Rafe no longer looked down on her as she summoned her will determined not to succumb to his dominance.

"We need to recover the Book of Realms," she said firmly, her eyes challenging him.

"You don't know what you are asking of me," he hissed, rage seeping through his teeth as he spat out the words.

She paused as she felt an unexpected wave of sorrow pass through him. "Then tell me," she whispered her hand reaching up to caress the side of his face.

Rafe winced at her touch as he realized he was no longer able to hide anything from her. His eyes clouded over, and his shoulders slumped as his body relaxed into the fatigue that suddenly flooded through them both.

Tears welled up in her eyes as she felt the mind-numbing sorrow flow through him again. He turned away from her, breaking the penetrating stare and the inexplicable hold, he had over her. She stood silently against the wall suddenly aware of how cold the stone was, its chill seeping into her skin through her thin shirt.

Seconds passed into minutes as she stood immobile against the wall watching him.

The air in the cavern was stifling as the heavy silence hung between them. She was just about to speak when she heard his voice penetrate the stillness.

"I told you my parents and brother died here but what I didn't tell you was how."

His shoulder's heaved as he took a long deep labored breath. "They were betrayed, betrayed by their own kind, murdered by another Warlician warrior."

She did not speak, stunned by this revelation as she had assumed that they died in the Great War, fighting, like many other Warlicians.

His voice grew hoarse as he continued. "Not long before the end of the Great War, the ranks of the Warlician warriors were torn apart by deceit. Your ancestor, Claaven Callathian, was Commander of The Order at the time and my father, Gareth Morrighann, his second in command. Vertigan Tierney was one of The Order's sentry leaders and a man Claaven entrusted with his very life. At the time, there were rumors suggesting that some Warlician warriors were manipulating elemental magic into dark magic, however, there was never any proof as to whom it was. You see magic is neither good nor evil, it becomes such through its manifestation and if a Warlician was breaking his oath in this way, it would be considered treason. My parents must have known something was askew because during the Great War, as they were fighting the ancient evil side by side, Vertigan and two other Warlician warriors slain them both along with my brother. I witnessed the massacre, but I was too late to save them. In my grief-filled rage, I killed the other two warriors. Vertigan ran, as the rest of my sentries closed in, escaping temporarily. We searched for him for days, the destruction from the Great War providing ample coverage for his treachery. Eventually, he was caught by Claaven, brought before the tribunal and sentenced to death. Claaven spared his life, but the trust was shattered. His punishment reflected that. Claaven banished Vertigan to the new world, your earth, where he was stripped of his magic and sentenced to live a mortal life. To my knowledge, no one ever heard from him again."

He stopped speaking and turned to look at her, his eyes glossed with the memory of his families' deaths. Her heart ached, but she remained silent for fear of interrupting his confession.

"There were whispers that dark magic existed in the Dead Lands, but no one knew for sure. The Great War was over, and the time of the Thanissia Universe was coming to an end. The war had taken its toll on all of us. Claaven never spoke of Vertigan again and I never found out the truth as to why he killed my family. Claaven saved my life more than once during battle so after his death I honored his memory by staying here to protect the magic and his legacy. I stayed—waiting for you."

His eyes softened as he whispered the last three words.

Her heart aching, she walked quickly to where he stood, wrapping her arms around his shoulders and looking deeply into his sorrow-filled eyes. She kissed his lips, her fingers finding their way into his long hair. She felt him tense under her touch as if he just realized he had shown her his greatest weakness. His hands reached up to her waist pushing her gently away as his demeanor shifted back to the strong, confident warrior.

"The etchings on the cavern walls revealed during my incantation to retrieve the Book of Realms confirms my suspicions that dark magic was practiced here and my parents died because of it. The elders had to have known this, it must be the reason they chose this specific spot to hide the Book of Realms. They hid it with light magic that in turn would be hidden behind the dark magic that already existed in this space."

His eyes opened wide as another realization slammed into him, "It must also be the reason they chose the Dead Lands as the place to capture the ancient evil, they used dark magic against it."

Suddenly, it all made sense to him, his parents must have found out about these caverns and the dark magic that Vertigan was practicing here. He killed them to keep his secret, but they must have already revealed what they knew to the high council and Claaven. As the realms were facing extinction, the elders must have used the dark magic to ensnare the ancient dark. Dark magic is unstable but strong and the ancient dark would not have expected it. It must be how they were able to defeat an entity much older than their magic. His parents had died, but their knowledge and sacrifice saved the realms from complete destruction.

He looked deeply into her eyes, a flicker of sadness still lingering in them. "I think I have always assumed, deep down, that my parent's murders bore the stain of dark magic, even though the existence of such magic was ever only a rumor. When I was confronted with its presence in the cavern room, it all became too real, and overwhelming. I'm sorry," he whispered.

She smiled, gently moving closer and standing on her tiptoes to kiss his lips. "You have nothing to be sorry for," she whispered back, her hand gently resting on his shoulder, the other hand holding his.

He pulled her in close, his hand snaking around her lower back, catching her off balance as she fell forward into him. Releasing his grip on her other hand, he cupped the back of her head, holding her gently against his chest.

His leather vest was cool against her cheek and through it, she could hear his heartbeat, a steady rhythmic thumping that seemed amplified by the damp coolness of the stone caverns. The late day sun beat down from above, bathing them in a column of bright sunlight. He kissed the top of her head as she closed her eyes listening as the beating of his heart fell into rhythm with her own.

CHAPTER 31

RAFE LIFTED THE TORCH HIGHER, its flickering orange flame casting irregular shadows along the cave walls as it doused the area in a soft warm glow. He had discovered the hiding place of the Book of Realms by reversing the ancient concealment spell and now he stood in the small room quietly watching as Dane studied the massive tome.

The book lay on a thick stone pedestal, its worn leather cover concealed by a heavy layer of dust and cobwebs. As she wiped the debris gently from its surface, he could see that the edges of its pages were yellowed and tattered with age. The thick spine was covered with tarnished metal its center emblazoned with delicate Celtic etchings.

He stood very still, his breathing syncing up with her as she listened intently to the old tome, its magic revealing the secrets contained within its pages. The book was very powerful, and he could feel that it sensed her presence, the archaic magic curious but cautious.

The Book of Realms was the keeper of all the knowledge in the Thanissia Universe, infused with the ancient magic of each of the races. It was a powerful weapon in the right hands, in the wrong hands it could mean—*the end of days.*

As he watched her magically bond with the ancient manuscript, he felt a new energy weave its magical essence around him. He could sense the ancestral ghosts that whispered to her, their long-forgotten voices once again activated by the awakening of their world. It was a most surreal feeling, this binding connection he shared with her. At this moment when all her senses were alert and active and the ancient magic energized every fiber of her being, it was as if he no longer had control over his own.

She reached softly for the ancient tome, her hand gently brushing the thick dust off its cover. A slight vibration ran through her fingertips as they grazed the worn leather. She touched the embossed symbol on its cover tracing the raised outline with her finger. It was a familiar symbol—the double pentacle surrounded by the five runes.

"What does this symbol represent," she asked.

She felt Rafe move in closer, standing slightly behind her, lowering the torch so that it illuminated the front of the tome. "That is the symbol of the Five Realms. It represents all the races and the elements that guide them."

She nodded, understanding now why it was engraved on the stone box that held the portal stones. It was the symbol that united all the different races and thus would unite the Arcanists.

Her curiosity peaked, she opened the front cover, a cloud of dust wafting into the air. The first part of the book was a detailed history of the Thanissia Universe, its creation, and descriptions of its multiple realms. From there the book detailed each individual race beginning with the oldest; the celestials. The pages contained race history, connection to their governing element, and how the opposing life forces contributed to a specific balance within the universe. She scanned the pages quickly hesitating only when she got to the section on the witches, the ancient sorcerers, and enchantresses—*her ancestors.*

After briefly reading through their history she flipped to the back of the book, searching for any mention of the prophecy. The final few pages contained information about the consortium of ancient Druids, the last of their kind, that lived among the peoples of *Athir*, the realm inhabited by the fae and elves.

The pages revealed that the Druid priests knew the elemental magic contained within the realms would survive the Great War although it would mark the end of the supernatural races. They feared that even in stasis, the Thanissia Universe would be enticing to any predators who may find their way into its dimension. Without the protection of its people, the magic would be vulnerable. Looking for answers as to the fate of the universe the Druid priests went to the Pool of Sight, a sacred place ripe with knowledge and insight. There, under the light of the Athirian moon, their worst fears were revealed—*the ancient dark would rise again.*

Flipping to the final page, she was confused to find that the only thing displayed on its yellowed parchment, was a language she did not recognize. The page was filled with a jumble of interesting strokes, curves, and dots.

"It is ancient Druid script," Rafe said moving in close behind her.

"Can you read it?"

He nodded, handing her the torch his brow deepening as he studied the strange language. His voice took on a somber tone as he recited the words aloud.

Our lands have been ravished by a dark evil and its defeat has cost our kind greatly. The time of magic has come to an end. Our lands are barren, the magic depleted. Stasis will heal the realms over time, but those that harness its elemental power will be no more. A new world has been born and in it, magic will be forgotten but the end of our time is not final.

It has been foreseen, by the Druid priests, ancient seers of the realms, that the ancient dark once defeated will rise again, bringing havoc to the new world and unleashing a new kind of end. Magic will return in these dark times but those able to wield its power will be few and only those born of ancient blood will have the power required to defeat the ancient dark once again.

Six in all will be chosen, their individual destinies tied to one another through a birthright written long ago. They will represent each of the fallen races and carry the sacred blood of the ancient immortals. They will be known as the Arcanists and will initiate the rebirth of the five realms as rightful heirs to the powerful elemental magic of their ancestors. Branded by these elements and linked by destiny, they will be led by a fierce warrior, the one whose blood is touched by both the ether and the earth, the first of her kind born to a family as old and powerful as our world itself. Her birth will signify the beginning of a destiny that will end in a fight for the very souls of mankind. Her ascension to immortality will mark the beginning of the Second Rising.

The Arcanists will be powerful, more so as they stand as one. They will have the ability to not only harness the power of the

elements but to control them and bend them to their will. But be fore-
warned—they will be marked by the shadow of separation, an ancient
essence that identifies a fractured destiny, of which either good or evil
can unfold. There will be an end to mankind if they fail to defeat the
ancient dark—an end that may come from their hands alone.

She looked at him, a puzzled look clouding her face.

"That's it?" She said bewildered by the lack of information on the prophecy. Flipping the pages back and forth she
looked for more, anything that would provide more answers
than questions. "How is this supposed to help?"

He could sense her aggravation. He grasped her shoulders, pushing a calming energy into her before responding.

"Prophecies are not directives Dane, they foretell of the
future, guide an individual, or shape a destiny. Seers from
our world interpret their visions as best they can, and the
result is often more of a puzzle than an answer. If the one
reading the prophecy is the one it is intended for, then it
will eventually reveal its truth."

Shaking her head in disgust she scanned the page again
looking for more clues. Under the flickering light of the
flame, she noticed something faint in the bottom corner of
the parchment. It seemed to fade in and out with the torchlight's glow. She grabbed the torch from his hand and held
it near the Book of Realms.

"Careful!" He shouted as the flame of the torch came
dangerously close to the page. "The book is ancient and
fragile; it could ignite quickly."

She moved the torch back a little further but concentrated the flame's glow across the bottom corner. As she
moved the light back-and-forth, something written on the
parchment appeared.

"Can you make that out?" She asked, pointing to the numbers and symbols that appeared and then disappeared.

"It is magic ink," he said. "The elders used it when passing confidential messages through different realms. Flame reveals its location but only one thing can bring it forward from the page."

She watched as he rummaged through his pockets, looking for something he obviously thought was there. A few seconds went by as he searched the numerous pockets in his pants and jacket, relief spreading across his face as he pulled a small polished yellow stone from his breast pocket.

"What is that?" She asked curiously.

"Fairy dust," he responded, holding his prize up in triumph. "Well, a fairy stone."

He lowered the stone to the pedestal, using his hand to wipe away the thick cobwebs that covered its edge before rubbing the fairy stone gently across the rock's surface. Tiny particles of yellow dust pooled onto the pedestal with every stroke until a small pile formed. He put the fairy stone back in his pocket and swept the fairy dust into his palm, carefully sprinkling it over the parchment where the magic ink was located. As it landed on the ink, the yellow powder twinkled, fizzled, and then turned black, sinking into the page and revealing the hidden Druid message.

15.[1.[[3.[[[1.(3.O

She sighed, frustrated that the revealed message was just as cryptic as the prophecy.

"What do you think it is?" She asked reviewing the line of numbers and symbols again, "A date?"

Rafe looked up from the parchment, frowning at her in confusion, his green eyes questioning. "Date?"

"Yes," she responded jotting down the message on a notepad she took from her backpack. "A period in time?"

"I do not understand this date you refer to," he stated, shaking his head.

She was about to provide further explanation, when she hesitated, noticing the deep frown on his face. He was a billion centuries old immortal who existed in another dimension long before man started tracking time and creating calendars. A date was just another way to track the passing of time, and time meant nothing to the inhabitants of the Thanissia Universe.

"Let me explain it another way. On earth, time is a very important aspect of daily life and man has created a way of tracking it in very small increments. Long ago, man tracked seasons by the moon phases so that they could hunt and plant their food. As man progressed, became educated, and inventive, time became more important to everyday life, so a calendar was designed, dissecting time into increments that compartmentalized their existence within the natural world. For mortals, time is important and every small amount of it matters. In my world time is tracked in variations of seconds, minutes, hours, days, years, decades, and centuries."

He looked at her, a small smile appearing on his face. "You mortals are a curious type. You hold on to time as if it is the very meaning of life."

"It's important to us because there is an end to that life." She reminded him. "A mortal life is finite in comparison to the life of an immortal which is why our sense of time is very different to yours."

"Our concept of time is very dissimilar, this is true," he acknowledged. "Sebastian must have told you why time has no importance to an immortal."

"Yes, he explained that when one lives a life with no end, charting time only slows it down."

"In a sense, yes. To us, time and space are one—a void to which all the answers and knowing belong. Although we understand the concept of time and feel its passing, time is not of consequence because it is so expansive. It does not exist to control our lives as it seemingly does for you, so tracking it is redundant."

He glanced back at the line of symbols and numbers that were revealed at the bottom corner of the page by the fairy dust. Tapping his finger on it in thought, he searched the recesses of his mind for a memory.

"I believe this is an ancient counting system," he said, recalling the old elvish structure of hierarchy.

"What do you mean counting system?"

"The elves were a proud race and their elders were much revered in their social system. The elvish counting system was a way to honor these elders. They would carve lines and dots into the trunks of the Elfire—trees that grew in the Sacred Vale of Irin. The Elfire was thought to be a gateway to the ethereal divine, a capsule for the life essences of those from their race who had passed from this world. Those carvings represented the length of the lifespan of each fallen elf. A dot signifies a starting point, the day an elf comes into being and the line indicates the portions of millennia—a section of an Elf's life cycle that has passed."

He grabbed the pen from her hand. "I will show you," he said, jotting down some lines and dots in a sequence. "The more lines the longer the lifespan."

She thought about the specific way the elves documented a life force's time in their realm prior to it moving to the ethereal divine. If the Druid priests used this counting system to foretell the time of the Second Rising, then all she had to do was figure out how to transfer this counting system into today's calendar.

Well, that should be easy! She thought, the sarcasm clear even in her own head.

Taking the pen back from him she began to separate the numbers and letters, using the intervals of millennia as a guide, pairing them with the smaller increments that man used in current time—year, decade, century. Trusting her instincts and the ancient knowledge building inside her she began to decipher the code.

After a long period, through which Rafe never said a word, Dane put down her pen and lifted the pad of paper, reading aloud her calculated guess.

"The 15th year, in the 1st century, of the 3rd millennium is the year 2016, in my world. The final two numbers and symbols, if representing the first new moon and the third full moon in that year, would be…"

She reached into her backpack and pulled out the Llewellyn's witches' pocket calendar that Stevie had gifted her at Christmas. Flipping to the first month of 2016, she scanned the days looking for the symbols that indicated the new and full moons. The first new moon was January 9th, her thirty-first birthday and the day of her second awakening. Flipping forward she counted the full moons, stopping when she got to the third one.

"If my translation of Druid code and an ancient elvish counting system are correct, the Second Rising would commence on March 23rd, 2016. We have a little more than two months to find all the others and reactivate all the Druidstones."

Rafe looked at her quizzically, her statement meaningless.

"We don't have a lot of time," she stated, "let's just leave it at that."

CHAPTER 32

THEY REACHED THE TOP OF the waterfall just as the sun began its descent toward the horizon. The sinking sun lit the landscape with an ebbing glow emphasizing the brutal starkness of the Dead Lands. Dane watched as heat waves on the horizon blurred the sweltering landscape, making everything slightly fuzzy as they rippled in the distance. Staring into the dusty ravine she felt the horizon alter slightly as its lifeless pulse intensified.

She squinted at the horizon. The heat waves seemed to move sideways as if something was interfering with their path, pushing them out of the way in an effort to move forward. She lifted her face up to the sky and closed her eyes, allowing her mind's eye to open, pushing her consciousness forward across the barren expanse—searching. There was something out there something hidden, something that didn't belong.

"We must go, Dane," Rafe said, his voice echoing across the ravine that separated the two contrasting landscapes.

"We need to get back to your world. Time is no longer on our side."

She opened her eyes at the sound of his voice, lifting her hand in acknowledgment but not moving, as she continued to search the distant horizon. She could sense the change in the Dead Land's energy as the heat waves continued to ebb and flow, distorted by the unseen interference. There was something coming across the Dead Lands toward them hidden by the haze dispensed by the sweltering heat. She could not see it, but she sensed its movement.

Squinting into the setting sun, she allowed her inner eye to focus her vision, pushing out her consciousness again. Slowly, the fiery orange gateway on the horizon began to shift, its vibrancy diminishing. From its hazy heat emerged one, two, five shadowy figures, the mysterious images drifting toward her over the dry simmering landscape. The figures flickered as the heat waves struggled to retain their space in the environment.

She could hear Rafe behind her calling her name, but she was unable to remove her eyes from the blurred figures. There was something else there, something behind the shadowy figures—*something dark*. She continued to stand very still, blocking out every other sound, emotion, and distraction pulsating through this world. Encasing herself in silence, she concentrated only on the figures that hovered in the distance, allowing the ancient magic inside her to explore. The figures kept moving forward, their silhouettes wavering as the heat from the horizon played with their energy.

Suddenly, the horizon began to change, like bubbling oil, a black cloud rose from the ground swallowing the figures in its darkness. A jolt shot through her as the ancient magic recognized a threat, blocking its attempt at entering her mind. Abruptly, the figures and the black cloud disappeared, the horizon barely visible as the last of the sun's rays vanished behind it.

She stood in the evening breeze, a feeling of foreboding surrounding her. Staring at the distant horizon, she watched as the blazing sun ebbed into its final descent, a chill creeping slowly down her spine. The ancient dark had tried to enter her mind again but this time her powers repelled it.

Turning away from the darkening distance she looked at Rafe. "We may already be running out of time."

He nodded, silently acknowledging his understanding.

They moved quickly down the side of the waterfall and through the dense forest as they made their way back to the barracks. Entering the city through the west gate, she felt a whisper pass through her mind, a warning. She felt him tense beside her, his emotions erratic as he too sensed something about the marketplace was different. Putting his finger to his lips in a silent signal he pointed toward the town center, grabbing her hand and pulling her into the shadows of the stone buildings.

Cautiously, they headed toward the fountain their backs skimming the cool stone of the town shops as they inched their way quietly forward. As they came to the final corner, he stopped and peered around the edge of the building. She heard his breath catch in his throat as she felt his confusion and disbelief turn to joy at what he saw.

Curious, she peeked around the corner.

There, standing by the fountain was a man, tall with broad shoulders. His curly brown hair was shaved short at the back and sides, the top an unruly mess of unkempt waves. His back was to them and all she could see was the long, black, hooded coat that ended just above his boots. He stood perfectly still; his shoulders hunched slightly as if he sensed something.

She glanced at Rafe trying silently to get his attention, but his eyes were trained on the stranger at the fountain. Without warning, he left the safety of the shadows and walked straight toward the man. Caught off guard she could only watch as he strode confidently toward the fountain. Just as she regained her composure and darted out into the sunlight to follow him, the stranger turned, his sword unsheathed and pointing directly at Rafe.

Shock vibrated throughout the marketplace as the two men's eyes locked and a surge of energy passed between them. She stopped abruptly, her head pounding as his memories flooded through her mind—*he knew this man.*

She opened her eyes, just in time to see the two men embrace.

"Brannon my brother...how...where," Rafe sputtered as he clutched the man tightly in a hug pounding his back enthusiastically. They said nothing for a few minutes, an awkward silence surrounding them as they stared in astonishment at one another.

Rafe found his voice first, "I thought you were dead," he admitted, as she felt relief flood through him.

"And I you, my old friend," Brannon replied his voice cracking with emotion. "It's good to see we were both wrong."

Rafe nodded in agreement, a big grin expanding across his face. She could feel that he was still clearly wrestling with the confusion surrounding his friend's sudden appearance but was overshadowed by the relief that pulsed through him.

"Where have you been?" He asked knowing that besides Tauria there was no one else on Dywen during stasis.

"I was caught in a portal between worlds," Brannon explained. "Stuck between here and Kaizi. As you know my patrol had been sent to the fire realm during the Great War, to engage the remaining demons that the ancient dark had unleashed there. My men were all lost and I the only survivor thanks to a Dragon Gypsy who saved my life. I was wounded and being hunted by the one demon left that we had not managed to kill. I had no idea there were any inhabitants of the fire realm left. He saved my life, and I owe him.

Rafe nodded, recognizing the debt that Brannon now owed to this individual. "Is he still alive, this Dragon Gypsy."

"Drow," Brannon noted. "I am not sure. After he saved me, he patched me up and pushed me through the portal, closing it behind me. I must have been passing back through the portal to Dywen when it was put into stasis, leaving me trapped in between time and space until the portal on this side opened up moments ago."

She could feel Rafe ache for his friend's predicament.

"I'm sorry," he said. "If I had known you were still alive, I would never have shut down the portal to the fire realm and put Dywen in stasis. I didn't know."

"There was no way you could have my friend. It is over now. I am back home and happy to see you."

Brannon slapped Rafe on the shoulder a warm smile spreading across his handsome face.

His skin was darker, but his green eyes were just as

bright. He was unshaven, a patchy scruff covering most of his square jawline. A deep-set brow gave him a slight natural scowl, offset by his huge warm grin. Two small silver rings pierced his bottom lip and a large Celtic tattoo covered most of the left side of his neck.

Now that she was closer, she could see that there were lines and patterns shaved into the short hair on the side of his head. Like Rafe, he was dressed all in black, the familiar Warlician symbol of The Order attached to the lapel of his long coat, and the same metal rune pendant tied to a leather string around his neck.

He turned as she walked toward them, his green eyes piercing hers, his brow furrowed as he held her gaze, watching curiously as she approached.

Stopping directly beside Rafe, who instinctively put his arm around her, she smiled at Brannon waiting for an introduction. Suddenly, Brannon's eyes widened, and his mouth fell open. Looking at Rafe and then back to her, he carefully assessed the two of them before his look of surprise turned into a smirk.

"You are bound," he said to Rafe, his eyes never leaving her face. She could feel him swell with pride beside her as his arm tightened around her waist.

"Yes, this is Dane. Dane this is my best friend Brannon Draagorn."

Brannon stuck out his hand, accepting hers in a firm handshake. "Very nice to meet YOU," he said a twinkle in his eye. "Never thought this one would settle down let alone bind in destiny with someone."

Looking back at Rafe he continued, "I assume we have a lot to catch up on then?"

Rafe smirked using the hand not around her waist to

clutch his friend by the shoulder. "You have no idea," he laughed.

They returned to the barracks where she helped Rafe make a stew for dinner. As they sat around the table eating and drinking a dusty bottle of red wine that he found in the kitchen cellar, they filled Brannon in on everything they knew. She could tell that he was overwhelmed at first, but as he digested what they were saying his disbelief turned into concern.

"So, the prophecy is true."

Rafe nodded. "Yes, it would seem so. We have little time. We must return to Dane's world to search for the other Arcanists."

"Then I shall come with you," Brannon said the strong, confident warrior very much alive in his response.

Rafe shook his head, smiling affectionately at him. "Thank you, my friend but you must stay here, rest, train, and get back to your full strength and power. We will need your help in the new world once the prophecy has come to pass and the Second Rising has commenced. Any immortals left in these realms will have to fight."

He paused for a moment, his eyes suddenly filling with mischief. "I could also use help with Tauria."

"Tauria!" Brannon exclaimed, apparently shocked by his request. "She's still here, on Dywen."

"Yes, and still in stasis," he responded.

"You want me to babysit your bratty little sister," Brannon huffed, his eyes widening as his mouth set into a grim line.

"She's not so little anymore, but she is just as bratty." They both laughed, banging the table with their hands as they shared an inside joke.

"Now that the magic is awakening what will happen to your sister?" She asked.

A shadow passed over Rafe's face. "Nothing quickly, I'm afraid. She is an immortal witch, but her magic is not strong like a Warlicians. Her stasis is deep. Her body will need to heal from the long sleep. It will take time before she is awake, and then she too will need to regain her strength."

She could feel the conflicting emotions surging through him as he contemplated leaving his sister on Dywen without him.

"But I am glad that Brannon is here to take care of her when she does wake."

"Nothing will happen to her Rafe. You need not worry. I will be here for Tauria when she wakes, and I am sure she will be back to her exasperating self when you return." Brannon said, smiling warmly at his friend.

"You are a good friend," Rafe responded, nodding his appreciation.

Dane smiled and squeezed his hand impressed by their comradery and the level of comfort and dedication there was between them. Their history must be long and inter-twined she thought as she watched the two warriors ease quickly back into their friendship.

CHAPTER 33

D ANE WOKE, HER BODY WRAPPED around Rafe's. It was early, and the sun was just peeking over the horizon. She tried to untangle herself, but he pulled her closer in his sleep, mumbling incoherently into her hair. It felt good in his warm embrace, her skin tingling where it touched his. She lay quietly, breathing in his intoxicating scent. His face was so peaceful when he slept, so different from the flurry of memories erupting in his eyes when awake.

Suddenly, she felt lightheaded. Her palms started to itch as a strange warmth began to build in them, a stinging sensation that flooded down through her fingertips. She glanced down at her hands. Underneath the skin there rippled a green light, its energy pulsing.

"Rafe," she whispered, uneasiness in her voice. He stirred beside her but did not wake. "Rafe!" she said, much louder this time, watching as the green light pulsed brighter under her skin, sparks sporadically spitting out into the air.

Stirred from unconsciousness by the sound of her voice,

he looked at her, his eyes flickering with affection and desire.

"Morning," he said, his voice thick with lust until he saw her panic-stricken face and felt the dread emanating from her. Pulling himself onto his elbows he asked. "What is it?"

She raised her hands, showing him the palms and the green light that flowed just below the surface.

To her surprise, he smiled and checked his own palms, showing her that his too pulsed with a green light. "Our magic is back."

Confused, she just stared at him waiting for an explanation.

He kissed her gently pulling her toward him as he raised his left palm, producing a perfect green sphere of light that pulsed erratically just above his hand.

"Energy balls," he explained. "The power of the Warlicians and our magical weapon." He lifted her hand placing it palm up. "Concentrate on the heat of the energy, feel it building in your palm, then mentally shape it into a ball and will it to come forth."

She did as she was told, and suddenly she too was holding a small ball of green energy that pulsated in her palm.

"You are a natural," he said kissing her again. "Now reverse it. Disperse the energy and pull it back into your hand."

His energy ball disappeared, the green glow flickering again under the skin of his palm.

Taking a deep breath, she concentrated, and did the same, feeling a slight pop as the energy withdrew back into her palm.

"See, a natural." He reiterated proudly. "This must mean that Dywen is fully re-energized. Warlician magic is extremely powerful and drains a lot of energy from the elements. Now that our powers have returned, we must teach you how to wield them."

Jumping from their bed, he went into the bathroom, washing up and quickly dressing.

"I will meet you in the kitchen," he said winking at her as he left the room, yelling for Brannon as he hurried down the hall.

She stared for a few more minutes at her palm as the green light glowing under her skin began to fade. Washing her hair and dressing in her last clean shirt she headed down the corridor toward the kitchen following the sound of Rafe and Brannon's excited voices.

She found them in the kitchen, igniting energy balls and laughing with glee, like two children with a new toy.

"It's been ages since I have been able to do this," Brannon said, his eyes shining brightly with joy.

Rafe agreed, throwing his energy ball into the air and catching it before it hit the ground. He turned to look at her when she walked in but his childish smile vanished when he saw her stoic expression.

"We were just practicing," he said coyly.

"Isn't there a better place to do that, than the kitchen?" she asked, helping herself to the porridge that sat in the middle of the table.

"We will go out to the training grounds after breakfast," he agreed. "You need to learn what your new power can do."

"Fine," she said trying to hide her smirk as the two big strong warriors tried to stifle their giggles as they headed out of the kitchen. Finishing her porridge, she cleaned up the breakfast dishes and headed outside to find them.

Rafe was in a serious discussion with Brannon when she arrived in the training area. As she approached, he looked up with a big smile. "Ready?"

"I guess." She said, looking around. He had moved three large targets into the training pit. Brannon jumped in, moving to the end and standing just to the left of targets. Rafe guided her to a position about thirty feet in front of them.

"The energy ball is a power that only Warlician warriors possess. It is a natural weapon and works in two ways. First, they can be used to destroy." He produced one in his palm and threw it toward the target, the green light exploded on impact, shattering the target into a dozen splintered pieces. "Second, it can be used to impede." Producing another energy ball, he cast it at the second target, the green sphere hitting the target with enough force to knock it over. The energy ball flew back through the air, returning to Rafe who caught it easily. "When you use the energy in this way, it will always return to you. The energy is a part of us. It responds to our individual will. Your intent is the key to how the energy reacts to the target. You try."

Moving backward he gestured for her to take down the final target.

Taking a step forward she took a deep breath, concentrating on the itchy warmth she felt in her hand, willing the energy forward until it formed a bright green ball of light that pulsed in her hand. She eyed the target in the distance, taking aim and throwing the ball with all her might, watching as it sailed effortlessly through the air, toppling the target at the other end and returning to her all in mere seconds.

She smiled at Rafe who was nodding at her in approval.

Brannon moved in to set up three new targets and then walked back to where she and Rafe stood.

"Can I knock down more than one at a time?" She asked him, feeling the power of her natural weapon surging in her hands.

He smirked, "Of course."

"Maybe you should get used to how the energy responds first Dane." Rafe retorted his voice a little too condescending for her liking.

Casting him a look of disdain, she quickly fired an energy ball through the air watching as it knocked over all three targets, arced back and flew directly at him, stopping inches from his face before returning to her hand.

He looked at her, his face a mask of irritation. He shot Brannon a similar look, who shrugged in response as he tried desperately to stifle a laugh.

She smiled weakly, feeling the annoyance surge through him at the stunt she had just pulled.

"Sorry," she mumbled.

"Let's see if your foresight is as acute."

Motioning for Brannon to go to the targets, he walked in the opposite direction leaving her directly in the middle of them.

She looked at him then at Brannon, wondering what he was up to.

"Warlician foresight is the reason we are so hard to fool and the most difficult immortal to kill. The ability for us to see our own fate prior to it happening has always given us an edge in battle. Tapping into this innate power will allow you to avoid many things. Concentrate on the surrounding environment, feel its energy. With practice, you will eventually be able to distinguish between what is harmless and what is a threat, helping you to avoid injury and harm, even death."

He motioned to the targets.

"Brannon is going to throw an energy ball gently at you. Stay facing me, do not turn around. Feel the energy moving toward you and then avoid its path. He will not harm you," he said, looking past Dane and staring harshly at Brannon. "Concentrate."

Closing her eyes, she allowed her inner eye to expand, searching the area. She felt a shift in her magic as her foresight activated. She sensed the energy of everything around her, and of those that drifted aimlessly on the air. Suddenly, a sensation ran through her as her senses heightened and an image appeared in her mind. She could see the green ball of light hurtling directly at her from behind. Quickly, she sidestepped the ball feeling the crackle of its energy fly by, inches from her head.

She opened her eyes to a grinning Rafe.

"Now we will try one from Brannon and me at the same time. Remember you must be careful as to where you move, know where the path is clear and where it is not."

He moved quickly to stand somewhere to her left just outside of her peripheral vision. She could feel the surrounding energy begin to change as once again Brannon's energy ball moved toward her. Stepping away from its trajectory, she turned directly into the path of Rafe's energy ball, just as it reached her.

With reflexes, she didn't know she possessed she reached up and caught his energy ball just before impact. The ball crackled in her grip its green energy warming her hand. She glanced at Rafe, a look of shock on his face. Turning to Brannon she saw that he too exhibited the same look.

"Impossible," he stammered, as he ran toward her. "It has to be because she is bound to you, Rafe. There is no other explanation. No Warlician can be killed by another's energy ball but to my knowledge, Warlician energy cannot be held by any other than the one to whom it belongs."

Rafe recalled his energy, gently inspecting her hand for any sign of trauma. There was not a mark on her.

"I guess your innate abilities are more refined than we thought," he said, completely baffled as to the depth of her newfound powers. "I suppose there is not much I can teach you that you don't already know instinctively, although there is one thing about our magic that you must truly understand and respect. The energy does not just come from inside us Dane, it is us. A part of our magical essence and because of that using it comes with a price."

He looked deep into her eyes as he continued, his emotions imploring her to understand the consequences. "The energy that is dispelled when we use our energy balls to destroy effectively weakens us overtime because it does not return to us like it does when we use it to impede. We can always regenerate the energy but the essence of ourselves that it contains, we can never get back. A recall is always the best way to use your energy as a weapon. If you must relinquish some of yourself permanently, make sure it is for the correct reason."

Kissing her forehead, he looked at Brannon. "I think we are done here."

It was late afternoon and Rafe had gone to check on Tauria before they left. She and Brannon were sitting in the garden, Farrimore perched gently on her shoulder. Since her binding with his master, Farrimore had been showing her much attention. He had taken to pulling her hair gently with his beak, she guessed as a sign of affection. He was a very loyal and charismatic bird, and she really enjoyed his company the past few days. In some way he filled the void not having Tyson around left.

Rafe returned with news that Tauria's stasis was beginning to wear off and that her skin color was returning. Brannon assured his friend once again that he would be here when she woke and would fill her in on everything.

"Can't wait to see how she reacts to your binding." He exclaimed, a chuckle filling the gardens.

"Maybe you should just keep that to yourself for now," Rafe warned, stressing his words with a stern look.

Brannon pouted but agreed to let Rafe and Dane be the ones to tell her.

She wondered silently how Rafe's sister was going to react to a woman coming so dramatically into her brother's life, especially when she brings the Second Rising with her.

"I think I will go have another look at the Book of Realms," she said, shooing Farrimore from her shoulder and standing up.

"I'll come with you," he responded, looking at Brannon and winking.

"And I will take a long walk around the barracks," Brannon responded, calling for Farrimore to follow as he sauntered outside, the setting sun's rays painting the evening sky with oranges, pinks, and purples.

Rafe grabbed her waist and pulled her in for a deep

sensual kiss, his tongue exploring her mouth, his touch igniting her skin. "Shall we look at the book later?" He asked, his voice husky with desire.

She smirked and rolled her eyes.

"I'll take that as a yes." Scooping her up into his strong arms, he carried her down the corridor into his bedroom.

An hour later, wrapped in a bedsheet, she sat at the small desk leafing through the pages of the book looking for anything that could help them find the others. Carefully, she turned the pages, the fragile parchment crinkling in displeasure as their crumbling edges scattered dusty pieces over the tabletop.

"There," said Rafe over her shoulder, pointing to the page she had just flipped to.

Written in an ancient script was a paragraph that detailed how the celestial would rise. It stated that she would appear as a harbinger of the future and a messenger from the past. She would be born of the ether to create balance and stability between the ancient powers. She would join with others, those who share a destiny. Her knowledge would guide them and together they would deliver fate upon the new world.

She gaped at the paragraph, shaking her head in exasperation and flipping through the next few pages looking for any other information that may help them in their search for the celestial and the other Arcanists.

"That makes us look like we are out to destroy the world?" She said pointing to the last line of the paragraph. "Why does this book consistently refer to us as evil?"

Picking up the massive tome, she shook it in frustration. "Show us something. Anything!"

The metal spine creaked, and the pages rustled as

suddenly a folded piece of paper fell from its depths. She stopped shaking the book, watching as it floated softly to the floor. Placing the Book of Realms back on top of the desk, she picked up the paper from where it had landed. Rafe's name was printed in bold black letters on the front.

"It's for you," she said, holding out the folded paper toward him.

He looked at the black ink scrawled across its face, recognizing Seri's handwriting immediately. Taking the piece of paper from her, he read it.

My dearest Rafe,

I will no longer be of physical form when you read this, but you need to be prepared for what is coming. I had a vision before my transcendence back into the ether, a vision about your future. Your destiny as a great warrior has yet to commence for your greatest battle lies in a future that does not yet exist. The time of mankind is where your destiny unfolds, in the new world known to us now as Earth. You are a part of the prophecy that foretells of the Second Rising but be forewarned, all will not go your way. For your destiny has a fatal end if you allow your emotions to rule your judgment. I tell you this for your destiny includes another. A daughter of the forgotten realms, the one whose bloodline is both Warlician and Celestial—one of the Arcanists, and the one fated for you. You will bind with her, your life force becoming forever linked with hers.

Heed this advice old friend, for there may come a time when her life is in peril and you will want to intervene. Your desire to save her will be overwhelming, but you must not, for her destiny is her own and you cannot interfere. For if you do, the cycle of fate will be forever broken, and the prophecy will unravel. You must resist the fate of the binding, the desire to protect her, for she is the key to our survival. Trust that she is strong and her destiny powerful. Trust in the power of fate. I send this warning across time as Claaven lost his life because he was unable to resist the emotional tie that bound us. You must not make the same fatal mistake. Heed my warning dear friend. For the prophecy must follow the path it is destined to take, or all will be lost.

Rafe took a deep breath handing the paper to Dane who read it quickly. "What does it mean?"

"It is of no significance now," he replied, his face emotionless as he tried to hide his anxious energy. She decided not to pursue it as she felt the conflicted emotions battle inside of him. He would tell her when he was ready. Scanning the note again, she saw an odd-looking script just below the note at the bottom of the page.

"What is this?" she asked, pointing to the dark ink.

"The language of the celestials,"

"Can you read it?"

"Yes,"

"Really? You know a lot of ancient languages," she teased.

"I know the languages of the realms, those that belong to the races I protected," he replied.

She nodded realizing that Rafe did not understand the futile banter of mortals. "What does it say?"

He looked at the thick black symbols frowning. "The celestial has the answers. Find her or all will be lost."

"So, we need to find the celestial before the others?"

"That would be my interpretation yes. Seri was very forthright; she would not include this unless it was of dire importance. The celestial must be found first."

"How? The passage in the Book of Realms is vague at best and gives us no clues as to who or where she is."

"We will find her when the time is right," he said, feeling that familiar tug as her frustration washed over him.

He leaned down and pressed his lips to her cheek feeling her heart lurch at his touch. "Let's go to bed," he whispered in her ear. It was late, and they had to make the journey back to her world tomorrow. They both needed rest but what he wanted more was to hold this beautiful, headstrong woman close to him. He needed to feel their hearts beating as one, for deep down he was afraid—afraid of what was to come and what he may lose because of it.

CHAPTER 34

THE PORTAL FELT DIFFERENT ON the return. This time Dane was pulling a tether with her, an invisible line that attached her energy to the ancient magic of Dywen. It was an odd sensation, like walking against a strong wind, the tether dragging behind her, resisting her attempts to move forward.

She could feel Rafe beside her, his physical body barely visible as the green light of the portal pulsed around him.

"You will get used to the sensation." His voice filled her mind. He had never used their Warlician connection to communicate with her telepathically and it was oddly eerie, especially with the portal encasing them in its throbbing green light.

He watched, as she struggled to pull along her connection to Dywen, remembering the first time he had gone through a portal. The drag behind him almost pulled him to his backside a few times but eventually, the tether became a part of him, a way for him to draw energy and knowledge from his homeland. The less his mind focused on the resistance, the less resistant the tether became until it was merely a twinge in his mind. She too would eventually absorb the tether's pull. Dane had proven to be innately powerful and profoundly capable wielding the ancient magic that flowed through her, and he had no doubt that this too she would master.

She glanced over at him, her eyes blazing with defiance and exhaustion. Composing herself she smiled, winked at him, and moved with a renewed confidence through the portal back to earth.

The brilliant green light pushed them out right at the base of the Elder Oak. Stumbling, she fell forward, her feet scrambling to find solid footing. She felt a strong hand on her elbow helping her to secure her trajectory and regain her balance.

"Steady," Sebastian said gently. "Take a moment to get your bearings. Portal walking can take a lot out of you when you haven't yet learned to absorb its effects."

Her head spun as Sebastian's face blurred in front of her eyes. She shook her head slowly bringing everything back into focus. "Why did I not feel like this when I went through to Dywen," she asked weakly.

"Mainly because you didn't belong to a higher plane like you do now. Immortality does not exist in the energy of this world only in our realms. The tether connecting you to the Thanissia Universe and the ancient magic is new. Your body must learn to adjust."

She could feel Rafe's energy beside her as she stood bent over, her hands resting on her knees, her eyes closed, as she waited for the strange sensations rushing through her to subside. His energy was not stable either, but he was handling it much better. As she pulled herself up to a prone position, she looked at him, his green eyes concerned.

"I'm OK," she reassured him.

"Did everything go as planned?" Sebastian asked.

"Well if you mean was my first meeting with Rafe contemptuous like you thought, then yes," she answered smiling uncomfortably. "He held a sword to my throat for a very long time without moving, it was quite impressive."

Rafe looked at her cocking his head slightly, "Sarcasm?"

She smiled and nodded approvingly, "you're getting it."

Sebastian ignored the banter. "I mean did anything happen that I did not predict. Anything that one may deem of importance?"

Rafe glanced at her, a dark shadow passing through his eyes as his jaw clenched and his fists balled. "The ancient dark knows who Dane is, it senses her essence. It tried to gain control of her mind not long after I found her."

"It was in her mind?" Sebastian's said, his voice unable to disguise his apprehension.

"Briefly. It seems her second awakening gave her powers beyond just those of the Warlician. It seems she is also a Timestopper." He hesitated, waiting for Sebastian to process this new information. He reached out and squeezed her hand.

"She will learn how to control the gateway to her mind."

A burst of energy exploded in the air around them surprising both them and Sebastian with not only its power but its veracity.

Sebastian gaped momentarily, his eyes going back and forth between the two of them before he regained his composure.

"A binding," he whispered, with a surprised curiosity. "Interesting, and I suppose better than him killing you."

"Thanks," she said still trying to regain her senses.

Rafe smirked, "It was a surprise to us as well."

Sebastian looked troubled, his mind seemingly searching for something in his memory.

"What is it?" She asked, acutely aware of the confused energy that now encircled him.

Returning from his own thoughts he looked at them both. "The binding is not part of the ancient prophecy. Only six destinies are to be intertwined. I am not sure how this will effect that which has already been written."

"Well surely our combined destiny is part of the larger one or it would not have happened, right?" She said looking at Rafe for support.

Sebastian's face darkened. "Possibly, I just pray your fate is not shadowing your ancestors."

"What do you mean?"

Rafe's eyes darkened as he scowled at Sebastian, a subtle caution.

"Claaven died because of his binding with Seri," he said as his eyes moved away from Rafe's glare and back to Dane.

She frowned, confusion masking the uneasy feeling building inside. "Seri's note, this is what she was warning you about." She said to Rafe.

He continued to scowl at Sebastian, obvious annoyance evident in his glare. "Yes," he whispered.

"Note?" Sebastian asked.

Rafe regained his composure. "Seri left me a message; it fell from the Book of Realms. A warning. She had seen a vision of me. My destiny in a distant future and my binding with Dane. She was warning me that if I took the same path as Claaven, allowing my emotions to interfere with destiny, all would be lost. The prophecy would unravel. The fate of mankind would suffer."

"And will you be able to heed this warning if the time comes? Allowing destiny to unfold as it is meant to."

Rafe scowled again, his heart pounding. "I must," he said looking directly at her, pain visible in his eyes.

She could feel the despair that flooded through him. She assumed from Seri's message that Claaven had died protecting her, but she did not know the details. "How did he die?"

The two warriors glanced at one another, a look passing between them as they shared a painful memory from the past.

Rafe shifted uncomfortably as he recalled the memory. "Vertigan Tierney, the man who murdered my family had a son, Darmond, a Warlician that we thought had perished in the Great War. Not long after Vertigan was captured and banished, Darmond reappeared, vengeance for what Claaven had done to his family the only thing driving him. He was half mad. Driven insane by the dark magic that stained his blood he attacked Seri, intent on killing her so that Claaven would have to live with the grief. He wanted him to endure his pain, know a loss so great you are consumed by it. As he aimed his energy ball at Seri, Claaven jumped in front of it ignoring his instincts, listening only to his emotions. The energy ball, like Darmond, was tainted with dark magic, it killed Claaven instantly. The effect of that magic on Seri would have been minimal, something Claaven would have known, but the heightened emotional connection between them due to their binding caused him to act irrationally. He did not think or rationalize he reacted, driven only by his love and devotion to her, and it cost him everything."

Sebastian moved toward her, his green eyes looking deep into her own. "Binding is intense and often results in carelessly driven emotional reactions. Seri must have felt the need to relay this message to Rafe because the consequences of him repeating this mistake would be more significant than just his death. Whatever Seri's reasons for leaving him that message she means for him to take heed."

Rafe was clearly uncomfortable with the discussion they were having; she could feel the anxiousness battling inside him.

"I will be fine. You know I can take care of myself, but if there does come a time when my destiny is at an end, promise me you will let me go, for it will be my choice."

"I will," he whispered.

She kissed him deeply feeling his heart pounding against her. His answer was not convincing and although she hoped it was a promise he could keep; she was determined to never find herself in a position where he had to make that choice.

CHAPTER 35

S EBASTIAN CLEARED HIS THROAT INTERRUPTING the
intimate connection between Dane and Rafe.

"There is much I need to tell you," he said his
eyes conveying a sense of urgency that she had not seen
before. "Much has happened here since the Druidstone was
activated. The magic of our realm is flowing through the
portal and the prophecy will soon begin to take hold in this
world. There is much we need to do."

Rafe interrupted, "First, we need to find the one that
carries the blood of the celestial. Seri made mention of the
importance of this in her message."

"Seri must have seen much before her transcendence,
and she speaks the truth, for I can already feel the celestial
that you seek."

"Feel her? But how?"

"It seems the celestial is in fact, not an ancestor of the
ancient bloodline but rather a fallen, and she has already
begun her ascent. I can sense her essence and the light
magic of the ether."

"A fallen? That is rare."

"It is, but I suspected this may be a possibility. My suspicions were the reason I tasked Dane with retrieving the Essence of Ether from Dywen. As you know the bloodlines of the celestials are unique and with their inability to exist without the life force of the ether, I was unsure as to how their kind would last through generations on earth. The Essence of Ether is her only chance."

"She will require it if she is to revert soon." Rafe acknowledged. "If you can sense her, we don't have much time. Seri was right we must find her quickly or all will be lost."

"Can someone fill me in?" She said impatiently her scowl directed at Sebastian. "Fallen? Reverting?"

"A fallen is a celestial from our universe who have lost their wings and transcended through time and space to exist in another universe as an inhabitant of a specific world. Here she would be a mere mortal." The tone of his voice echoed the importance of this rare process. "A fall is normally only initiated in crisis, making it an extremely rare occurrence and a decision the Guardian of Deities never undertakes without great consideration, as it is both an extraordinary honor and an extreme sacrifice for the celestial who falls. Eventually, the reason for a celestial's fall will come to pass, at which point they will begin to revert. A transformation that is required for the celestial to fulfill their destiny."

She looked at both warriors, curious about the celestial's transformation. "What is she reverting to?"

"Her true self," Rafe answered. "The celestial she was before the fall."

Sebastian nodded in agreement, a knowing look passing

between them, an unspoken understanding of what those words meant.

She cleared her throat reminding the two ancient warriors that there was another person in their midst who required more information. "If she reverts will she also regain her magic?"

"Yes," Rafe said.

"You told me the Arcanists must enter the portal of their ancestral homes and reactivate the Druidstones before they are able to obtain magic and accept their birthright."

"I thought this to be true for all of you," Sebastian agreed. "But I was wrong. Because she is a fallen, she does not have a birthright to claim. She is already immortal, sent to earth by the Guardian to wait, hidden as a mortal among you. She won't know who she truly is, as her memories were blocked when she fell to earth, but these too will return, along with all her powers and knowledge of the past. I can sense her now because the process has already begun. Soon she will begin to remember and when she does, she will immediately convert into her true form."

She was stunned by this disclosure. Numerous questions began running through her head, one of which bubbled up to her lips before she could stop it. "What the hell does her true form look like, exactly?"

Two sets of green eyes narrowed, as both warriors looked at her, a small smirk turning up one side of Sebastian's mouth as they shared yet another knowing look.

"Mortals have put their own name to what celestials look like. To your kind, she would look like an angel, although not the ethereal type that mortals have conjured to combat their fear of death. Celestials are ancient sentinels—warriors in their own right."

Suddenly, a vivid image of Paul Bettany, as Michael in the movie *Legion,* appeared in her mind. Massive black wings stretched out behind him, his strong muscular body covered in ancient symbols and script, wielding a gun and knife—the ultimate warrior angel. The image ignited a subtle panic as she imagined a hysteria breaking out if the celestial transformed in public.

"What if she reverts in front of mortals?"

Rafe frowned. "We can only hope that she does not and that we find her before her transformation is complete. But if she does no mortal will be a match for her, even in her weakened form."

"Not exactly what I meant," she responded, eyeing Rafe with irritation.

Sebastian interjected his voice tense. "With what is coming, a mortal seeing a celestial is the least of our problems. Do you have the elixir?"

"Yes," Rafe answered pulling the small vial from his breast pocket.

"She will cease to exist without it, you must hurry and discover her identity."

Her attention peaked at this new information. Her voice unintentionally dropping to a whisper. "What do you mean she will cease to exist?"

"Falling for a celestial is traumatic but not permanent. Unfortunately, they cannot exist on a mortal plane, not in their true form, anyway. Their life force is not just tethered to their realm like ours, it is made up of the ether itself. Without the elixir, her physical form will disintegrate, and her life force will disperse into an atmosphere that has no magical properties to sustain it. It is why she had to become mortal when she fell to earth, it is the only way for them to exist in this world. A world without magic is difficult enough for immortals like us to survive in, for a celestial in their true form, surviving in a mortal world is impossible. The 'Essence of Ether' is her only chance.

"This must be what Seri meant when she said, find her or all will be lost," Rafe interjected. "If the celestial's life force disperses, the remaining Arcanists will not link, they will be rendered incomplete and the prophecy will unravel, all hope of defeating the ancient dark will be lost."

"If you can feel her essence does this mean she is near?" She asked.

"No, my light stasis only allows me to feel the Arcanists once the birthright has been passed on. You are different as your second awakening provided you the telepathy that only Warlician warriors possess. Once that ancient gift was bestowed on you, I was able to communicate with you through our shared gift—as you know."

She rolled her eyes remembering the dreams and the strange occurrences that happened at the Elder Oak.

Sebastian pretended to ignore her slight. "Now that the magic of Dywen has been ignited the Thanissia Universe is beginning to awaken. The ether is coming back to life which in turn has triggered the start of the celestial's journey back to her purest form. I can feel her essence because my light stasis is also born from the ether but locate her I cannot. That is something only you can do."

"She could be anywhere, they all could! How am I supposed to find them?"

"Do not be alarmed," he said his calm, strong voice soothing her fraying nerves. "You may find they are closer than you think for destiny has a way of bringing those that share a similar one together. The blood of the witch, warrior, and celestial run through you Dane. Use your powers, awaken the ancient bloodlines—believe in yourself, believe in them."

She nodded, feeling the magic of the ancients as it swirled around her. A familiar sensation ignited her skin as Rafe's hand touched her own.

"We must go, Dane," he said softly, his voice echoing through the clearing as the night sky pressed down on them. "We don't have much time. The celestial's transformation back to purity will not take long now that the ether is awakening. We must find her."

"There is something else," Sebastian said his tone betraying him as he tried to remain calm.

The hair on her arms stood up as Sebastian's uneasiness drifted toward her, an anxious energy that crept into the furthest reaches of her mind. She felt the inklings of dread begin to build in her stomach as a strange hollowness saturated the night air. She stared at him anxiously, but if he sensed the apprehension, he wasn't acknowledging it.

"Shortly after you went through the portal, I felt something, a flash of darkness, something lurking in the physical plane. It disappeared before I could identify it, but it stirred something deep in my memory. I have sensed it briefly, a few more times since but never long enough to recognize it, until a few hours ago."

His hand sub-consciously gripped the handle of his sword. "A dark witch is here in Brighton Hill."

The air exploded around her with a mix of emotions, all of which were flooding from Rafe.

"Are you sure?" He growled.

"Yes. Her magical energy is tainted with the mark of the necromancer."

"Who is she?" He hissed.

Sebastian stiffened. "At first, I was not sure, as dark magic is extremely rare in this world and those that succumb to its dark power usually do so in seclusion. Even Brighton Hill's violent past and negative energy are not enticing enough for a dark witch to risk detection."

He hesitated, briefly glancing at Rafe, with empathy. "Although I didn't recognize her energy initially, the imprint of the dark witch is familiar to me, but it has been a very long time since I have felt that aura. At first, I thought I must be mistaken about her identity, for that family blood-line has long been extinguished but the more I focused, the more recognizable her energy became. The dark witch is an ancestor of Vertigan Tierney."

Rafe's energy exploded through the clearing at hearing the name of the man who murdered his family.

Instantly she was overwhelmed by the anger that raged through him. She whirled around to look at him, but his face was passive, only a fleeting glimpse of sorrow and hatred passing through his eyes.

Sebastian must have sensed the rage, immediately going to his side and putting a hand on his shoulder.

"You must not allow hate to be your undoing."

He nodded, as he quickly controlled his flailing emotions. "Why is she here?"

"There can be only one reason she is in Brighton Hill, practicing dark magic in the open. She wants *revenge*."

"Dane?" Rafe asked. Sebastian nodded.

Her heart began to thump. The air hung heavy as the word revenge reverberated in her head.

"Revenge, for what?" she whispered. "What could she possibly have against me? I don't know any dark witches."

The words were barely off her lips before a sinking feeling came over her.

Lilith, she thought.

"She must have figured out your heritage. That you are a descent of the Callathian family. How I do not know, but it is really the only explanation." Sebastian said.

Rafe's eyes flashed with darkness. A deep-seated fury only visible for a second before he managed to regain control of his emotions again. She could feel the sudden surge of resentment, his seething rage ramming through her before he managed to push it back to the depths of his being where it would continue to fester in silence.

"A dark witch, bent on revenge, means nothing good," he said, his voice tight with anger.

Sebastian nodded in agreement. "This is true."

She thought about Lilith and the venom that spewed from her lips the last time they had crossed paths. It was obvious then her hatred was real, but what exactly her intentions, she had not made clear. Just her vow to be Dane's undoing.

A slow creeping chill ran over the surface of her skin as a feeling of dread erupted to the surface.

"We met," she whispered.

Feeling her energy shift, Rafe came up behind her wrapping his strong arms around her waist protectively.

"I'm fine," she said giving him a reassuring smile but thankful that she would not have to face Lilith alone.

"I know."

"Whatever she has planned there is no way for her to know about the prophecy or that you are now immortal and have gained ancient powers," Sebastian stated.

"She is a new witch and her dark powers are limited;

she is no match for you Dane. She is nothing more than a nuisance even at her most powerful. My fear is that her unrelenting desire to exact revenge will cause history to repeat. Like her ancestor Vertigan, her dark magic may unwittingly fuel the ancient dark, luring him toward it, and if the ancient dark feeds off the dark magic, its powers may intensify at a much quicker rate. The prophecy may come to pass sooner than foretold."

Rafe's arm tightened around her waist, his energy growing heavy with an emotion she was having a hard time identifying. "The dark magic may have to be dealt with then," he stated, his eyes darkening.

Sebastian's eyes locked with his, a knowing look passing between them again. "It may. Yes"

Dane need not be privy to the special bond that these two ancient warriors held to understand exactly what they were not saying. For the emotion that now encompassed Rafe was that of a man prepared to kill.

CHAPTER 36

THE NIGHT SKY HELD A chill, a dampness that seeped through your skin and settled in your bones. It was early evening, and she was anxious to get home. She wanted to take a hot shower before she could think about how she was going to find the celestial. She was gathering their bags when she heard Rafe's voice.

"There is something else, something written in the Book of Realms." He said, once again in control of his emotions.

"You have been reading the ancient tome?" Sebastian questioned, his tone expressing concern and disapproval.

"Yes, well the parts Dane could not. Those that were written in the languages of our universe." He explained, feeling slightly uncomfortable under Sebastian's stern stare. He was sure that the rules of the past no longer held weight, but Sebastian had always been rigid when it came to The Order and the laws of their people.

"There was a page, regarding the prophecy, written in old Druid script. It detailed what we already knew, but it was the final warning that was worrisome."

"What warning did it give?" Sebastian asked inquisitively as Dane moved back to join them.

The air in the clearing became heavy as the silence of anticipation seeped into their midst. He had not fully discussed the meaning of the warning with her, and he was now about to reveal something she may not want to know.

"The Druid priests said the Arcanists will not only have the power to harness the elements but physically control them—bend them to their will. They are to be marked with the shadow of separation, the sign of fractured destinies."

Sebastian's eyes widened at his revelation. "Dual unwritten destinies?"

"Precisely."

She watched as both warriors cast her baleful looks. "What is the shadow of separation?"

Sebastian looked at her, his expression pained. "It is a credence found in the lore of the fire realm. The dragon gypsies believed those who bore the mark of the shadow of separation were destined for either good or evil—their destiny broken and not yet written. They believed there to be a point in one's journey where a major decision or choice would set them on a path from which there was no return. Once that fateful choice had been made the destiny to which it does not lead would be forever closed, leaving only the chosen path and any consequences that would unfold. The shadow of separation is said to sound like a clock ticking down to the precise moment when the individual's destiny is finally written."

Her face darkened as a memory surfaced. "I heard a ticking when I became immortal."

"I heard it then as well," Rafe said. "When Dane accepted her birthright, and she collapsed at the Druidstone. I didn't realize what it was until I read the Druid prophecy."

"You had already experienced the binding?"

"Yes."

Sebastian nodded. "Then it is true, your destiny is much more complex than we initially realized."

Her confusion was apparent in her voice, "So I, the Arcanists, we all have the possibility of turning evil?"

"The shadow of separation is never that black and white. It is not a matter of your path being simply good or evil, it is more about the repercussions of a choice, a choice that may very well be the only one that can be made at the time. We often make difficult decisions, many of which render outcomes that ripple negatively. A fractured destiny does not indicate the Arcanists will simply become evil or be consumed by dark magic, it can mean that their choice, whatever it may be, may have an unfavorable outcome. Consequences that may be the better of two evils. The shadow of separation is a unique destiny and is different for any who are marked, but those that are, usually have destinies that are far-reaching."

She shook her head thinking about the passage in the book and the final line—the warning.

"In the Book of Realms, it was written that the end of mankind could come at the hands of the Arcanists, is that far-reaching enough?!"

Sebastian looked once again at Rafe, worry furrowing his brow. "We cannot try to decipher what the Druid warning actually means, any more than we can try to inter-pret how to change the outcome. If you fail to defeat the ancient dark, the end of mankind is imminent, so we must not dwell on what is written. We can only proceed as we must; find the other Arcanists, open the remaining portals, and reactivate all the Druidstones."

Rafe nodded in agreement, looking at her in support. She too acknowledged the task at hand, giving a faint smile to the two ancient warriors in hopes that it would hide the dread that simmered inside her.

Dane pulled the keys from her jacket pocket and unlocked the Trax, the beep of the security system causing Rafe to stop suddenly, his eyes narrowing. She grinned and opened the rear gate, motioning for him to put his bag in the back.

"Get in," she said watching with amusement as he stared bewildered at the big black metal machine sitting in front of him.

"It's a vehicle," she said, knowing that he had no idea what that meant. "It will take us to places in this world, faster and easier than walking. It's how mortals get around."

She walked to the passenger side and opened the door, her hand taking his, gently guiding him toward the front. On her instruction, he climbed tentatively inside, sitting cautiously in the seat and wincing visibly as she slammed the door shut. Hurrying around to the driver's side, she giggled to herself, amused that she was involved with a man that knew nothing about the modern world and its technology.

She started the engine, glancing over at Rafe as it roared to life. His eyes narrowed. His jaw clenched, but he remained calm, refusing to acknowledge her. Putting it in reverse she backed out of the parking spot and just for fun accelerated, turning the wheel quickly so that the Trax's wheels spun sideways, throwing the vehicle around until they were facing the opposite direction.

She burst out laughing at his face, her amusement stifled as he turned a dark scowl her way.

"Sorry," she said meekly, a giggle escaping her lips as she drove out of the trailhead parking lot toward home.

They were almost to her house when she suddenly pulled to the side of the road and quickly exited the vehicle. Opening the back, she retrieved something from her backpack and then walked quickly to the passenger side. Grinning at Rafe she opened his door but was greeted only with his stoic expression, a reminder that he was still not amused by her earlier antics.

Reaching into the glove compartment she pulled out a folded map, motioning for him to follow as she stepped out in front of the Trax where the headlights pierced the darkness. Unfolding the map, she laid it out on the road, smoothing its creases.

"We are back in my world now."

He leaned casually against the vehicle's wheel hub watching her, the dark night shrouding him in shadows.

"Let's see what modern magic can do," she whispered, leaning over the map.

She pulled a long silver chain from her pocket, a clear crystal hanging from one end attached to an intricate silver filigree clasp. Holding the crystal over the center of the map she recited an incantation under her breath, focusing her energy on the crystal and the map. Slowly, the crystal began to swing, moving back and forth across the map like a pendulum. As the movement intensified the crystal's swaying began to morph changing the direction of its swing into a circular pattern, its trajectory getting tighter and tighter as she moved it over the map's surface.

"You are scrying," he said, as the crystal zeroed in on its target. "For the celestial?"

She nodded, her focus never wavering from the task at hand. Suddenly, the crystal dropped, its weight pulling down hard on the delicate silver chain, landing with a thud on an area to the left of the map.

"Where in this world is she?" He asked, curious as to what her modern magic had revealed.

"Oh, this is not a world map," she answered, a glint appearing in her eye as she looked at him. "It's a town map, she is here in Brighton Hill."

Rafe moved to her side quickly, his eyes dropping down to the map as he scanned the area where the crystal had landed. "Do you know this place?"

She nodded, "Very well."

Checking the map again to make sure she was reading it correctly she stared at the crystal, astonished at where it had landed. The tip of the crystal was pointing to a spot she herself had circled on this very map a few years ago when she and Stevie had first moved back to Brighton Hill and were looking at properties to purchase—*It was Stevie's house!*

Stunned by the crystal's revelation, she quickly gathered up the map, determined to get some answers tonight.

Glancing over at Rafe, the beam of the Trax's headlights highlighting his frame, she surveyed his clothes. His tight black cloth pants were tucked into worn knee-high leather boots. His strong chiseled torso and arms, covered only by a dark sleeveless shirt and a thick leather vest, were covered in tattoos. The head of his sword, strapped to his left side, glinted in the headlights. A thick leather strap snaked up his left arm, its leather wrapping itself around his forearm from wrist to elbow. The crest of the Warlician warrior was attached to the left shoulder of his vest and a small blade was sheathed at his ankle. He looked just like a warrior from a fantasy movie and completely out of place in her world.

"We will need to stop at my house first," she said, getting back into the Trax and waiting patiently for him to climb back in.

"We need to make you look a little more like you belong here."

He frowned but nodded tersely in agreement.

A few minutes later she pulled into her townhome, thankful that the neighbor's homes closest to her residence were both shrouded in darkness. Pulling into her garage she waited until the door closed behind them before climbed out of the Trax. Rafe followed her into the house, surprised when she flipped the light switch and the residence was awash with light.

"It's called electricity."

His eyes searched her home, looking for something familiar and comforting in the surroundings. Her modern townhome was nothing like castles, town shops, barracks, or residences of his time, and she could feel his apprehension as he took in the unfamiliar surroundings.

She laid her backpack on the kitchen counter and glanced up at the large metal clock that hung on the far wall—ten-fifty. Gabby and Stevie should still be up, but even if they weren't she needed to find out why the crystal had pointed to her house. She didn't have time to introduce Rafe to the amenities of this world or ease him into the strangeness of it all, he would just have to trust her.

"We need to find you something to wear," she said moving to the back bedroom and pulling a large cardboard box from the closet. Rummaging through the contents she pulled out some clothes and handed them to him. "These should fit you."

His brow furrowed as he inspected the items she had given him.

"You will look more like you belong in the modern world," she explained, planting a kiss on his cheek and leaving him to change.

She was standing at the kitchen counter, after having changed herself, trying to devise a reasonable explanation as to why she was showing up at Stevie's so late when Rafe walked into the room. Her breath caught in her throat. The clothes she had given him were Mason's—her ex. Remnants left behind after their failed romance, but he certainly hadn't looked as good in them.

The black Henley shirt stretched over Rafe's muscular torso perfectly. He had pushed the sleeves up so that his tattoos were visible giving the casual look an edgy feel. The faded jeans hung from his hips, the denim curving seductively over his butt and then falling straight down to his black combat boots. He had tied the boot knife and sheath to his belt, but his sword was nowhere to be seen. Her eyes traveled back up to his handsome face, his long wavy hair tousled, making his overall appearance even sexier and more appealing.

His green eyes penetrated her. "You approve," he asked, a small smirk played on his lips.

She raised her eyebrow as a familiar surge of desire ran

through her body. She knew he could feel the effect he had on her both emotionally and physically so the question he posed was in fact rhetorical.

"Let's go," her raspy voice choked out as she glanced at her watch.

Pulling her eyes away from his intense gaze she headed toward the front door feeling a slight sting of satisfaction as she passed through his energy. She reached into the hall closet and removed a slightly worn army-green cargo jacket, handing it to him. "Immortal or not, you need to look like you belong here, and it's cold out."

He shrugged. Taking the jacket from her he put it on, nonchalantly pulling the collar up so the front tips peeked out through the waves of his shoulder-length hair. Desire swept through her once again as she looked at this beautiful immortal warrior hidden under Gap, Levi, and Abercrombie. *How was she going to explain him to her parents and friends?*

CHAPTER 37

I T WAS ALMOST TEN-THIRTY WHEN Gabby said
goodnight to Stevie and headed toward her bedroom,
dragging her tired aching body up the hallway. She
had not been feeling well for a few days and she longed for
a peaceful night's sleep. The strange illness had begun a few
hours after Dane had left town for her photo shoot in the
Catskills and she had been steadily declining since. At first,
she thought it was just a headache, but then her body
started to ache. Her muscles became weak and sore, and
she was both physically and mentally drained. She'd lost
most of her appetite and was constantly distracted.

Dragging herself into the bathroom, she checked her
temperature again surprised that it was still registering as
normal. The flu would be the only explanation, or a cold
maybe but without a fever, congestion, or nausea, those
illnesses didn't seem plausible. She leaned against the vanity
to steady the spinning room—the dizziness was new and
not welcomed.

Putting the thermometer back in the drawer she took

out her toothbrush, looking at herself in the mirror. Her pale skin looked deathly under the harsh glow of the vanity lights and it had a purple tint to its undertone. Dark circles underlined her eyes, and her lips were dry and cracked, adding to the unappealing face that stared back at her.

Lack of sleep was certainly not helping matters either. The dreams had become relentless the last couple of nights. Each morning she would wake exhausted as an onslaught of images and memories filled her head. She'd written down most of what she remembered but her exhaustion was interrupting her memory, and she was having a difficult time with her recall.

Her mind was tired and overloaded with images, words, memories, none of which she recognized as her own. If it was her past trying to surface, she was not sure she wanted it back.

She could hear Stevie moving around in the next room.

Crawling into bed, she curled up tightly under the cozy blankets, a shiver sending a chill across her skin. She heard the bedroom door squeak as it was pushed gently open, Tyson's head appearing gingerly around the corner. It was odd to see Tyson in her room at night as he always stayed with Diego and Stevie when they looked after him, only coming into her room in the morning.

"Well hi there Ty," she whispered, a yawn muffling her words. "Are you going to sleep with me tonight?"

He stood in the doorway, his big brown eyes staring.

"Come on," she said, patting the bed beside her. He lumbered in, climbing awkwardly onto the bed and curling up beside her, his head resting on her stomach, one paw slung over her leg.

Turning out the bedside lamp she closed her eyes and

listened to Tyson's breathing, the rhythmic sound lulling her to sleep, as the fatigue that had haunted her for the past few days overwhelmed her.

The clock in the living room struck eleven-thirty. The metrical ticktock echoed through the dark house. The moon hung high in the night sky like a silver beacon blazing against a pitch-black backdrop. Its beams sent a shimmering radiance cascading down over the rooftop and an eerie stillness fell over the house. As the moonlight seeped through the window, a golden hue igniting Gabby's room in a ghostly glow.

Tyson whined, as she tossed and turned, her lips moving as she mumbled inaudible words. He watched her cautiously, his ears pressed tightly against his head, his body shaking as her sleep continued to be disrupted. Suddenly, she sat upright, her abrupt movement startling Tyson who darted to the corner and cowered. Bursting into tears she jumped from the bed and ran from the room, the moonlight ebbing in response.

The knocking became more frantic as Stevie struggled to wake from her deep sleep. At first, she thought she was still dreaming but as the knocking intensified, she realized that the pounding was coming from her bedroom door.

"Stevie?" A hoarse voice whispered from the other side.

Recognizing Gabby's voice immediately, she fought to shake off the remaining remnants of sleep. Wiping her eyes, she looked at the bedside clock. The glow of the full moon seeping through the curtains illuminated the face—it was almost midnight.

"Stevie, are you awake?"

There was a hint of panic just underneath the breathy way she said her name, and Stevie knew something was wrong.

"Come in, Gabby," she croaked sitting up in bed and reaching for the sweatshirt she had laid on the chair earlier. There was a slight chill in the air, and she shivered as she reached to turn on the light.

The house was unusually quiet, a deafening silence, snuffing out the normal night sounds. Suddenly she felt extremely uneasy, a feeling that was reinforced as an agitated and tearful Gabby walked tentatively through the door, a very worried bullmastiff on her heels.

Her skin was extremely pale, all color had disappeared from her cheeks and the dark circles surrounding her teary blue eyes made her look hollow. The room seemed to get cooler as she entered, and Stevie shivered again, her skin exploding with goosebumps.

"Gabby, you look terrible, are you OK?" She asked, noting her disheveled appearance and the strange look that cast a shadow across her features.

She stood in the middle of Stevie's room, tears slowly spilling down her face, her hands shaking as she shifted her weight from one foot to the other. Getting out of bed, she walked quickly over to her friend, taking her hands in her own and searching deep into her scared eyes. "Gabby what is it? What has gotten you so upset?"

"I had another dream Stevie, but it was different this time. It was so real, and I knew things, things that make no sense to me now that I am awake but were so familiar in the dream. I think I'm going crazy."

There was a fear in her eyes that Stevie had never seen before.

"Calm down and tell me about it," she said guiding her friend over to the bed, urging her to sit on the edge.

"There was a light," Gabby said softly, taking a deep breath. "It was so bright, it blocked out everything else around it. I felt calm, relaxed, and safe in its presence, the warmth of it was soothing. It just blazed there right in front of me and then there was a voice, coming from the light, speaking a strange language, one that I somehow understood. It told me that I must go, that I am needed elsewhere, that I am part of a larger destiny."

Her hands began to shake as Stevie held them tightly in her own. "It's OK."

Tears welled up in her eyes again. She took a deep breath, calming herself, giving Stevie, an apprehensive look before continuing.

"The light started to get smaller like it was moving away from me but then I realized it was not the light moving it was me! I was falling, falling from a very high place and I could hear the wind as it rushed past my ears, feel its caressing touch as I fell backward through the dark. I reached out my arms and shifted my weight so that I could turn myself around. Now facing my descent, I saw the clouds and stars below me in the night sky getting larger as I hurtled toward them."

She hesitated for a minute trying to slow her breathing, panic rising inside. She locked eyes with Stevie, the contact providing her with courage.

"I wasn't scared, Stevie. I was falling through the night

sky and I felt comfortable like I had done it a million times before. Minutes passed and then suddenly, as the clouds dispersed, I could see the ground below coming up quickly toward me. It was a heavily wooded area and a soft blanket of fresh snow lay on the ground making it more visible in the dark. As I neared the ground, I arched my back and pulled up my shoulders readying myself to slow my descent, but they didn't come out, I tried harder to push them from my back but—they were no longer there."

Her grip tightened around Stevie's hands as those words came out of her mouth, tears spilling down her cheeks as she relived every moment of her dream.

"What was not there?" Stevie asked quickly, confusion and panic now visible in her own voice as she could feel the fear penetrating from her friend's pores.

Gabby's eyes grew wide, her demeanor shifting. She sat up straight pushing her chin out and looking at Stevie directly in the eyes.

"My wings," she uttered.

The room collapsed into a deathly quiet as her words echoed off the stagnant air that seemed to have quickly filled the area. Stevie could feel a shift in the temperature as the air in the room suddenly plummeted. She watched in awe as small white puffs of air escaped from Gabby's mouth. She sensed the surrounding energy changing as it morphed into something stronger and more confident.

Gabby seemed to slip into her own world, oblivious to her presence, vacant eyes staring across the room as she whispered to herself. "It is real."

Stevie heard the whispered words but was unable to respond, as she watched the surreal scene unfolding before her, her mind not fully grasping the reality. She realized she was holding her breath but dare not move, not even to inhale. From the corner of her eye she could see Tyson and Diego sitting like statues across the room, both sets of eyes fixed on Gabby.

She continued to stare at her friend as a golden light began seeping from her skin surrounding her in a strange ethereal glow. She couldn't decipher the look that lingered on Gabby's face—relief, confusion, rapture—but there was a strange peacefulness that seemed to embrace her.

Stevie saw movement out of the corner of her eye and involuntarily looked that way, the reflex movement allowing her to breathe once again. There standing in her bedroom door was Dane, her eyes fixed on Gabby, her mouth set in a grim line. Behind her, stood a man that she did not recognize, his long dark hair framed his handsome face; his light green eyes penetrated the room as they moved quickly from Stevie to Gabby. She could see the markings of tattoos peeking out from his shirt collar and cuffs, and he wore a strange pendant tied to a leather string around his neck.

Stunned by their sudden late-night appearance in her bedroom but still unable to utter a word she continued to gape in disbelief, gazing back at Gabby who still sat calmly in a glowing golden aura at the end of her bed.

Unexpectedly, Dane's calm voice broke the unnerving stillness that had saturated the room.

"Gabby?" She said, watching closely as the golden aura surrounding her friend pulsed in response.

Gabby turned to face the voice that had spoken her name, smiling as she saw who it was.

"You're back," she said softly, warmth generating in her steely gaze. Her once bright blue eyes were now a soft liquid gold, flecks of silver and lavender sparkled in the irises reminding Dane of the multitude of galaxies she had observed in Dywen's night sky. She could feel Rafe close behind her, his composed energy pulsating around him, calming her nerves. She could also sense his awe, a genuine respect for the woman sitting in a golden aura on Stevie's bed, her liquid eyes watching them intently—*for he too knew who she was.*

"I believe you were looking for me," Gabby said, a knowing gaze passing between them.

"I was." Smiling in agreement as the familiar surge of ancient magic ignited inside her, its curiosity peaked by Gabby's presence. Her disbelief overwhelmed her as her mind struggled to grasp the reality of those two words, and how they related to her friend. The prophecy, the history of the realms, the words that Seri had written, all suddenly collided with one simple fact. The celestial, the one that fell to earth, the one she was tasked to find, had in fact been in her life all along—Gabriella Winters was one of the Arcanists.

As that veracity took hold in her mind, the golden aura around Gabby surged, exploding into shimmering beams of light that pulsated throughout the room, sending Stevie and the dogs scurrying to her side. The golden light expanded, creating a shimmering fog, a subtle mist that filled the room, encasing all of them in its vitality.

As the golden mist hovered around them, she could feel an ancient energy come forth. Its power was unmistakable. It moved toward her through the mist, drenched with the essence of an archaic past.

Suddenly, she could hear Gabby's voice echoing around them, confident and resolute, the ancient energy throbbing as she spoke.

"The time of the Second Rising has begun."

As Gabby's words hung in the air, Dane's head began to throb. Her magic racing through her veins as she felt a malevolent presence invade her senses. A cold darkness chilled her skin and the stench of decaying rot surrounded her as the deathly rattle of its haunting laughter filled her mind.

END OF BOOK 1

ACKNOWLEDGMENTS

This book came to life thanks to my husband, Dale who allowed me to dream and provided me with the time and space to develop that dream. Michelle, Deb, Margo, and Kim, your friendship inspires not only my creativity but my life. This book would not have been possible if not for all of you. To my Parson Russell Terrier, Ike, thanks for sleeping under my writing desk and keeping me company. And to everyone else who influenced this book, whether you know it or not, your impact on my life helped create these characters, and worlds. To my overactive subconscious, thanks for all the great ideas even though you kept me up many nights —*dreaming is creating.*

ABOUT THE AUTHOR

Jaci Miller is a dark fantasy author originally from Ontario, Canada. She graduated from University of Phoenix with a BA in English and has worked in both the legal and real estate mortgage businesses. Jaci enjoys paddle boarding, yoga, and her Peloton. She currently resides in Vermont, with her husband, Dale and their Parson Russell Terrier, Ike.

The Scrying Trilogy

The Scrying

The Hallowed

The Arcana

The Dark Kingdom Trilogy

coming 2020/21

Short Stories

Neverland: The Iron Fortress

The Dark Season (republishing 2020)

Printed in Great Britain
by Amazon